"**ANDRE NORTON** has been writing top flight SF for more than forty years and, unlike many of her craft, has been true almost completely to her first love. . . . Her work has not received the critical acclaim of others, perhaps because she is incomparable, perhaps because the sheer quality is so overwhelming, perhaps because of her consistently superior workmanship. . . .

"**THE BOOK OF ANDRE NORTON** is a sampler for the uninitiated and a delightful reminiscence for the seasoned.

"Ms. Norton pleasures mostly with her undiminished confidence in man and an essay, *On Writing Fantasy*, gives some of her professional thoughts.

"But there, too, is much good reading: the minor classic, *The Toads of Grimmerdale*, a piece about a woman who learns that revenge is not sweet when one is dealing with alien beings; a chilling little tale, *Mousetrap*, that teaches the danger of losing one's temper on a world where you don't know the rules; a tribute to cats, *All Cats Are Gray*, which shows that aliens likewise should not underestimate the intelligence of a slightly mangy tomcat. There's more. . . ."

The Jackson Sun

Andre Norton

The Book
of
ANDRE NORTON

Original Title:
*The Many Worlds of
ANDRE NORTON*

EDITED BY ROGER ELWOOD

DAW BOOKS, INC.
DONALD A. WOLLHEIM, PUBLISHER

1301 Avenue of the Americas
New York, N. Y.   10019

Library of Congress Catalogue Number: 74-10980

ACKNOWLEDGMENTS

"The Toads of Grimmerdale" is from *Flashing Swords*, Vol. II, Copyright 1973 by Dell Publishing Co.

"London Bridge" is from *Fantasy and Science Fiction*, October 1973, Copyright 1973 by Mercury Press, Inc.

"On Writing Fantasy" is from the *Dipple Chronicle*, November/December 1971.

"Mousetrap" is from *Fantasy and Science Fiction*, June 1954, Copyright 1954 by Mercury Press.

"All Cats Are Gray" is from *Fantastic Universe*, August-September 1953, Copyright 1953 by Ziff-Davis Publishing Company.

"The Long Night of Waiting," is from *Long Night of Waiting and Other Stories*, Copyright 1973 by Aurora Publishing Co.

"The Gifts of Asti," Copyright 1949 by Andre Norton.

"Long Live Lord Kor!" is from *Worlds of Fantasy*, July 1970, Copyright 1970 by Galaxy Publishing Co.

"Andre Norton: Loss of Faith" is from the *Dipple Chronicle*, November/December 1971.

FIRST PRINTING, OCTOBER 1975

4 5 6 7 8 9

Contents

Introduction

By DONALD A. WOLLHEIM

IN lists of leading science fiction writers such as might be compiled by academics or fan experts, it is probable that the name of Andre Norton would be missing, whereas such writers as Robert Heinlein, Poul Anderson, Arthur C. Clarke, John Brunner and others would be certainly present. Yet if these list compilers would take librarians and booksellers into investigation, they would discover that the name of Andre Norton would be right up there in any top ten list.

Why then would they have omitted her in their original off-the-top-of-the-head listings? It would be for a number of reasons. For one, Andre Norton has but rarely graced the pages of the standard science fiction magazines. Her novels are not serialized in the newsstand pulps. And she has written but a handful of short stories and novelettes as compared with the others' output.

For another thing, she never made herself the object of self-promotion. She does not attend conventions; she rarely, if ever, speaks at gatherings of any sort; and her novels do not push themselves to promote any sort of special pleading of the kind likely to attract controversy and debate.

Then also the greater part of her science fiction has been composed of novels written for hard-cover publishers as works for "young adults" and not promoted or even offered among the science fiction shelves of the adult fiction sections of book shops. Yet any bookseller could tell you that wherever her science fiction books are sold, however they may be labelled, they sell well, they sell steadily, they remain in print for years and years.

A couple of decades ago, during the founding days of the

paperback publishing enterprise known as Ace Books, when I was its editor, I took a chance. I have always felt that if a book was enjoyable to me as science fiction then it would be enjoyable to the readers I sought to cater to. I published Andre Norton's first science fiction novel, a book packaged by its hard-cover publishers as a juvenile, called *Star Man's Son*. I published it in paperback with a new title, *Daybreak—2250 A.D.* I avoided all reference to it as a novel for younger readers. I presented it simply as a darned good novel for anybody who reads science fiction. It was so accepted and it has been selling steadily as such ever since.

Subsequently this has been true for all her science fiction and her marvelous worlds of fantasy too, regardless of how the hard-cover publishers first offered them. The world of science fiction and fantasy readers, the same people who devour Anderson and Simak and Farmer and Niven, also buy and read everything by Andre Norton they can get their hands on.

While they may spend a lot of time discussing the sociology and speculations of the other writers, Andre Norton they read for pleasure. This is not to say that her works lack the depth of the others, because they do not. But it is that these depths form part of the natural unobtrusive background of her novels whereas one's nose is, as it were, forceably shoved into the special pleading that the others so often project into their novels.

Andre Norton thought of herself as writing for young people; from the start she had an instinctive understanding of modern youth that many of her contemporaries and predecessors in juvenile fiction lacked. She knew that you did not have to write down to them; she knew that you did not have to explain the elementary details or futurology of infinity or other-worldly lore to them. She knew that the youth of today was already self-oriented to what came to their older contemporaries as "future shock."

So quite calmly she could speak of colonized planets and the problems of people living on them; she could write of alien beings, friendly and unfriendly; she could bring to the imagination the feel of what an alien mind could be, of what a wholly nonhuman intelligence might desire, or what unsolved mysteries the galaxy may very well hold for us.

She does this as part of a background in which flesh and blood humans develop—young people indeed, but not so young as not to be able to assume responsibilities for themselves, their causes, their loved ones. She could place a story in the grim setting of a ghetto for the dispossessed of a cosmic war—and her readers would understand. She could bring forth the thrill and commerce of space trade, of corporations and "free traders" and do it so that it all came alive, rang true. She could set a human being down alone on an alien landscape and make that alienness felt, make the reader live just what it had to be like.

She knows and loves animals and she utilizes her own feeling for the other living beasts of our Earth to place them or their like on other worlds and other futures—and she brings the magic of communication between man and his old allies of our terrestrial heritage into a reality desired by the legendry of mankind's rise, but possibly capable of achievement only through the knowledge of the ways of genetic structuring and mental revision.

So it is that Andre Norton quietly, without fanfare, but always with love, moved into the ranks of the top science fiction writers. Perhaps she herself was unaware of this—she never sought this aim. One feels that her intent was to tell wonderful stories of far-off worlds, of strange and often fearful futures, of dimensions beyond our own, of magic and witchcraft made possible through the advance of science, but she never sought Hugos or Nebulas or the paraphernalia of self-glorification.

That her books sell continuously in hard covers and in the millions in paperbacks is evidence that she succeeded in this. Most readers take her for granted. Of course they will buy and read the next Andre Norton book; of course they want to wander her wonder worlds and listen to her tales of witches and wise women and wonder-working beasts and courageous young men and women with pride and courage. It is our good fortune, all of us, that Andre Norton herself enjoys the telling. One feels that her contentment is in our contentment—that she herself enjoys her wonder tales of things to come and of things "elsewhere," that she is in personal harmony with the living things of Earth that go on four feet or on wings, and that she is happy in that she has managed to bring some of that harmony to the rest of the human sphere.

She is herself primarily an observer from afar rather than a participant. You will, as I said earlier, not find her at conventions or bumbling around at literary gatherings, nor expounding any special theories at academic halls.

Andre Norton is at home telling wonder stories.

She is telling us that people are marvelously complex and marvelously fascinating. She is telling us that all life is good and that the universe is vast and meant to enhance our life to infinity. She is weaving an endless tapestry of a cosmos no man will ever fully understand, but among whose threads we are meant to wander forever to our personal fulfillment.

Basically this is what science fiction has always been about. And because she has always understood this, her audience will continue to be as ever-renewing and as nearly infinite as her subjects.

The Toads of Grimmerdale

I

THE drifts of ice crusted snow were growing both taller and wider. Hertha stopped to catch her breath, ramming the butt of the hunting spear she had been using as a staff into the one before her, the smooth shaft breaking through the crust with difficulty. She frowned at the broken hole without seeing it.

There was a long dagger at her belt, the short hafted spear in her mittened hand. And, under her cloak, she hugged to her the all too small bundle which she had brought with her out of Horla's Hold. The other burden which she carried lay within her, and she forced herself to face squarely the fate that had been brought upon her.

Now her lips firmed into a line, her chin went up. Suddenly she spat with a hiss of breath. Shame—why should she feel shame? Had Kuno expected her to whine and wail, perhaps crawl before him so he could "forgive" her, prove thus to his followers his greatness of spirit?

She showed her teeth as might a cornered vixen, and aimed a harder blow at the drift. There was no reason for her to feel shame, the burden in her was not of wanton seeking. Such things happened in times of war. She guessed that when matters worked so Kuno had not been backward himself in taking a woman of the enemy.

It remained that her noble brother had sent her forth from

11

Horla's Hold because she had not allowed his kitchen hags to brew some foul potion to perhaps poison her, as well as what she bore. Had she so died he could have piously crossed hands at the Thunderer's Altar and spoken of Fate's will. And all would have ended neatly. In fact she might believe that perhaps that had been his true intention.

For a moment Hertha was startled at the grim march of her thoughts. Kuno—Kuno was her *brother!* Two years ago she could not have thought so of him or any man! When yet the war had not nearer the Hold. But that was long before she set out the Landendale. Before she knew the world as it was and not as she had believed it.

Hertha was glad she had been able to learn her lesson quickly. The thin-skinned maid she had once been could not have fronted Kuno, could not have taken this road—

She felt the warmth of anger, a sullen, glowing anger, as heating as if she carried a small brazier of coals under her cloak's edge. So she went on, setting her rough boots firmly to crunch across the drift edge. Nor did she turn to look back down at that stone walled keep which had sheltered those of her blood for five generations. The sun was well westward, she must not linger on the trail. Few paths were broken now, times in number she must halt and use the spear to sound out the footing. But it was easy to keep in eye her landmarks of Mulma's Needle and the Wyvern's Wing.

Hertha was sure Kuno expected her to come creeping woefully back to accept his conditions. She smiled wryly. Kuno was so very certain of everything. And since he had beaten off the attack of a straggling band of the enemy trying to fight their way to the dubious safety of the coast, he had been insufferable.

The Dales were free in truth. But for Kuno to act as if the victories hard won there were his alone—! It had required all the might of High Hallack, together with strange allies from the Waste, to break the invaders, to hunt and harry them back to the sea from which they had come. And that had taken a score of years to do it.

Trewsdale had escaped, not because of any virtue, but by chance. But because fire and sword had not riven, there was no reason to cry upon unbroken walls as gamecocks. Kuno had harried men already three-quarters beaten.

She reached the divide, to plod steadily on. The wind had been at work here, and her path was free of snow. It was very old, that road, one of the reminders to be found all across the dale land that her own people were late comers. Who had cut these ways for their own treading?

The well weathered carvings at the foot of the Wyvern's Wing could be seen easily now. So eroded they were by time that none could trace their meaning. But men—or intelligent beings—had shaped them to a purpose. And that task must have been long in the doing. Hertha reached out her mittened fingers to stroke one of the now vague curves. She did not believe they had any virtue in themselves, though the field workers did. But they marked well her road.

Down slope again from this point, and now the wind's lash did not cut at her. Though again, snow drifted. Two tens of days yet to the feast of Year Turn. This was the last of the Year of the Hornet, next lay the Year of the Unicorn, which was a more fortunate sign.

With the increase of snow, Hertha once more found the footing dangerous. Bits of broken crust worked in over the tops of her boots, even though she had drawn tight their top straps, and melted clamily against her foot sacks. She plodded on as the track entered a fringe of scrub trees.

Evergreens, the foliage was dark in the dwindling light. But they arose to roof over a road, keep off the drifts. And she came to a stream where ice had bridged from one stony bank to the other. There she turned east to gain Gunnora's Shrine.

About its walls was a tangle of winter killed garden. It was a low building, and an archway faced her. No gate or door barred that and she walked boldly in.

Once so inside the outer wall she could see windows, round as the eyes of some great feline regarding her sleepily. Those flanking a door by which hung a heavy bell-pull of wrought metal in the form of Gunnora's symbol of a ripened grain stalk entwined with a fruit-laden branch.

Hertha leaned her spear against the wall that her hand might be free for a summons pull. What answered was not any peal of bell, rather an odd, muted sound as if some one called in words she did not understand. That, too, she accepted, though she had not been this way before, and had only a few whispered words to send her here.

The leaves of the door parted. Though no one stood there to give her house greeting, Hertha took that for an invitation to enter. She moved into gentle warmth, a fragrance of herbs and flowers. As if she had, in that single step, passed from the sure death of mid-winter into the life of spring.

With the warmth and fragrance came a lighting of heart, so that the taut lines in her face smoothed a little, and her aching shoulders and back lost some of the stiffening tension.

What light there was issued from two lamps, set on columns, one right, one left. She was in a narrow entry, its walls painted with such colors as to make her believe that she had truly entered a garden. Before her those ranks of flowers rippled and she realized that there hung a curtain, fashioned to repeat the wall design. Since there still came no greeting, she put out her hand to the folds of the curtain.

But before she could finger it, the length looped a side of itself, and she came into a large room. There was a table there with a chair drawn up to it. Before that place was set out dishes, some covered as if they held viands which were to be kept warm, a goblet of crystal filled with a green liquid.

"Eat—drink—" a voice sighed through the chamber.

Startled, Hertha looked about the room, over her shoulder. No one—. And now that hunger of which she had hardly been aware awoke full force. She dropped the spear to the floor, laid her bundle beside it, let her cloak fall over both, and sat down in the chair.

Though she could see no one, she spoke:

"To the giver of the feast, fair thanks. For the welcome of the gate, gratitude. To the ruler of this house, fair fortune and bright sun on the morrow—" The formal words rang a little hollow here. Hertha smiled at a sudden thought.

This was Gunnora's shrine. Would the Great Lady need the well wishing of any mortal? Yet it seemed fitting that she make the guest speech.

There was no answer, though she hoped for one. At last, a little hesitatingly, she sampled the food spread before her and found it such fare as might be on the feast table of a Dales Lord. The green drink was refreshing, yet warming, with a subtle taste of herbs. She held it in her mouth, trying to guess which gave it that flavor.

When she had finished, she found that the last and largest covered basin held warm water on the surface of which floated petals of flowers. Flowers in the dead of winter! And beside it was a towel, so she washed her hands, and leaned back in the chair, wondering what came next in Gunnora's hall.

The silence in the room seemed to grow the greater. Hertha stirred. Surely there were priestesses at the Shrine? Some one had prepared that meal, offered it to her with those two words. She had come here for a purpose, and the need for action roused in her again.

"Great Lady," Hertha arose. Since she could see no one, she would speak to the empty room. There was a door at the other end of the chamber but it was closed.

"Great Lady," she began again. She had never been deeply religious, though she kept Light Day, made the harvest sacrifices, listened respectfully to the Mount of Astron at Morn Service. When she had been a little maid, her foster mother had given her Gunnora's amulet and later, according to custom, that had been laid on the house altar when she came to marriageable age. Of Gunnora's mysteries she knew only what she had heard repeated woman to woman when they sat apart from the men. For Gunnora was only for womankind and when one was carrying ripening seed within one, then she listened—

For the second time her words echoed. Now her feeling of impatience changed to something else—awe, perhaps, or fear? Yet Gunnora did not hold by the petty rules of men. It did not matter when you sought her if you be lawful wife or not.

As Hertha's distrust grew, the second door swung silently open—another invitation. Leaving her cloak, bundle, spear where they lay, the girl went on. Here the smell of flowers and herbs was stronger. Lazy curls of scented smoke arose from two braziers standing at the head and foot of a couch. And that was set as an altar at the foot of a pillar carved with the ripened grain, the fruited branch.

"Rest—" the sighing voice bade. And Hertha, the need for sleep suddenly as great as her hunger had been, moved to that waiting bed, stretched out her wearied and aching body. The curls of smoke thickened, spread over her as a coverlet. She closed her eyes.

She was in a place of half light in which she sensed others coming and going, busied about tasks. But she felt alone, lost. Then one moved to her and she saw a face she knew, though a barrier of years had half dimmed it in her mind.

"Elfreda!" Hertha believed she had not called that name aloud, only thought it. But her foster-mother smiled, holding out her arms in the old, old welcome.

"Little dove, little love—" The old words were as soothing as healing salve laid on an angry wound.

Tears came as Hertha had not allowed them to flow before. She wept out sore hurt and was comforted. Then that shade who was Elfreda drew her on, past all those about their work, into a place of light in which there was Another. And that one Hertha could not look upon directly. But she heard a question asked, and to that she made truthful answer.

"No," she pressed her hands to her body," what I carry I do not want to lose."

Then that brightness which was the Other grew. But there was another question and again Hertha answered:

"I hold two desires—that this child be mine alone, taking of no other heritage from the manner of its begetting, and of him who forced me so. And, second, I wish to bring to account the one who will not stand as its father—"

There was a long moment before the reply came. Then a spear of light shot from the center core of the radiance, traced a symbol before Hertha. Though she had no training in the Mysteries yet this was plain for her reading.

Her first prayer would be answered. The coming child would be only of her, taking naught from her ravisher. And the destiny for it was auspicious. But, though she waited, there was no second answer. The great One—was gone! But Elfreda was still with her, and Hertha turned to her quickly:

"What of my need for justice?"

"Vengeance is not of the Lady." Elfreda shook her veiled head. "She is life, not death. Since you have chosen to give life, she will aid you in that. For the rest—you must walk another road. But—do not take it, my love—for out of darkness comes even greater dark."

Then Hertha lost Elfreda also and there was nothing, only the memory of what happened in that place. So she fell into deeper slumber where no dreams walked.

She awoke, how much later she never knew. But she was renewed in mind and body, feeling as if some leachcraft had been at work during her rest, banishing all ills. There was no more smoke rising from the braziers, the scent of flowers was faint.

When she arose from the couch, she knelt before the pillar, bowing her head, giving thanks. Yet still in her worked her second desire, in nowise lessened by Elfreda's warning.

In the outer room there was again food and drink waiting. And she ate and drank before she went forth from Gunnora's house. There was no kin far or near she might take refuge with. Kuno had made loud her shame when he sent her forth. She had a few bits of jewelry, none of worth, sewn into her girdle, some pieces of trade money. Beyond that she had only a housewife's skills, and those not of the common sort, rather the distilling of herbs, the making of ointments, the fine sewing of a lady's teaching. She could read, write, sing a stave—none of these arts conducive to the earning of one's bread.

Yet her spirit refused to be darkened by hard facts. From her waking that sense of things about to come right held. And she thought it best that she limit the future to one day ahead at a time.

In the direction she now faced lay two holdings. Norden-dale was the first. It was small and perhaps in a state of disorder. The lord of the dale and his heir had both fallen at the battle of Ruther's Pass two years gone. Who kept order there now, if there was any who ruled, she did not know. Beyond that lay Grimmerdale.

Grimmerdale! Hertha set down the goblet from which she had drained the last drop. Grimmerdale—

Just as the shrine of Gunnora was among the heights near the ancient road, so did Grimmerdale have a place of mystery. But no kind and welcoming one if rumor spoke true. Not of her race at all, but one as old as the ridge road. In fact perhaps that road had first been cut to run there.

Hertha tried to recall all she had heard of Grimmerdale. Somewhere in the heights lay the Circle of the Toads. Men had gone there, asked for certain things. But ill report they had received all they asked for. What had Elfreda warned? That Gunnora did not grant death—that one must follow another path to find that. Grimmerdale might be the answer.

She looked about her, almost in challenge, half expecting to feel condemnation in the air of the room. But there was nothing.

"For the feast, my thanks," she spoke the guesting words, "for the roof, my blessing, for the future all good, as I take my road again."

She fastened the throat latch of her cloak, drew the hood over her head. Then with bundle in one hand and spear in the other, went out into the light of day, her face to the ridges behind which lay Grimmerdale.

On the final slope above Nordendale, she paused in the afternoon to study the small settlement below. It was inhabited, there was a curl of smoke from more than one chimney, the marks of sleds, of foot prints in the snow. But the tower keep showed no such signs of life.

How far ahead still lay Grimmerdale she had no knowledge, and night came early in the winter. One of those cottages below was larger than the rest. Nordendale had once been a regular halt for herdsmen with wool from mountain sheep on their way to the market at Komm High. That market was of the past, but the inn might still abide, at least be willing to give her shelter.

She was breathing hard by the time she trudged into the slush of the road below. But she had been right, over the door of the largest cottage hung a wind battered board, its painted device long weathered away, but still proclaiming this an inn. She made for that, passing a couple of men on the way. They stared at her as if she were a fire-drake or wyvern. Strangers must be few in Nordendale.

The smell of food, sour village ale, and too many people too long in an unaired space, was like a smothering fog as she came into the common room. There was a wide hearth at one end, large enough to take a good sized log, and fire burned there, giving off a goodly heat.

A trestle table with flanking benches, and a smaller one stacked with tankards, settles by the hearth, were the only furnishings. As Hertha entered a wench in a stained smock and kirtle, two men on a hearth settle, turned and stared with the same astonishment she had seen without.

She pushed back her hood and looked back at them with that belief in herself which was her heritage.

"Good fortune to this house."

For a moment they made no answer at all, seemingly too taken back at seeing a stranger to speak. Then the maid servant came forward, wiping her hands on her already well be-spattered apron.

"Good fortune—" Her eyes were busy taking in the fine material of Hertha's cloak, her air of ease. She added quickly—"Lady. How may we serve you?"

"With food—a bed—if such you have."

"Food—food we have, but it be plain, coarse feeding, lady," the girl stammered. "Let me but call mistress—"

She ran to an inner door, bolting through it as if Hertha was minded to pursue her.

But she rather laid aside her spear and bundle, threw back the edges of her cloak and went to stand before the hearth, pulling with her teeth at mitten fastenings, to bare her chilled hands. The men hunched away along the settle, mum-mouthed and still staring.

Hertha had thought her clothing plain. She wore one of

the divided riding skirts, cut shorter for the scrambling up
and down of hill—and it was now shabby and much worn,
yet very serviceable. There was an embroidered edge on her
jerkin, but no wider than some farm daughter might have.
And her hair was tight braided, with no band of ribbon or
silver to hold it so. Yet she might be clad in some festival fin-
ery the way they looked upon her. And she stood as im-
passive as she could under their stares.

A woman wearing the close coff of a matron, a loose
shawl about her bent shoulders, a kirtle, but little cleaner
than the maid's, looped up about her wide hips and thick
thighs, bustled in.

"Welcome, my lady. Thrice welcome! Up you, Henkin,
Fim, let the lady to the fire!" The men pushed away in a
hurry at her ordering.

"Malka says you would bid the night. This roof is hon-
ored."

"I give thanks."

"Your man—outside? We have stabling—"

Hertha shook her head, "I journey alone and on foot." At
the look on the woman's face she added, "In these days we
take what fortune offers, we do not always please ourselves."

"Alas, lady, that is true speaking if such ever came to ear!
Sit you down!" She jerked off her shawl and used it to dust
along the settle.

Later, in a bed spread with coverings fire warmed, in a
room which manifestly had been shut up for some time, Hertha lay in what comfort such a place could offer and mused
over what she had learned from her hostess.

As she had heard, Nordendale had fallen on dreary times.
Along with their lord and his heir, most of their able bodied
men had been slain. Those who survived and drifted back
lacked leadership and had done little to restore what had
been a prosperous village. There were very few travelers
along the road, she had been the first since winter closed in.
Things were supposed to be somewhat better in the east and
south and her tale of going to kinsmen there had seemed
plausible to those below.

Better still she had news of Grimmerdale. There was another inn there, a larger place, with more patronage, which
the mistress here spoke of wistfully. An east-west road, now
seeing much travel with levies going home, ran there. But the
inn-keeper had a wife who could not keep serving maids,
being of jealous nature.

Of the Toads she dared not ask, and no one had volunteered such information, save that the mistress here had warned against the taking farther of the Old Road, saying it was better to keep to the highway. Though she admitted that was also dangerous and it was well to be ready to take to the brush at the sighting of some travelers.

As yet Hertha had no more than the faint stirrings of a plan. But she was content to wait before she shaped it more firmly.

II

The inn room was long but low, the cross beams of its ceiling not far above the crown of a tall man's head. There were smoking oil lamps hanging on chains from those beams. But the light those gave were both murky and limited. Only at the far corner where a carven screen afforded some privacy were there tallow candles set out on a table. And the odor of their burning added to the general smell of the room.

That was crowded enough to loosen the thin-lipped mouth of Uletka Rory as her small eyes darted hither and yon, missing no detail of service or lack of service, as her two laboring slaves limped and scuttled between benches and stools. She herself waited upon the candle lit table, a mark of favor. She knew high blood when she saw it.

Not that in this case she was altogether right, in spite of her years of dealing with travelers. One of the men there, yes, was the younger son of a dale lord. But his family holding had long since vanished in the red tide of war, and no one was left in Corriedale to name him master. One had been Master of Archers for another lord, promoted hurriedly after three better men had been killed. And the third, well, he was not one who talked, and neither of his present companions knew his past.

Of the three he was the middle in age. Though that, too, could not be easily guessed, since he was one of those lean, spare-framed men who once they begin to sprout beard hair can be any age from youth to middle years. Not that he went bearded now—his chin and jaws were as smooth as if he had scraped them within the hour, displaying along the jaw line the seam of a scar which drew a little at one lip corner.

He wore his hair cropped closer than most, also, perhaps because of the heavy helm now planted on the table at his right hand. That was battered enough to have served through

the war. And the crest it had once mounted was splintered
down to a meaningless knob, though the protective bowl was
unbreached.

His mail shirt, under a scuffed and worn tabbard, was
whole. And the plain hilted sword in his belt sheath, the war
bow now resting against the wall at his back, were the well
kept tools of a professional. But if he was mercenary he had
not been successful lately. He wore none of those fine buckles
or studs which could be easily snapped off to pay for food or
lodging. Only when he put out his hand to take up his tankard did the candle light glint on something which was not
dull steel or leather. For the bowguard on his wrist was true
treasure, a wide band of cunningly wrought gold set with
small colored stones, though the pattern of that design was so
complicated that to make anything of it required close study.

He sat now sober faced, as if he were deep in thought, his
eyes half veiled by heavy lids. But he was in truth listening,
not so much to the half drunken mumblings of his companions, but to words arising here and there in the common
room.

Most of those gathered there were either workers on the
land come in to nurse an earthen mug of home brewed bar-
ley beer and exchange grumbles with their fellows, or else
drifting men-at-arms seeking employment, with their lords
dead, or ruined so that they had to release the men of their
levies. The war was over, these were the victors. But the land
they turned to was barren, largely devastated, and it would
take much time and energy to win back prosperity for High
Hallack.

What the invaders from overseas had not early raped,
looted for ship loads sent back to their own lands, they had
destroyed in a frenzy when the tide of war began to wash
them away. He had been with the war bands in the smoking
port, sent to mop up desperate enemies who had fallen back
too late to find their companions had taken off in the last
ships, leaving them to be ground between the men of the
dales and the sullen sea itself.

The smoke of the port had risen from piles of supplies set
burning, oil poured over them and torches applied to the
spoilage. The stench of it had been near enough to kill a
man. Having stripped the country bare, and this being the
midwinter, the enemy had made a last defiant gesture with
that great fire. It would be a long cold line of days before the
coming of summer, and even then men would go pinched of

belly until harvest time—if they could find enough grain to plant, if sheep still roamed the upper dales, or cattle, wild now, found forage in the edges of the Waste—to make a beginning of new flocks and herds.

There were many dales swept clean of people. The men were dead in battle, the women either fled inland if they were lucky, or else slaving for the invaders overseas—or dead also. Perhaps those were the luckiest of all. Yes, there had been a great shaking and leveling, sorting and spilling.

He had put down the tankard. Now his other hand went to that bowguard, turning it about, though he did not look down at it, but rather stared at the screen and listened.

In such a time a man with boldness, and a plan, could begin a new life. That was what had brought him inland, kept him from taking service with Fritigen of Summersdale. Who would be Master of Archers when he could be more, much more?

The invaders had not reached this Grimmerdale, but there were other lands beyond with darker luck. He was going to find one of those—one where there was no lord left to sound the war horn. If there was a lady trying to hold a heritage, well, that might even fit well with his ambitions. Now his tongue showed for an instant on his lower lip, flicking across as if he savored in anticipation some dish which pleased him. He did not altogether believe in an over-ride of good or ill fortune. In his calculations a man mostly made his own luck by knowing what he wanted and bending all his actions toward that end. But he had a feeling that this was the time when he must move if he were ever to bring to truth the dream which had lain in him since early boyhood.

He, Trystan out of nowhere, was going to end Lord Trystan of some not inconsiderable stretch of land—with a keep from his home and a dale under his rule. And the time to move was here and now.

"Fill!" His near companion, young Urre, pounded his tankard on the table top so that one of the candles shook, spattering hot grease. He bellowed an oath and threw his empty pot beyond the screen to clatter across the flagstones.

The lame pot boy stooped to pick it up, casting a frightened look at Urre and a second at his scowling mistress who was already on her way with a tray of freshly filled tankards. Trystan pushed back from the table. They were following a path he had seen too many nights. Urre would drink himself sodden, sick not only with the rank stuff they called drink back here in the hills, but also with his life, wherein he could only bewail what he had lost, taking no thought of what might be gained.

Onsway would listen attentively to his mumbling, willing to play leigeman as long as Urre's money lasted, or he could use his kin ties to win them food and lodging at some keep. When Urre made a final sot of himself, Onsway would no longer wallow in the sty beside him. While he, himself, thought it time now to cut the thread which had brought them this far in uneasy company. Neither had anything to give, and he knew now that traveling longer with them he would not do.

But he was not minded to quit this inn soon. Its position on the highway was such that a man could pick up a wealth of information by just sitting and listening. Also—here he had already picked out two likely prospects for his own purposes. The money pouch at his belt was flat enough, he could not afford to spin a coin before the dazzled eyes of an archer or pike man and offer employment.

However, there were men like himself to be found, rootless man who wanted roots in better circumstances than they had known, men who could see the advantage of service under a rising man with opportunities for rising themselves in his wake. One did not need a large war band to overawe masterless peasants. Half a dozen well armed and experienced fighting men at his back, a dale without a lord, and he would be in!

Excitement awoke in him as it did everytime his plan reached that place in his thoughts. But he had learned long since to keep a tight rein on his emotions. He was a controlled man, abstemious to a degree astounding among his fellows, though he did what he could to conceal that difference. He could loot, he could whore, he could kill—and he had—but always calculatingly.

"I'm for bed," he arose and reached for his bow, "the road this day was long—"

Urre might not have heard him at all, his attention was fixed on the tray of tankards. Onsway nodded absently, he was watching Urre as he alway did. But the mistress was alert to the hint of more profit.

"Bed, good master? Three bits—and a fire on the hearth, too."

"Good enough." He nodded, and she screeched for the pot

boy who came at a limping waddle, wiping his grimed hands on the black rags of an apron knotted about him.

It seemed that while the inn gave the impression of space below, on the second floor it was much more cramped. At least the room into which Trystan tramped was a narrow slit of space with a single window covered by a shutter heavily barred. There was a litter of dried rushes on the floor and a rough bed frame on which lay a pile of bedding as if tossed. The hearth fire promised did not exist. But there was a legged brazier with some glowing coals which gave off a little heat, and a stool beside a warp-sided chest which did service as a table. The pot boy set the candle down on that and was ready to scuttle away when Trystan, who had gone to the window, hailed him.

"What manner of siege have you had here, boy? This shutter has been so long barred it is rusted tight."

The boy cringed back against the edge of the door, his slack mouth hanging open. He was an ugly lout, and looked half-witted into the bargain, Trystan thought, but surely there was something more than just stupidity in his face, when he looked to the window there was surely fear also.

"Thhheee tooods—" His speech was thick. He had lifted his hands breast high, was clasping them so tightly together that his knuckles stood out as bony knobs.

Trystan had heard the enemy called many things, but never toads, nor had he believed they had raided into Grimmerdale.

"Toads?" He made a question of the word.

The boy turned his head away so that he looked neither to the window nor Trystan. It was very evident he planned escape. The man crossed the narrow room with an effortless and noiseless stride, caught him by the shoulder.

"What manner of toads?" He shook the boy slightly.

"Toodss—Thhhee toods—" the boy seemed to think Trystan should know of what he spoke. "They—that sit 'mong the Standing Stones—that what do men evil." His voice, while thick no longer sputtered so. "All men know the Toods o' Grimmerdale!" Then, with a twist which showed he had had long experience in escaping, he broke from Trystan's hold and was gone. The man did not pursue him.

Rather he stood frowning in the light of the single candle. Toads—and Grimmerdale—together they had a faintly familiar sound. Now he set memory to work. Toads and Grimmerdale—what did he know of either?

The dale was of importance, more so now than in the days before the war when men favored a more southern route to the port. That highway had fallen almost at once into invader hands, and they had kept it forted and patrolled. The answer then had been this secondary road, which heretofore had been used mainly by shepherds and herdsmen. Three different trails from up country united at the western mouth of Grimmerdale.

However had he not once heard of yet a fourth way, one which ran the ridges, yet was mainly shunned, a very old way, antedating the coming of his own people? Now—he nodded as memory supplied answers. The toads of Grimmerdale! One of the many stories about the remnants of those other people, or things, which had already mostly faded from this land so that the coming of man did not dislodge them, for the land had been largely deserted before the first settlement ship arrived.

Still there were places in plenty where certain powers and presences were felt this day, where things could be invoked—by men who were crazed enough to summon them. Had the lords of High Hallack not been driven at the last to make such a bargain with the unknown when they signed solemn treaty with the Were Riders? All men knew that it had been the aid of those strange outlanders which had broken the invaders at the last.

Some of the presences were beneficial, others neutral, the third dangerous. Perhaps not actively so in these days. Men were not hunted, harried, or attacked by them. But they had their own places, and the man who was rash enough to trespass there did so at risk.

Among such were the Standing Stones of the Toads of Grimmerdale. The story went that they would answer appeals, but that the manner of answer sometimes did not please the petitioner. For years now men had avoided their place.

But why a shuttered window? If, as according to legend the toads (people were not sure now if they really *were* toads) did not roam from their portion of the dale, had they once? Making it necessary to bolt and bar against them? And why a second story window in this fusty room?

Moved by a curiosity he did not wholly understand, Trystan drew his belt knife, pried at the fastenings. They were deeply bitten with rust, and he was sure that this had not been opened night or day for years. At last they yielded to his efforts, he was now stubborn about it, somehow even a little angry.

Even though he was at last able to withdraw the bar, he had a second struggle with the warped wood, finally using sword point to lever it. The shutters grated open, the chill of the night entered, making him aware at once of how very odorous and sour was the fug within.

Trystan looked out upon snow and a straggle of dark trees, with the upslope of the dale wall beyond. There were no other buildings set between the inn and that rise. And the thick vegetation showing dark above the sweep of white on the ground suggested that the land was uncultivated. The trees there were not tall, it was mainly brush alone, and he did not like it.

His war trained instincts saw there a menace. Any enemy could creep in its cover to within a spear cast of the inn. Yet perhaps those of Grimmerdale did not have such fears and so saw no reason to grub out and burn bare.

The slope began gradually and shortly the tangled growth thinned out, as if someone had there taken the precautions Trystan thought right. Above was smooth snow, very white and unbroken in the moonlight. Then came outcrops of rock. But after he had studied those with an eye taught to take quick inventory of a countryside, he was sure they were not natural formations but had been set with a purpose.

They did not form a connected wall. There were wide spaces between as if they had served as posts for some stringing of fence. Yet for that purpose they were extra thick.

And that first row led to a series of five such lines, though more distantly they were close together. Trystan was aware of two things. One, bright as the moon was, it did not, he was sure, account for all the light among the stones. There was a radiance which seemed to rise either from them, or the ground about them. Second, no snow lay on the land from the point where the lines of rock pillar began. Above the stones also there was a misting, as if something there bewildered or hindered clear sight.

Trystan blinked, rubbed his hand across his eyes, looked again. The clouding was more pronounced when he did so. As if whatever lay there increased the longer he watched it.

That this was not of human Grimmerdale, he was certain. It had all signs of being one of those strange places where old powers lingered. And that this was the refuge or stronghold of the "toads" he was now sure. That the shutter had been bolted against the weird sight he could also understand, and he rammed and pounded the warped wood back into place, though he could not reset the bar he had levered out.

Slowly he put aside mail and outer clothing, laying it across the chest. He spread out the bedding over the hide webbing. Surprisingly the rough sheets, the two woven covers were clean. They even (now that he had drawn lungfuls of fresh air to awaken his sense of smell) were fragrant with some kind of herb.

Trystan stretched out, pulled the covers about his ears, drowsy and content, willing himself to sleep.

He awoke to a clatter at the door. At first he frowned up at the cobwebbed rafters above. What had he dreamed? Deep in his mind there was a troubled feeling, a sense that a message of some importance had been lost. He shook his head against such fancies and padded to the door, opened it for the entrance of the elder serving man, a dour-faced, skeleton thin fellow who was more cleanly of person than the pot boy. He carried a covered kettle which he put down on the chest before he spoke.

"Water for washing, Master. There be grain-mush, pig cheek, and ale below."

"Well enough." Trystan slid the lid off the pot. Steam curled up. He had not expected this small luxury and he took its arrival as an omen of fortune for the day.

Below the long room was empty. The lame boy was washing off table tops, splashing water on the floor in great scummy drollops. His mistress stood, hands on her hips, her elbows out-spread like crooked wings, her sharp chin with its two haired warts outthrust as a spear to threaten the other woman before her, well cloaked against the outside winter, but with her hood thrown back to expose her face.

That face was thin with sharp features which were lacking in any claim to comeliness since the stretched skin was mottled with unsightly brown patches. But her cloak, Trystan saw, was good wool, certainly not that of a peasant wench. She carried a bundle in one hand, and in the other was a short hafted hunting spear, its butt scarred as if it had served her more as a journey staff than a weapon.

"Well enough, wench. But here you work for the food in your mouth, the clothing on your back." The mistress shot a single glance at Trystan before she centered her attention once more on the girl.

Girl, Trystan thought she was. Though by the Favor of Likerwolf certainly her face was not that of a dewy maid, being rather enough to turn a man's thoughts more quickly to other things when he looked upon her.

"Put your gear on the shelf yonder," the mistress gestured. "Then to work, if you speak the truth on wanting that."

She did not watch to see her orders obeyed, but came to the table where Trystan had seated himself.

"Grain-mush, Master. And a slicing of pig jowl—ale fresh drawn—"

He nodded, sitting much as he had the night before, fingering the finely wrought guard about his wrist, his eyes half closed as if he were still wearied, or else turned his thoughts on things not about him.

The mistress stumped away. But he was not aware she had returned, until someone slid a tray onto the table top. It was the girl. Her shrouding of cloak was gone, so that the tight bodices, the pleaded skirt could be seen. And he was right, she did not wear peasant clothes. That was a skirt divided for riding, though it had now been shortened enough to show boots, scuffed and worn, straw protruding from their tops. Her figure, was thin, yet shapely enough to make a man wonder at the fate which wedded such to that horror of a face. She did not need her spear for protection, all she need do was show her face to any would-be ravisher and she would be as safe as the statue of Gunnora the farmers carried through their fields at first sowing.

"Your food, Master." She was deft, far more so than the mistress, as she slid the platter of crisp browned mush, the pink sliced thin meat, onto the board.

"Thanks given," Trystan found himself making civil answer as he might in some keep were one of the damsels there noticing him in courtesy.

He reached for the tankard and at that moment saw her head sway, her eyes wide open rested on his hand. And he thought, with a start of surprise, that her interest was no slight one. But when he looked again, she was moving away, her eyes downcast as any proper serving wench.

"There will be more, Master?" she asked in a colorless voice. But her voice also betrayed her. No girl save one hold bred would have such an accent.

There had been many upsets in the dales. What was it to him if some keep woman had been flung out of her soft nest to tramp the roads, serve in an inn for bread and a roof?

With her face she could not hope to catch a man to fend for her—unless he be struck blind before their meeting.

"No," he told her. She walked away with the light and soundless step which might have equalled a forest hunter's, the grace of one who sat at high tables by right of blood.

Well, he, too, would sit at a high table come next year's end. Of that he was certain as if it had been laid upon him by some Power Master as an unbreakable greas. But it would be because of his own two hands, the cunning of his mind. And as such his rise would be worth more than blood right. She had come down, he would go up. Seeing her made him just more confident of the need for moving on with his plan.

III

The road along the ridges was even harder footing after Nordendale Hertha discovered. There were gaps where landslides had cut away sections, making the going very slow. However she kept on, certain this was the only way to approach what she sought.

As she climbed and slid, edged with caution, even in places had to leap recklessly with her spear as a vaulting pole, she considered what might lie ahead. In seeking Gunnora she had kept to the beliefs of her people. But if she continued to the shrine of the Toads she turned her back on what safety she knew.

Around her neck was hung a small bag of grain and dried herbs, Gunnora's talisman for home and hearth. Another such was sewn into the breast of her undersmock. And in the straw which lined each boot were other leaves with their protection for the wayfarer. Before she had set out on this journey she had marshalled all she knew of protective charms.

But whether such held against alien powers, she could not tell. To each race its own magic. The Old Ones were not men and their beliefs and customs must have been far different. That being so did she now tempt great evil?

Always when she reached that point she remembered. And memory was as sharp as any spur on a rider's heel. She had been going to the abbey in Lethendale, Kuno having suggested it. Perhaps that was why he had turned from her, feeling guilt in the matter.

Going to Lethendale, she must ever remember how that journey was, every dark part of it. For if she did not hold that in mind, then she would lose the booster of anger for her courage. A small party because Kuno was sure there was naught to fear from the fleeing invaders. But after all it was not the invaders she had had to fear.

There had come a rain of arrows out of nowhere. She could hear yet the bubbling cry of young Jannesk as he fell from the saddle with one through his throat. They had not even seen the attackers, and all the men had been shot down in only moments. She had urged her mount on, only to have him entangle feet in a trip rope. She could remember only flying over his head thereafter—

Until she awoke in the dark, her hands tied, looking out into a clearing where a fire burned between rocks. Men sat about it tearing at chunks of half roasted meat. *Those* had been the invaders. And she had lain cold, knowing well what they meant for her when they had satisfied one appetite and were ready—

They had come to her at last. Even with tied hands she had fought. So they had laughed and cuffed her among them, tearing at her garments and handling her shamefully, though they did not have time for the last insult and degradation of all. No, that was left for some—some *man* of her own people!

Thinking on it now made rage rise to warm her even though the sun had withdrawn from this slope and there was a chill rising wind.

For the ambushers had been attacked in turn, fell under spear and arrow out of the dark. Half conscious she had been left lying until a harsh weight on her, hard, bruising hands brought her back to terror and pain.

She had never seen his face, but she had seen (and it was branded on her memory for all time) the bowguard encircling the wrist tightened as a bar across her throat to choke her unconscious. And when she had once more stirred she was alone.

Someone had thrown a cloak over her nakedness. There was a horse nearby. There was for the rest only dead men under a falling snow. She never understood why they had not killed her and been done with it. Perhaps in that little skirmish her attacker had been over-ridden by his companions. But at the time she had been sorely tempted to lie where she was and let the cold put an end to her. Only the return of that temper which was her heritage roused her. Somewhere living was the man who should have been her savior and in-

stead had rift from her what was to be given only as a free
gift. To bring him down, for that she would live.

Later, when she found she carried new life, yes, she had
been tempted again—to do as they urged, rid herself of that.
But in the end she could not. For though part of the child
was of evil, yet a part was hers. Then she recalled Gunnora
and the magic which could aid. So she had withstood Kuno's
urging, even his brutal anger.

She held to two things with all the stubborn strength she
could muster—that she would bear this child which must be
hers only, and that she would have justice on the man who
would never in truth be its father. The first part of her desire
Gunnora had given, now she went for answer to the second.

At last night came and she found a place among the rocks
where she could creep in, the stone walls giving refuge from
the wind, a carpet of dried leaves to blanket her. She must
have slept, for when she roused she was not sure where she
was. Then she was aware of the influence which must have
brought her awake. There was an uneasiness in the very air
about her, a tension as if she stood on the verge of some
great event.

With the spear as her staff, Hertha came farther into the
open. The moon showed her unmarked snow ahead, made
dark pits of her own tracks leading here. With it for a light
she started on.

A wan radiance, having no light of fire, shown in the distance. It came from no torch either, she was sure. But it
might well mark what she sought.

Here the Old Road was unbroken, though narrow. She
prodded the snow ahead, lest there be some hidden crevice.
But she hurried as if to some important meeting.

Tall shapes arose, stones set on end in rows. For the outer
lines there were wide spaces between, but the inner ones
were placed closer and closer together. She followed a road
cut straight between these pillars.

On the crest of each rested a small cone of light, as if
these were not rocks but giant candles to light her way. And
the light was cold instead of warm, blue instead of orange-
red as true flame. Also here the moonlight was gone, so that
even though there was no roof she could see, yet it was shut
away.

Three stone rows she passed, then four more, each with
the stones closer together, so that the seventh brought them

touching to form a wall. The road dwindled to a path which led through a gate therein.

Hertha knew that even had she wanted to retreat, now she could not. It was as if her feet were held to the path and that moved, bearing her with it.

So she came into a hexagon shaped space within the wall. There was a low curbing of stone to fence off the centermost portion and in each angle blazed a flame at ground level. But she could go no farther, just as she could not draw away.

Within the walled area were five blocks of green stone. Those glistened in the weird light as if they were carved of polished gems. Their tops had been squared off to give seating for those who awaited her.

What she had expected Hertha was not sure. But what she saw was so alien to all she knew that she did not even feel fear, but rather wonder that such could exist in a world where men also walked. Now she could understand why these bore the name of toads, for that was the closest mankind could come in descriptive comparison.

Whether they went on two limbs or four, she could not be sure the way they hunched upon their blocks. But they were no toads in spite of their resemblance. Their bodies were bloated of paunch, the four limbs seemingly too slender beside that heaviness. Their heads sat upon narrow shoulders with no division of neck. And those heads were massive, with large golden eyes high on their hairless skulls, noses which were slits only, and wide mouths stretching above only a vestige of chin.

"Welcome, Seeker—"

The words rang in her head, not her ears. Nor could she tell which of the creatures spoke then.

Now that Hertha had reached her goal she found no words, she was too bemused by the sight of those she had sought. Yet it seemed that she did not have to explain, for the mind speech continued:

"You have come seeking our aid. What would you, daughter of men, lose that which weighs your body?"

At that Hertha found her tongue to speak.

"Not so. Though the seed in me was planted not by lawful custom, but in pain and torment of mind and body, yet will I retain it. I shall bear a child who shall be mine alone, as Gunnora has answered my prayers."

"Then what seek you here?"

"Justice! Justice upon him who took me by force and in shame!"

"Why think you, daughter of men, that you and your matters mean aught to us who were great in this land before your feeble kind came, and who will continue to abide even after man is again gone? What have we to do with you?"

"I do not know. Only I have listened to old tales, and I have come."

She had an odd sensation then. If one could sense laughter in one's mind, she was feeling it. They were amused, and, knowing that, she lost some of her assurance.

Again a surge of amusement, and then a feeling as if they had withdrawn, conferred among themselves. Hertha would have fled but she could not. And she was afraid as she had not been since she faced horror on the road to Lethendale.

"Upon whom ask you justice, daughter of men? What is his name, where lies he this night?"

She answered with the truth. "I know neither. I have not even seen his face. Yet—" she forgot her fear, knew only that hate which goaded her on, "I have that which shall make him known to me. And I may find him here in Grimmerdale since men in many now pass along this road, the war being ended."

Again that withdrawal. Then another question.

"Do you not know that services such as ours do not come without payment? What have you to offer us in return, daughter of men?"

Hertha was startled. She had never really thought past making her plea here. That she had been so stupid amazed her. Of course there would be payment! Instinctively she dropped her bundle, clasped her hands in guard over where the child lay.

Amusement once more.

"Nay, daughter of men. From Gunnora you have claimed that life, nor do we want it. But justice can serve us, too. We shall give you the key to that which you wish, and the end shall be ours. To this do you agree?"

"I do." Though she did not quite understand.

"Look you—there!" One of the beings raised a forefoot and pointed over her shoulder. Hertha turned her head. There was a small glowing spot on the surface of the stone pillar. She put out her hand and at her touch a bit of stone loosened so she held a small pebble.

"Take that, daughter of men. When you find him you seek,

see it lies in his bed at the coming of night. Then your justice will fall upon him—here! And so you will not forget, nor think again and change your mind, we shall set a reminder where you shall see it each time you look into your mirror."

Again the being pointed, this time at Hertha. From the forelimb curled a thin line of vapor. That curdled to form a ball which flew at her. Though she flinched and tried to duck, it broke against her face with a tingling feeling which lasted only for a second.

"You shall wear that until he comes hither, daughter of men. So will you remember your bargain."

What happened then she was not sure, it was all confused. When she was clear-headed again dawn was breaking and she clawed her way out of the leaf carpeted crevice. Was it all a dream? No, her fingers were tight about something, cramped and in pain from that hold. She looked down at a pebble of green-grey stone. So in truth she had met the Toads of Grimmerdale.

Grimmerdale itself lay spread before her, easy to see in the gathering light. The lord's castle was on the farther slope, the village and inn by the highway. And it was the inn she must reach.

Early as it was there were signs of life about the place. A man went to the stable without noticing her as she entered the courtyard. She advanced to the half open door, determined to strike some bargain for work with the mistress, no matter how difficult the woman was reputed to be.

The great room was empty when she entered. But moments later a woman with a forbidding face stumped in. Hertha went directly to her. The woman stared at her and then grinned, maliciously.

"You've no face to make trouble, wench, one can be certain of that," she said when Hertha asked for work. "And it is true that an extra pair of hands is wanted. Not that we have a purse so fat we can toss away silver—"

As she spoke a man came down the steep inner stair, crossed to sit at a table half screened from the rest. It was almost as if his arrival turned the scales in Hertha's favor. For she was told to put aside her bundle and get to work. So it was she who took the food tray to where he sat.

He was tall, taller than Kuno, with well set, wide shoulders. And there was a sword by his side, plain hilted, in a worn scabbard. His features were sharp, his face thin, as if he might have gone on short rations too often in the past.

Black hair peaked on his forehead and she could not guess his age, though she thought he might be young.

But it was when she put down her tray and he reached out for an eating knife that it seemed the world stopped for an instant. She saw the bowguard on his wrist. And her whole existence narrowed to that metal band. Some primitive instinct of safety closed about her, she was sure she had not betrayed herself.

As she turned from the table she wondered if this was by the power of the Toads, that they had brought her prey to her hand so. What had they bade her—to see that the pebble was in his bed. But this was early morn, and he had just risen, what if he meant not to stay another night, but would push on? How could she then carry out their orders? Unless she followed after, somehow crept upon him at nightfall.

At any rate he seemed in no hurry to be up and off if that was his purpose. Finally, with relief, she heard him bargain with the mistress for a second night's stay. She found an excuse to go above, carrying fresh bedding for a second room to be made ready. And as she went down the narrow hall she wondered how best she could discover which room was his.

So, intent was she upon this problem that she was not aware of someone behind her, until an ungentle hand fell on her shoulder and she was jerked about.

"Now here's a new one—" The voice was brash and young. Hertha looked at a man with something of the unformed boy still in his face. His thick yellow hair was uncombed, and his jaw beard stubbled, his eyes red-rimmed.

As he saw her clearly he made a grimace of distaste, shoved her from him with force, so she lost her balance and fell to the floor.

"As leave kiss a toad!" He spat. But the trail of spittle never struck her. Instead hands fell on him, slammed him against the other wall. While the man of the bowguard surveyed him steadily.

"What's to do?" The younger man struggled. "Take your hands off me, fellow!"

"Fellow, is it?" observed the other. "I am no liege man of yours, Urre. Nor are you in Roxdale now. As for the wench, she's not to blame for her face. Perhaps she should thank what ever Powers she lights a candle to that she has it. With such as you ready to lift every skirt they meet."

"Toad! She is a toad-face—" Urre worked his mouth as if he wished to spit again, then something in the other's eyes must have warned him. "Hands off me!" He twisted and the other stepped back. With an oath Urre lurched away, heading unsteadily for the stair.

Hertha got to her feet, stooped to gather up the draggle of covers she had dropped.

"Has he hurt you?"

She shook her head dumbly. It had all been so sudden, and that *he*—this one—had lifted hand in her defense dazed her. She moved away as fast as she could, but before she reached the end of the passage she looked back. He was going through a door a pace away from where the one called Urre had stopped her. So—she had learned his room. But toad face? That wet ball which had struck her last night—what had it done to her?

Hertha used her fingers to trace any alteration in her features. But to her touch she was as she had always been. A mirror—she must find a mirror! Not that the inn was likely to house such a luxury.

In the end she found one in the kitchen, in a tray which she had been set to polishing. Though her reflection was cloudy, there was no mistaking the ugly brown patches on her skin. Would they be so forever, a brand set by her trafficking with dark powers, or would they vanish with the task done? Something she had remembered from that strange voiceless conversation made her hope the latter was true.

If so, the quicker she moved to the end, the better. But she did not soon get another chance to slip aloft. The man's name was Trystan. The lame pot boy had taken an interest in him and was full of information. Trystan had been a Marshal, and Master of Archers—he was now out of employment, moving inland probably to seek a new lord. But perhaps he was thinking of raising a war band on his own, he had talked already with other veterans staying here. He did not drink much, though those others with him, Urre, who was son to a dale lord, and his leigeman ordered enough to sail a ship.

Crumbs, yes, but she listened eagerly for them, determined to learn all she could of this Trystan she must enmesh in her web. She watched him, too, given occasion when she might do so without note. It gave her a queer feeling to so look upon the man who had used her so and did not guess now she was so near.

Oddly enough, had it not been for the evidence of the bowguard and she would have picked him last of those she saw beneath this roof. Urre, yes, and two or three others, willing to make free with her until they saw her face clearly. But when she had reason to pass by this Trystan he showed her small courtesies, as if her lack of comeliness meant nothing. He presented a puzzle which was disturbing.

But that did not change her plan. So, at last, when she managed close to dusk to slip up the stairway quickly, she sped down the hall to his room. There was a huddle of coverings on the bed. She could not straighten those, but she thrust the pebble deep into the bag-pillow and hurried back to the common room where men were gathering. There she obeyed a stream of orders, fetching and carrying tankards of drink, platters of food.

The fatigue of her long day of unaccustomed labor was beginning to tell. And there were those among the patrons who used cruel humor to enlighten the evening. She had to be keen witted and clear eyed to avoid a foot slyly thrust forth to trip her, a sudden grab at her arm to dump a filled patter or tray of tankards. Twice she suffered defeat and was paid by a ringing buffet from the mistress's hand for the wasting of food.

But at length she was freed from their persecution by the mistress (not out of any feeling for her, but as a matter of saving spillage and spoilage) and set to the cleaning of plates in a noisome hole where the stench of old food and greasy slops turned her stomach and made her so ill she was afraid she could not last. Somehow she held out until finally the mistress sourly shoved her to one of the fireside settles and told her that was the best bed she could hope for. Hertha curled up, so tired she ached, while the rest of the inn people drifted off to their holes and corners—chambers were for guests alone.

The fire had been banked for the night, but the hearth was warm. Now that she had the great room to herself, though her body was tried, her mind was alert, and she rested as best she could while she waited. If all went well, surely the stone would act this night, and she determined to witness the action. Beyond that she had not planned.

Hertha waited for what seemed a long time, shifting now and then on her hard bed. Near to hand were both her cloak and the spear staff, her boots new filled with fresh straw, were on her feet.

She was aware of a shadow at the head of the stairs, of steps. She watched and listened. Yes, she had been right—

this was the man Trystan, and he was walking toward the door. Whirling her cloak about her, Hertha rose to follow.

IV

She clung to the shadow of the inn wall for fear he might look behind. But he strode on with the sure step of a man on some mission of such importance his present surroundings had little meaning, rounding the back of the inn, tramping up slope.

Though a moon hung overhead, there was also a veiling of cloud. Hertha dropped farther and farther behind, for the brambles of the scrub caught at her cloak, the snow weighted her skirt, and the fatigue of her long day's labor was heavy on her. Yet she felt that she must be near to Trystan when he reached his goal. Was it that she must witness the justice of the Toads? She was not sure any more, concentrating all her effort on the going.

Now she could see the stones stark above. They bore no candles on their crests this night, were only grim blots of darkness. Toward them Trystan headed as straight a line as the growth would allow.

He reached the first line of stones, not once had he looked around. Long since Hertha abandoned caution. He was almost out of sight! She gathered up her skirts, panting heavily as she plunged and skidded to where he had disappeared.

Yes, now she could see him, though he was well ahead. But when he reached that final row, the one forming a real wall, he would have to move along it to the entrance of the Old Road. While she, already knowing the way, might gain a few precious moments by seeking the road now. And she did that, coming to better footing with her breath whistling through her lips in gasps.

She had no spear to lean on and she nursed a sharp pain in her side. But she set her teeth and wavered on, between those rows of stones, seeing the gate ahead and framed in it a dark figure. Trystan was still a little before.

There came a glow of light, the cold flames were back on pillar top. In its blue radiance her hands looked diseased and foul when she put them out to steady herself as she went.

Trystan was just within the gate of the hexagon. He had not moved, but rather stared straight ahead at whatever awaited him. His sword was belted at his side, the curve of his bow was a pointing finger behind his shoulder. He had come fully armed, yet he made no move to draw weapon now.

Hertha stumbled on. That struggle up slope had taken much of her strength. Yet in her was the knowledge that she must be there. Before her now, just beyond her touching even if she reached forth her arm, was Trystan. His head was uncovered, the loose hood of his surcoat lay back on his shoulders. His arms dangled loosely at his sides. Hertha's gaze followed to the source of his staring concentration.

There were the green blocks. But no toad forms humped upon them. Rather lights played there, weaving in and out in a flickering dance of shades of blue, from a wan blight which might have emanated from some decaying bit on a forest floor, to a brilliant sapphire.

Hertha felt the pull of those weaving patterns, until she forced herself (literally so forced her heavy hands to cover her eyes) not to look upon the play of color. When she did so there was a sensation of release. But it was plain her companion was fast caught.

Cupping her hands to shut out all she could of the lights, she watched Trystan. He made no move to step across the low curbing and approach the blocks. He might have been turned into stone himself, rapt in a spell which had made of him ageless rock. He did not blink an eye, nor could she even detect the rise and fall of his chest in breathing.

Was this their judgment then, the making of a man into a motionless statue? Somehow Hertha was sure that whatever use the Toads intended to make of the man they had entrapped through her aid it was more than this. Down inside her something stirred. Angrily she fought against that awakening of an unbidden thought, or was it merely emotion? She drew memory to her, lashed herself with all shameful, degrading detail. This had he done to her, and this, and this! By his act she was homeless, landless, a nothing, wearing even a toad face. Whatever came now to him, he richly deserved it. She would wait and watch, and then she would go hence, and in time, as Gunnora had promised, she would bear a son or daughter who had none of this father—none!

Still watching him, her hands veiling against the play of the ensorcelling light, Hertha saw his lax fingers move, clench into a fist. And then she witnessed the great effort of that gesture, and she knew that he was in battle, silent though he stood. That he fought with all his strength against what held him fast.

That part of her which had stirred and awakened, grew stronger. She battled it. He deserved nothing but what would come to him here, he deserved nothing from her but the justice she had asked from the Toads.

His hand-fist arose, so slowly that it might have been chained to some great weight. When Hertha looked from it to his face, she saw the agony that was causing him. She set her shoulders to the rock wall, had she but a rope she would have bound herself there, that no weakness might betray her plan.

Strange light before him and something else, formless as yet, but with a cold menace greater than any fear born of battle heat. For this terror was rooted not in any ordinary danger, but grew from a horror belonging by rights far back in the beginnings of his race. How he had come here, whether this be a dream or not, Trystan was not sure. And he had no time to waste on confused memory.

What energy he possessed must be used to front that which was keeping him captive. It strove to fill him with its own life, and that he would not allow, not while he could summon will to withstand it.

Somehow he thought that if he broke the hold upon his body, he could also shatter its would-be mastery of his mind and will. Could he act against its desires, he might regain control. So he set full concentration on his hand—his fingers. It was as if his flesh was nerveless, numb—But he formed a fist. Then he brought up his arm, so slowly that, had he allowed himself to waver, he might have despaired. But he knew that he must not relax his intense drive of will centered in that simple move. Weapons—what good would his bow, his sword, be against what dwelt here? He sensed dimly that this menace could well laugh at weapons forged and carried by those of his kind.

Weapons—sword—steel—there was something hovering just at the fringe of memory. Then for an instant he saw a small, sharp mind picture. Steel! That man from the Waste side dale who had set his sword as a barrier at the head of his sleeping roll, his dagger, plunged point deep in the soil at his feet the night they had left him on the edge of very ancient ruins with their mounts. Between cold iron a man lay safe, he said. Some scoffed at his superstition, others had nodded agreement. Iron—cold iron—which certain old Powers feared.

He had a sword at his belt now, a long dagger at his

hip—iron—talismen? But the struggle for possession of his fist, his arm, was so hard he feared he would never have a chance to put the old belief to the proof.

What did they want of him, those who abode here? For he was aware that there was more than one will bent on him. Why had they brought him? Trystan shied away from questions. He must concentrate on his hand—his arm!

With agonizing slowness he brought his hand to his belt, forced his fingers to touch the hilt of his sword.

That was no lord's proud weapon with a silvered, jeweled hilt, but a serviceable blade nicked and scratched by long use. So that the hilt itself was metal, wound with thick wire to make a good grip which would not turn in a sweating hand. His finger tips touched that and—his hand was free!

He tightened hold instantly, drew the blade with a practiced sweep, and held it up between him and that riot of blending and weaving blue lights. Relief came, but it was only minor he knew after a moment or two of swelling hope. What coiled here could not be so easily defeated. Always that other will weighted and plucked at his hand. The sword blade swung back and forth, he was unable to hold it steady. Soon he might not be able to continue to hold it at all!

Trystan tried to retreat even a single step. But his feet were as if set in a bog, entrapped against any move. He had only his failing hand and the sword, growing heavier every second. Now he was not holding it erect as if on guard, but doubled back as if aimed at his own body!

Out of the blue lights arose a tendril of wane, phosphorescent stuff which looped into the air and remained there, its tip pointed in his direction. Another weaved up to join it, swell its substance. A third came, a fourth was growing—

The tip which had been narrow as a finger, was now thickening. From that smaller tips rounded and swelled into being. Suddenly Trystan was looking at a thing of active evil, a grotesque copy of a human hand, four fingers, a thumb too long and thin.

When it was fully formed it began to lower towards him. Trystan, with all his strength, brought up the sword, held its point as steady as he could against that reaching hand.

Again he knew a fleeting triumph. For at the threat of the sword, the hand's advance was stayed. Then it moved right, left, as if to strike as a foeman's point past his guard. But he was able by some miracle of last reserves to counter each attack.

Hertha watched the strange duel wide-eyed. The face of her enemy was wet, great trickles of sweat ran from his forehead to drip from his chin. His mouth was a tight snarl, lips flattened against his teeth. Yet he held that sword and the emanation of the Toads could not pass it.

"You!"

The word rang in her head with a cold arrogance which hurt.

"Take from him the sword!"

An order she must obey if she was to witness her triumph. Her triumph? Hertha crouched against the rock watching that weird battle—sword point swinging with such painful slowness, but ever just reaching the right point swinging with such painful slowness, but ever just reaching the right point in time so that the blue hand did not close. The man was moving so slowly, why could the Toads not beat him by a swift dart past his guard? Unless their formation of the hand, their use of it, was as great an effort for them as his defense seemed to be for him.

"The sword!" That demand in her mind hurt.

Hertha did not stir. "I can not!" Did she cry that aloud, whisper it. Or only think it? She was not sure. Nor why she could not carry through to the end that which had brought her here—that she did not understand either.

Dark—and her hands were bound. There were men struggling. One went down with an arrow through him. Then cries of triumph. Someone came to her through shadows. She could see only mail—a sword—

Then she was pinned down by a heavy hand. She heard laughter, evil laughter which scorched her, though her body shivered as the last of her clothing was ripped away. Once more—

NO! She would not remember it all! She would not! They could not make her—but they did. Then she was back in the here and now. And she saw Trystan fighting his stumbling, hopeless battle, knew him again for what he was.

"The sword—take from him the sword!"

Hertha lurched to her feet. The sword—she must get the sword. Then he, too, would learn what it meant to be helpless and shamed and—and what? Dead? Did the Toads intend to kill him?

"Will you kill him?" She asked them. She had never foreseen the reckoning to be like this.

"The sword!"

They did not answer, merely spurred her to their will. Death? No, she was certain they did not mean his death. At least not death such as her kind knew it. And—but—

"The sword!"

In her mind that order was a painful lash, meant to send her unthinking to their service. But it acted otherwise, alerting her to a new sense of peril. She had evoked that which had no common meeting with her kind. Now she realized she had loosed that which not even the most powerful man or woman she knew might meddle with. Trystan could deserve the worse she was able to pull upon him. But that must be the worst by men's standards—not this!

Her left hand went to the bag of Gunnora's herbs where it rested betwen her swelling breasts. Her right groped on the ground, closed about a stone. Since she touched the herb bag that voice was no longer a pain in her head. It faded like a far-off calling. She readied the stone—

Trystan watched that swinging hand. His sword arm ached up into his shoulder. He was sure every moment he would lose control. Hertha bent, tore at the lacing of her bodice so that herb bag swung free. Fiercely she rubbed it back and forth on the stone. What so pitiful an effort might do—

She threw the rock through the murky air, struck against that blue hand. It changed direction, made a dart past him. Knowing that this might be his one chance, Trystan brought down the sword with all the force he could muster on the tentacle which supported the hand.

The blade passed through as if what he saw had no substance, had been woven of his own fears. There was a burst of palid light. Then the lumpish hand, that which supported it, was gone.

In the same moment he discovered he could move and staggered back. Then a hand fell upon his arm, jerking him in the same direction. He flailed out wildly at what could only be an enemy's hold, broke it. There was a cry and he turned his head.

A dark huddle lay at the foot of the door frame stone. Trystan advanced the sword point, ready, as strength flowed once more into him, to meet this new attack. The bundle moved, a white hand clutched at the pillar, pulled.

His bemused mind cleared. This was a woman! Not only that, but what had passed him through the air had not been flung at him, but at the hand. She had been a friend and not an enemy in that moment.

Now from behind he heard a new sound, like the hiss of a disturbed serpent. Or there might be more than one snake voicing hate. He gained the side of the woman, with the standing rocks at his back, looked once more at the center space.

That tentacle which had vanished at the sword stroke might be gone, but there were others rising. And this time those did not unite to form hands, but rather each produced something like unto a serpent head. And they arose in such numbers that no one man could hope to front them all. Though he must try.

Once more he felt a light weight upon his shoulder, he glanced to the side. The woman was standing, one hand tight to her breast, the other resting on his upper arm now. Her hood over-shadowed her face so he could not see that. But he could hear the murmur of her voice even through the hissing of the pseudo-serpents. Though he could not understand the words, there was a rhythmatic flow as if she chanted a battle song for his encouragement.

One of the serpent lengths swung at them, he used the sword. At its touch the thing vanished. But one out of dozens, what was that? Again his arm grew heavy, he found movement difficult.

Trystan tried to shake off the woman's hold, not daring to take hand from his sword to repell her.

"Loose me!" he demanded, twisting his body.

She did not obey, nor answer. He heard only that murmur of sound. There was a pleading note in it, a frantic pleading, he could feel her urgency, as if she begged of some one aid for them both.

Then from here her fingers dug into his shoulder muscles, there spread downward along his arm, across his back and chest, a warmth, a loosing—not of her hold, but of the bonds laid on him here. And within the center space the snake heads darted with greater vigor. Now and then two met in midair, and when they did they instantly united, becoming larger.

These darted forth, striking at the two by the gate, while Trystan cut and parried. And they moved with greater speed so he was hard put to keep them off. They showed no poison fangs, nor did they even seem to have teeth within their open jaws. Yet he sensed that if those mouths closed upon him or the woman they would be utterly done.

He half turned to beat off one which had come at him

from an angle. His foot slipped and he went to one knee, the sword half out of his grasp. As he grabbed it tighter he heard a cry. Still crouched, he slewed around.

The serpent head at which he had struck had only been a ruse. For his lunge at it carried him away from the woman. Two other heads had captured her. To his horror he saw that one had fastened across her head, engulfing most of it on contact. The other had snapped its length of body about her waist. Gagged by the one on her head she was quiet, nor did she struggle as the palid lengths pulled her back to the snakes' lair. Two more reached out to fasten upon her, no longer heeding Trystan, intent on their capture.

He cried out hoarsely, was on his feet again, striking savagely at those dragging her. Then he was startled by a voice which seemed to speak within his head.

"Draw back, son of men, lest we remember our broken bargain. This is no longer your affair."

"Loose her!" Trystan cut at the tentacle about her waist. It burst into light, but another was already taking its place.

"She delivered you to us, would you save her?"

"Loose her!" He did not stop to weigh the right or wrong of what had been said, he only knew that he could not see the woman drawn to that which waited. That he might not do and remain a man. He thrust again.

The serpents' coils were moving faster, drawing back into the hexagon. Trystan could not even be sure she still lived, not with that dreadful thing upon her head. She hung limp, not fighting.

"She is ours! Go you—lest we take more for feasting."

Trystan wasted no breath in argument, he leaped to the left, mounting the curb of the hexagon. There he slashed into the coils which pulled at the woman. His arms were weak, he could hardly raise the sword, even two-handed, and bring it down. Yet still he fought stubbornly to cut her free. And little by little he thought that he was winning.

Now he noted that where the coils tightened about her they did not touch her hand where it still rested clasping something between her breasts. So he strove the more to cut the coils below, severing the last as her head and shoulders were pulled over the edge of the curb.

Then it seemed that, tug though they would, the tentacles could not drag her wholly in. As they fought to do so Trystan had his last small grant of time. He now hewed those which imprisoned her head and shoulders. He saw those rising for new holds. But, as she so lay, to do their will they must cross across her breast to attack, and that they apparently could not do.

Wearily he raised the blade and brought it down again, each time sure he could not do so again. But at last there was a moment when she was free of them all. He flung out his left hand, clasped here where it lay between her breasts, heaved her back and away.

There was a sharp hissing from the serpent things. They writhed and twisted. But more and more they sank to the ground, rolled there feebly. He got the woman on his shoulder, tottered back, still facing the enemy, readied as best he could be for another attack.

V

It would seem that the enemy was spent, at least the snakes did not strike outward again. Watching them warily, Trystan retreated, dared to stop and rest with the woman. He leaned above her to touch her cheek. To his fingers the flesh was cold, faintly clammy. Dead? Had the air been choked from her?

He burrowed beneath the edges of her hood, sought the pulse in her throat. He could find none, so he tried to lay his hand directly above her heart. In doing so he had to break her grip on what lay between her breasts. When he touched a small bag there, a throbbing, a warmth spread up his hand, so he jerked hastily away, before he realized this was not a danger but a source of energy and life.

Her heart still beat. Best get her well away while those things in the hexagon were quiescent. For he feared their defeat was only momentary.

Trystan dared to sheath his sword, leaving both arms free to carry the woman. For all the bulk of her cloak and clothing, she was slender, less than the weight he had expected.

Now his retreat was that of a coastal sea crab, keeping part attention on the stew pot of blue light at his back, as well as on the footing ahead. And he drew a full breath again only when he had put two rings of the standing stones between him and the evil those guarded.

Nor was he unaware that there was still something dragging on him, trying to force him to face about. That he battled with a firm will and his sense of self preservation, his teeth set, a grimace of effort stiffening mouth and jaw.

One by one he pushed past the standing stones. As he went the way grew darker, the weird light fading. He was beginning to fear that he could no longer trust his own sight. Twice he found himself off the road, making a detour around a pillar which seemed to sprout before him, heading so back the way he had come.

Thus he fought both the compulsion to return and the tricks of vision, learning to fasten his attention on some point only a few steps ahead, and wait until he had passed that before he set another goal.

He came at last, the woman resting over his shoulder, into the clean night, the last of the stones behind him. Now he was weak, so weary that he might have made a twenty-four hour march and fought a brisk skirmish at the end of it. He slipped to his knees, lowered his burden to the surface of the old road, where, in the open, the wind had scoured the snow away.

There was no moon, the cloud cover was heavy. The woman was now only a dark bulk. Trystan squatted on his heels, his hands dangling loose between his knees, and tried to think coherently.

Of how he had come up here he had no memory at all. He had gone to bed in the normal manner at the inn, first waking to danger when he faced the crawling light in the hexagon. That he had also there fought a danger of the old time he had no doubt at all. But what had drawn him there?

He remembered the forcing open of the inn window to look up slope. Had that simple curiosity of his been the trigger for this adventure? But that those of the inn could live unconcerned so close to such a peril—he could hardly believe that. Or because they had lived here so long, were the descendants of men rooted in Grimmerdale, had they developed an immunity to dark forces?

But what had the thing or things in the hexagon said? That she who lay here had delivered him to them. If so—why? Trystan hunched forward on his knees, twitched aside the hood edge, stooping very close to look at her. Though it was hard to distinguish more than just the general outline of her features in this limited light.

Suddenly her body arched away from him. She screamed with such terror as startled him as she pushed against the road under her, her whole attitude one of such agony of fear as held him motionless. Somehow she got to her feet. She had only screamed that once, now he saw her arms move under the hindering folds of her cloak. The moon broke in a thin sliver from under the curtain of the cloud, glinted on what she held in her hand.

Steel swung in an arc for him. Trystan grappled with her before that blade bit into his flesh. She was like a wild thing, twisting, thrusting, kicking, even biting as she fought him. At length he handled her as harshly as he would a man, striking his fist against the side of her chin so her body went limply once more to the road.

There was nothing to do but take her back to the inn. Had her experience in that nest of standing stones turned her brain to see enemies all about her? Resigned, he ripped a strip from the hem of her cloak, tied her hands together. Then he got her up so she lay on his back, breathing shallowly, inert. So carrying her he slipped and slid, pushed with difficulty through the scrub to the valley below and the inn.

What the hour might be he did not know, but there was a night lantern burning above the door and that swung open beneath his push. He staggered over to the fireplace, dropped his burden by the hearth and reached for wood to build up the blaze, wanting nothing now so much as to be warm again.

Hertha's head hurt. The pain seemed to be in the side of her face. She opened her eyes. There was a dim light, but not that wan blue. No, this was flame glow. Someone hunched at the hearth setting wood lengths with expert skill to rebuild a fire. Already there was warmth which her body welcomed. She tried to sit up. Only to discover that her wrists were clumsily bound together. Then she tensed, chilled by fear, watching intently him who nursed the fire.

His head was turned from her, she could not see his face, but she had no doubts that it was Trystan. And her last memory—him looming above her, hands outstretched—to take her again as he had that other time! Revulsion sickened her so she swallowed hurriedly lest she spew openly on the floor. Cautiously she looked around. This was the large room of the inn, he must have carried her back. That he might take pleasure in a better place than the icy cold of the old road? But if he tried that she could scream, fight—surely someone would come—

He looked to her now, watching her so intently that she felt he read easily every one of her confused thoughts.

"I shall kill you," she said distinctly.

"As you tried to do?" He asked that not as if it greatly mattered, but as if he merely wondered.

"Next time I shall not turn aside!"

He laughed. And with that laughter for an instant he seemed another man, one younger, less hardened by time and deeds. "You did not turn aside this time, mistress, I had a hand in the matter." Then that half smile which had come with the laughter faded, and he regarded her with narrowed eyes, his mouth tight set lip to lip.

Hertha refused to allow him to daunt her and glared back. Then he said:

"Or are you speaking of something else, mistress? Something which happened before you drew steel on me? Was that—that *thing* right? Did I march to its lair by your doing?"

Somehow she must have given away the truth by some fraction of change he read in her face. He leaned forward and gripped her by the shoulders, dragging her closer to him in spite of her struggles, holding her so they were squarely eye to eye.

"Why? By the Sword Hand of Karther the Fair, why? What did I ever do to you, girl, to make you want to push me into that maw? Or would any man have sufficed to feed those pets? Are they your pets, or your masters? Above all, how comes humankind to deal with *them*? And if you so deal, why did you break their spell to aid me? Why, and why, and why?"

He shook her, first gently, and then, with each question, more harshly, so that her head bobbed on her shoulders and she was weak in his hands. Then he seemed to realize that she could not answer him, so he held her tight as if he must read the truth in her eyes as well as hear it from her lips.

"I have no kinsman willing to call you to a sword reckoning," she told him wearily. "Therefore I must deal as best I can. I sought those who might have justice—"

"Justice! Then I was not just a random choice for some purpose of theirs! Yet, I swear by the Nine Words of Min, I have never looked upon your face before. Did I in some battle slay close kin—father, brother, lover? But how may that be? Those I fought were the invaders. They had no women save those they rift from the dales. And would any daleswoman extract vengeance for one who was her master-by-force? Or is it that, girl? Did they take you and then you found a lord to your liking among them, forgetting your own blood?"

If she could have Hertha would have spat full in his face for that insult. And he must have read her anger quickly.

"So that is not it. Then why? I am no ruffler who goes about picking quarrels with comrades. Nor have I ever taken any woman who came not to me willingly——"

"No?" She found speech at last, in a wrath-hot rush of words. "So you take no woman unwillingly, brave hero? What of three months since on the road to Lethendale? Is it too usual a course of action with you that it can be so lightly put out of mind?"

Angry and fearful though she was, she could see in his expression genuine surprise.

"Lethendale?" he repeated. "Three months since? Girl, I have never been that far north. As to three months ago——I was Marshal of Forces for Lord Ingrim before he fell at the siege of the port."

He spoke so earnestly that she could almost have believed him, had not that bowguard on his wrist proved him false.

"You lie! Yes, you may not know my face. It was in darkness you took me, having overrun the invaders who had first made me captive. My brother's men were all slain. For me they had other plans. But when aid came——then still I was for the taking——as you proved, Marshal!" She made of that a name to be hissed.

"I tell you, I was at the port!" He had released her and she backed against the settle, leaving a good space between them.

"You would swear before a Truth Stone it was me? You know my face, then?"

"I would swear, yes. As for your face——I do not need that. It was in the dark you had your will of me. But there is one proof I carry ever in my mind since that time."

He raised his hand, rubbing fingers along the old scar on his chin, the fire gleamed on the bowguard. That did not match the plainness of his clothing, how could anyone forget seeing it?

"That proof being?"

"You wear it on your wrist, in plain sight. Just as I saw it then, ravisher——your bowguard!"

He held his wrist out, studying the band, "Bowguard! So that is your proof, that made you somehow send me to the Toads." He was half smiling again, but this time cruelly and with no amusement. "You did send me there, did you not?" He reached forward and, before she could dodge, pulled the hood fully from her head, stared at her.

"What have you done with the toad face, girl? Was that some trick of paint, or some magicking you laid on yourself? Much you must have wanted me to so despoil your own seeming to carry through your plan."

She raised her bound hands, touched her cheeks with cold fingers. This time there was no mirror, but if he said the loathesome spotting was gone, then it must be so.

"They did it—" she said, only half comprehending. She had pictured this meeting many times, imagined him saying this or that. He must be very hardened in such matters to hold to this pose of half amused interest.

"They? You mean the Toads? But now tell me why, having so neatly put me in their power, you were willing to risk your life in my behalf? That I can not understand. For it seems to me to traffic with such as abide up that hill is a fearsome thing and one which only the desperate would do. Such desperation is not lightly turned aside—so—why did you save me, girl?"

She answered with the truth. "I do not know. Perhaps because the hurt being mine, the payment should also be mine—that, a little, I think. But even more—" she paused so long he prodded her.

"But even more, girl?"

"I could not in the end leave even such a man as you to *them!*"

"Very well, that I can accept. Hate and fear and despair can drive us all to bargains we repent of later. You made one and then found you were too human to carry it through. Then later on the road you chose to try with honest steel and your own hand—"

"You—you would have taken me—again!" Hertha forced out the words. But the heat in her cheeks came not from the fire but from the old shame eating her.

"So that's what you thought? Perhaps, given the memories you carry, it was natural enough." Trystan nodded. "But now it is your turn to listen to me, girl. Item first—I have never been to Lethendale, three months ago, three years ago— never! Second: this which you have come to judge me on," he held the wrist closer, using the fingers of his other hand to tap upon it. "I did not have three months ago. When the invaders were close pent in the port during the last siege, we had many levies from the outlands come to join us. They had mopped up such raiding bands as had been caught out of there when we moved in to besiege.

"A siege is mainly a time of idleness, and idle men amuse themselves in various ways. We had only to see that the enemy did not break out along the shores while we waited for the coasting ships from Handelsburg and Vennesport to arrive to carry them from the sea. There were many games of chance played during that waiting. And, though I am supposed by most to be a cautious man, little given to such amusements, I was willing to risk a throw now and then.

"This I so won. He who staked it was like Urre, son to some dead lord, with naught but ruins and a lost home to return to if and when the war ended. Two days later he was killed in one of the sorties the invaders now and then made. He had begged me to hold this so that when luck ran again in his way he might buy it back, for it was one of the treasures of his family. In the fighting I discovered it was not only decorative, but useful. Since he could not redeem it, being dead, I kept it—to my disfavor it would seem. As for the boy—I do not even know his name—for they called him by some nickname. He was befuddled with drink half the time, being one of the walking dead—"

"Walking dead?" His story carried conviction, not only his words but his tone, and the straight way he told it.

"That is what I call them. High Hallack has them in many—some are youngsters such as Urre, the owner of this," again he smoothed the guard. "Others are old enough to be their fathers. The dales have been swept with fire and sword. Those which were not invaded have been bled of their men, of their crops—to feed both armies. This is a land which can now go two ways. It can sink into nothingness from exhaustion, or there can rise new leaders to restore and with will can courage build again.

It seemed to Hertha that he no longer spoke to her, but rather voiced his own thoughts. As for her, there was a kind of emptiness within, as if something she carried had been rift from her. That thought sent her bound hands protectively to her belly.

The child within her—who had been its father? One of the lost ones, some boy who had had all taken from him and so became a dead man with no hope in the future, one without any curb upon his appetites. Doubtless he had lived for the day only, taken ruthlessly all offered during that short day. Thinking so, she again sensed that queer light feeling. She had not lost the child, this child which Gunnora promised would be hers alone. What she had lost was the driving need for justice which had brought her to Grimmerdale—to traffic with the Toads.

Hertha shuddered, cold to her bones in spite of her cloak, of the fire. What had she done in her blindness, her hate and horror? Almost she had delivered an innocent man to that she dared not now think upon. What has saved her from that at the very last, throw that stone rubbed with Gunnora's talisman? Some part of her refusing to allow such a foul crime?

And what could she ever say to this man who had now turned his head from her, was looking into the flames as if therein he could read message runes? She half raised her bound hands, he looked about with a real smile from which she shrank as she might from a blow, remembering how it might have been with him at this moment.

"There is no need for you to go bound. Or do you still thirst for my blood?" He caught her hands, pulled at the cloth tying them.

"No," Hertha answered in a low voice. "I believe you. He whom I sought is now dead."

"Do you regret that death came not at your hand?"

She stared down at her fingers resting again against her middle, wondering dully what would become of her now. Would she remain a tavern wench, should she crawl back to Kuno? No! At that her head went up again, pride returned.

"I asked, are you sorry you did not take your knife to my gamester?"

"No."

"But still there are dark thoughts troubling you—"

"Those are none of your concern." She would have risen, but he put out a hand to hold her where she was.

"There is an old custom. If a man draw a maid from dire danger, he has certain rights—"

For a moment she did not understand, when she did her bruised pride strengthened her to meet his eyes.

"You speak of maids—I am not such."

His indrawn breath made a small sound, but one loud in the silence between them. "So that was the why! You are no farm or tavern wench are you? So you could not accept what he had done to you. But have you no kinsman to ride for your honor?"

She laughed raggedly. "Marshal, my kinsman had but one wish, that I submit to ancient practices among women so that he would not be shamed before his kind. Having done so I would have been allowed to dwell by sufferance in my own home, being reminded not more than perhaps thrice daily of his great goodness."

"And this you would not do. But with your great hate against him who fathered what you carry——"

"No!" Her hands went to that talisman of Gunnora's. "I have been to the shrine of Gunnora. She has promised me my desire, the child I bear will be mine wholly, taking nothing from *him!*"

"And did she also send you to the Toads?"

Hertha shook her head. "Gunnora guards life. I knew of the Toads from old tales. I went to them in my blindness and they gave me that which I placed in your bed to draw you to them. Also they changed my face in some manner. But—that is no longer so?"

"No. Had I not known your cloak, I should not have known you. But this thing in my bed—Stay you here and wait. Only promise me this, should I return as one under orders, bar the door in my face and keep me here at all cost!"

"I promise."

He went with the light footed tread of one who had learned to walk softly in strange places because life might well depend upon it. Now that she was alone her mind returned to the matter of what could come to her with the morn. Who would give her refuge—save perhaps the Wise Women of Lethendale. It might be that this Marshal would escort her there. Though what did he owe her, except such danger as she did not want to think on. But although her thoughts twisted and turned she saw no answer except Lethendale. Perhaps Kuno would some day—no! She would make no plan leading in that path!

Trystan was back holding two sticks such as were used to kindle brazier flames. Gripped between their ends was the pebble she had brought from the Toads' hold. As he reached the fire he hurled that bit of rock into the heart of the blaze.

He might have poured oil upon the flames so fierce was the answer as the pebble fell among the logs. Both shrank back.

"That trap is now set at naught," he observed. "I would not have any other fall into it.

She stiffened, guessing what he thought of her for the setting of the same trap.

"To say I am sorry is only mouthing words, but——"

"To one with such a burden, lady, I can return that I understand. When one is driven by a lash one takes any way to free oneself. And in the end you did not suffer that I be taken."

"Having first thrust you well into the trap! Also—you should have let them take me then as they wished. It would only have been fitting."

"Have done!" He brought his fist down on the seat of the settle beside which he knelt. "Let us make an end to what is past. It is gone. To cling to this wrong or that, keep it festering in mind and heart, is to cripple one. Now, lady," she detected a new formality in his voice, "where do you go, if not to your brother's house? It is not in your mind to return there, I gather."

She fumbled with the talisman. "In that you are right. There is but one place left—the Wise Women of Lethendale. I can beg shelter from them." She wondered if he would offer the escort she had no right to ask, but his next question surprised her.

"Lady, when you came hither, you came by the Old Road over ridge, did you not?"

"That is so. To me it seemed less dangerous than the open highway. It has, by legend, those who sometimes use it, but I deemed those less dangerous than my own kind."

"If you came from that direction you must have passed through Nordendale—what manner of holding is it?"

She had no idea why he wished such knowledge, but she told him of what she had seen of that leaderless dale, the handful of people there deep sunk in a lethargy in which they clung to the ruins of what had once been thriving life. He listened eagerly to what she told him.

"You have a seeing eye, lady, and have marked more than most, given such a short time to observe. Now listen to me, for this may be a matter of concern to both of us in the future. It is in my mind that Nordendale needs a lord, one to give the people heart, rebuild what man and time have wasted. I have come north seeking a chance to be not just my own man, but to have a holding. I am not like Urre who was born to a hall, and drinks and wenches now to forget what ill tricks fortune plays.

"Who my father was—" he shrugged, "I never heard my mother say. That he was of no common blood, that I knew, though in later years she drudged in a merchant's house before the coming of the invaders for bread to our mouths and clothing for our backs. When I was yet a boy I knew that the only way I might rise was through this—" he touched the hilt of his sword. "The merchant guild welcome no nameless man, but for a sword and a bow there is alway a ready market. So I set about learning the skills of war as thoroughly as any man might. Then came the invasion and I went from Lord to Lord, becoming at last Marshal of Archers. Yet always before me hung the thought that in such a time of upheaval, with the old families being killed out, this was my chance.

"Now there are masterless men in plenty, too restless after years of killing to settle back behind any plough. Some will turn outlaw readily, but with a half dozen of such at my back, I can take a dale which lies vacant of rule, such as this Nordendale. The people there need a leader, I am depriving none of lawful inheritance, but will keep the peace and defend it against outlaws—for there will be many such now. There are men here, passing through Grimmerdale, willing to be hired for such a purpose. Enough so I can pick and choose at will."

He paused and she read in his face that this indeed was the great moving wish of his life. When he did not continue she asked a question:

"I can see how a determined man can do this thing. But how does it concern me in any way?"

He looked to her straightly. She did not understand the full meaning of what she saw in his eyes.

"I think we are greatly alike, lady. So much so that we could walk the same road, to the profit of both. No, I do not ask an answer now. Tomorrow—" he got to his feet stretching, "no, today. I shall speak to those men I have marked. If they are willing to take liege oath to me, we shall ride to Lethendale, where you may shelter as you wish for a space. It is not far—"

"By horse," she answered in relief, "perhaps two days west."

"Good enough. Then having left you there, I shall go to Nordendale—and straightway that shall cease to be masterless. Allow me say three score days, and I shall come riding again to Lethendale. Then you shall give me your answer as to whether our roads join or no."

"You forget," her hands pressed upon her belly, "I am no maid, nor widow, and yet I carry—"

"Have you not Gunnora's promise upon that subject? The child will be wholly yours. One welcome holds for you both."

She studied his face, determined to make sure if he meant

that. What she read there—she caught her breath, her hands rising to her breast, pressing hard upon the talisman.

"Come as you promise to Lethendale," she said in a low voice. "You shall be welcome and have your answer in good seeming."

London Bridge

"Just another deader—" Sim squatted to do a search.

Me, I don't dig deaders much. No need to. There're plenty of den-ins and stores to rummage if you need a pricker or some cover-ups. Of course, I took that stunner I found by what was left of the dead Fuzz's hand. But that was different, he wasn't *wearing* it. Good shooter too; I got more'n a dozen con-rats before it burned out on me. Now I didn't want to waste any time over a deader, and I said so, loud and clear.

Sim told me to cool the air. He came back with a little tube in his hand. I took one look at that and gave him a sidesweep, took his wrist at just the right angle. The tube flew as straight as a beam across the stalled wiggle-walk and into a blow duct.

"Now what in blue boxes did you want to do that for?" Sim demanded. Not that he squared up to me over it. By now he knows he can't take me and it's no use to try. "I could have traded that to an Up—real red crowns and about ten of them!"

"What trade? Those hazeheads haven't got anything we want and can't get for ourselves."

"Sure, sure. But it's kinda fun showing them a haul like that and seeing 'em get all hot."

"Try it once too often and you'll take a pricker where it won't do you any good. Anyway, we're not here to scrounge."

The city's big. I don't know anybody who's ever gotten all over it. You would walk your feet raw trying since all the wiggle-walks cut out. And some of it's deathtraps—what with Ups who have lost any thinking stuff which ever was between their dirty ears, or con-rats. Those get bigger and bolder every time we have a roundup to kill them off. The arcs have shut off in a lot of places, and we use flashes. But those don't show much and they die awfully quick. So we don't go off the regular paths much. Except because of this matter of the Rhyming Man, which was why Sim and I were trailing now. I didn't much like the look ahead. A lot of arcs were gone, and the shadows were thick between those which were left. Anything could hide in a doorway or window to jump us.

We're immune, of course, or we wouldn't be kicking around at all. When the last plague hit, it carried off most of the cits. All the oldies went. I must have been nine—ten—I don't know. You forget about time where the ticks can tell you the hour but not the day or year. I had a good tick on my wrist right now, but it couldn't tell me what day it was, or how many years had gone by. I grew a lot, and sometimes when I got a fit to do something different, I went to the lib and cut into one of the teachers. Most of the T-casts there didn't make much sense. But I'd found a couple in the histro-division on primitives (whatever those were) which had some use. There was Fanna—she got excited about some casts which taught you about how to take care of someone who got hurt. Because of that Sim was walking beside me today. But, as I say, most of the stuff on the tapes was useless to us now.

There are twenty of us, or were 'til the Rhyming Man came around. Some don't remember how it was before the plague. They were too young then. And none of us remember back to before the pollut-die-off. Some of us have paired off for den-in—Lacy and Norse, Bet and Tim. But me, I'm not taking to den-in with some fem yet. There's too much to see and do, and a guy wants to be free to take off when he feels like it. Course I have to keep an eye on Marsie. She's my sister—she was just a baby in the plague days—and she's still young enough to be a nuisance—like believing in the Rhyming Man. Like he's something out of a tape. I mean—that he's going to take good children Outside.

Maybe there was an Outside once. There's so much about it in the tapes, and why would anyone want to spend good time making up a lot of lies and taping them? But to go Outside—no one has for longer than I've been around.

Marsie, she's like me, she digs the tapes. I can take her with me, and she'll sit quiet, not getting up and running out like most littles just when I get interested. No, she'll sit quiet with a teacher. I found some tapes of made-up stories—they showed the Outside and animals moving on their own and making noises before you squeezed them. Marsie, she had a fur cat I found and she lugged it everywhere. She wanted it to come alive and kept thinking she could find a way to make it. Kept asking Fanna how you could do that. Littles get awfully set on things sometimes and near burn your ears out asking why—why—why—

That was before the Rhyming Man. We heard about him later. Our territory runs to the double wiggle-walk on Balor, and there we touch on Bart's crowd's hangout. They're like us—not Ups. Once in a while we have a rap-sing with them. We get together for con-rat roundups and things like that. But we don't live cheek by cheek. Well, some time back Bart came over on a mission—a real important search. He had this weirdo story about a couple of their littles going off with the Rhyming Man.

Seems like one of his fems saw part of it. She must have been solid clear through between the ears not to guess it was trouble. She heard his singing first, and she thought someone was running a tape, only it didn't sound right. Said the littles were poking around down in the streets—she could see them through a window. All of a sudden they stood up and stopped what they were doing, then went running off. She didn't think of it again—because Bart's crowd's like us, they don't have any Ups in their territory. He keeps scouts out to make sure of that.

But when it came feed time, those two didn't show. Then the fem shoots out what she saw and heard. So they send out a mission, armed. Though Bart couldn't see how Ups could have got through.

Those littles, they never did find them. And the next day two more were gone. Bart rounded them up, kept them under cover. But three more went and with them the fem he had set with a stunner on guard. So now he wanted to know what gives, and if we had anything to tell him. He was really sky climbing and shadow watching by the time he got to us. Said now a couple more fems were missing. But he had two guys who had seen the Rhyming Man.

What Bart told us sounded like an Up was loose. But for an Up to do the same thing all the time, that wasn't in curve at all. Seems he wore this bright suit—all sparkling—and danced along singing and waving. Bart's boys took straight shots at him (with burners). And they swore that the rays just bounced off him, didn't even shake him.

We organized for a roundup quick and combed as much as you can comb with all the den-ins up and down. There was nothing at all. Only, when we came back—two more littles were gone. So Bart's crowd packed up and moved over to our side of the double wiggle-path and settled in a block front, downside from our place. But he was tearing mad, and now he spent most of his time over in his old territory hunting. He was like an Up with a new tube of pills, thinking only of one thing, getting the Rhyming Man.

Though right now I could understand it, how he felt, I mean, because Marsie was gone. We'd warned all our littles and fems good after Bart told us the score. They weren't to go on any search—not without a guy with them. But Marsie had gone to the tape lib this morning with Kath and Don. Don came back by himself saying they had heard some funny singing and that the girls had run away so he could not find them.

We rounded up all the littles and fems and posted a guard like an Up raid was on. Jak and Tim took out one way, Sim and I the other. The lib was empty. We searched there first. And whoever had been there couldn't have doubled back toward us. Too many had the path in good sight. So we went the other way and that took us into deep territory. Only I knew we were going right by what I found just a little while ago and had tucked in my belt now—Marsie's cat.

And if she'd dropped *that*—! I kept my hand on my pricker. Maybe you couldn't finish the Rhyming Man with a burner, but let me get close enough, and I'd use a pricker and my own two hands!

The deep territories are places to make a guy keep watching over his shoulder. They're always so quiet, and you keep coming across deaders from the old days, mostly just bones and such—but still they're deaders. And all those windows—you get an itchy feeling between your shoulders that someone just looked at you and ducked away when you turned around. With a hundred million places for a loony Up to hide out we had no chance at all of finding him. Only I wasn't going to give up as long as I could keep walking—knowing he had Marsie.

Sim had been marking our way. It's been done—getting lost—even keeping to paths we know. But we were coming into a place I'd never seen, big buildings with straight walls, no windows in them. There were a couple of wide doors—and one was open.

"Listen!" Sim pawed my arm. But he needn't have, I heard it too.

> *London bridge is broken down.*
> *Broken down, broken down,*
> *My fair lady.*
>
> *How shall we build it up again?*
> *Up again, up again?*
> *My fair lady.*
>
> *Build it up with silver and gold.*
> *Silver and gold, silver and gold.*
> *My fair lady.*

I had it now, pointed with my pricker—"In there." Sim nodded and we went through the open door.

> *Silver and gold will be stole away,*
> *Stole away, stole away,*
> *My fair lady.*

Odd, the sound didn't seem to get any louder, but it wasn't fading away either, just about the same. We were in a big wide hall with a lot of openings off on either side. There were lights here, but so dim you had to take a chance on your path.

> *Build it up with iron and steel,*
> *Iron and steel, iron and steel,*
> *My fair lady.*

Still ahead as far as I could tell.

> *Iron and steel will rust away,*
> *Rust away, rust away,*
> *My fair lady.*
>
> *Build it up with wood and clay,*
> *Wood and clay, wood and clay.*
> *My fair lady.*

All at once the singing was loud and clear. We came out on a balcony above a place so big that most of the den-ins I knew could be packed into it with room to spare. There was light below but it shone up from the floor in a way I had never seen before.

"There he is!" Again I didn't need Sim to point him out. I saw the blazing figure. Blaze he did, blue and gold, like he was a fire, but the wrong color. And he was dancing back and forth as he sang:

> *Wood and clay will wash away,*
> *Wash away, wash away,*
> *My fair lady.*
>
> *Build it up with stone so strong,*
> *Stone so strong, stone so strong.*
> *My fair lady.*
>
> *Hurrah, it will hold for ages long,*
> *Ages long, ages long.*
> *My fair lady.*

At the end of each verse he would bend forward in a jerky little bow, and those listening would clap their hands and laugh.

Because Marsie and Kath were not the only littles down there. There were four others I had never seen before. And none of them were Up brats.

The Rhyming Man jigged around. When he stopped and they all yelled for more, he shook his head and waved his hands as if he couldn't talk but could make motions they could understand. They all got up and formed a line and began to hop and skip after him. The floor was all laid out in squares of different colors. And, as those were stepped on, lights flashed underneath. It was as if the littles were playing a game. But I couldn't understand it.

Then the Rhyming Man began that singing again:

> *Erry, Orrey, Ickery Ann*
> *Fillison, follison, Nicholas John*
> *Queevy, quavey, English Navy*
> *One, two, three, out goes—*
> *She, he, she, he, she, she, he!*

Like he was shooting off a burner, he pointed his finger at each little in line. And, as he did so (it was like an Up dream), they just weren't there any more!

Marsie! I couldn't jump over that balcony. I'd go splat

down there, and that wouldn't do Marsie any good, if she was still alive. But I began running along, trying to find some way down, and there was no way down. Only what would I do when I got there, because now the Rhyming Man was gone also.

Sim pounded along behind me. We were about halfway around that place—still no way down. Then I saw it ahead and I guess I more fell than footed it down those inner stairs. When I came charging out on the empty floor—nothing, nothing at all!

I even got down and felt the squares where they had been standing, pounded on those, thinking those might be doors which opened to drop them through. But the blocks were tight. Then I began to wonder if I had tripped out like an Up—without any pills. I just sat there holding my head, trying to think.

"I saw them, they were here—then they weren't." Sim kicked at one of the squares. "Where did they go?"

If he saw it, too, then I hadn't tripped. But there had to be an answer. I made myself try to remember everything I had seen—that crazy song, them marching, then another crazy song—

I stood up. "They got out somehow. And if there's a door it can be opened." I couldn't just be wild mad, I had to think, and straight now. No use of just wanting to grab the Rhyming Man and pound his head up and down on the floor.

"Listen here, Sim. We've got to find out what happened. I'm staying here to look around. You cut back and get the rest of the guys, bring them here. When he comes out, I want that Rhyming Man!"

"Staying here by yourself mightn't be too good an idea, Lew."

"I can take cover. But I don't want to miss him when he comes back. Then I can trail him until you catch up." It might not be too bright, but it was the best plan I had. And I intended going over that flooring until something did happen and we could find the way in to wherever Marsie and the rest of the littles were.

Sim went off. I knew he was glad to get out of that place, but he'd be back. Sim had never back-footed yet on any mission. Meanwhile, I'd better get busy.

I closed my eyes. Sometimes if you think about a thing hard enough you see it like a picture in your mind. Now— the six littles—and then, in front of them, the Rhyming Man jiggling back and forth, his suit all bright and shining—singing about London bridge—

Opening my eyes again I studied the blocks. The littles had been sitting, or squatting, there, there, and there. And he had been over there. I raised my hand to point as if I were showing it all to someone else.

London bridge? London was another city—somewhere—not near here. When the cities were all sealed against the bad air—well, for a while they talked to each other with T-casts. Then it wasn't any use—every one had it all just as bad.

Cities died when their breathers broke—those that had been the worst off in the beginning. In others—who knows what happened? Maybe we were lucky here, maybe we weren't. But our breathers had kept on going—only the plaques hit and people died. After all the oldies died, there was a lot more air.

But London was a city once. London bridge? A bridge to another city? But how could one step off a block onto a bridge you couldn't see, nor feel? Silver and gold—we wore silver and gold things—got them out of the old stores. My tick was gold.

The whole song made a kind of sense, not that that helped any. But that other thing he had sung, after they had moved around on the blocks—I closed my eyes trying to see that march, and I moved to the square Marsie had stood on right at the last, following the different-colored blocks just as I had seen her do.

Yeah, and I nearly lost my second skin there. Because those blocks lit up under my feet. I jumped off—no lights. So the lights had meaning. Maybe the song also—

I was almost to the block where the Rhyming Man had been, but before I reached it, he was back! He was flashing blue and gold in a way to hurt your eyes, and he just stood there looking at me. He had no stunner nor burner, not even a pricker. I could have cut him down like a con-rat. Only if I did that, I'd never get to Marsie, I had to have what was in his mind to do that.

Then he gave me one of those bows and said something, which made no more sense than you'd get out an Up high on red:

> *Higgity, piggity, my black hen—*
> *She lays eggs for gentlemen.*

I left my pricker in my belt, but that didn't mean I couldn't take him. I'm light but I'm fast, and I can take any guy in our crowd. It's mostly thinking, getting the jump on the other. He was still spouting when I dived at him.

It was like throwing myself head first into a wall. I never laid a finger on him, just bounced back and hit the floor with a bang which knocked a lot of wind out of me. There he was, standing as cool as drip ice, shaking his head a little as if he couldn't believe any guy would be so dumb as to rush him. I wanted a burner then—in the worst way. Only I haven't had one of those for a long time.

> *One, two, three, four,*
> *Five, six, seven.*
> *All good children*
> *Go to Heaven.*

> *One, two, three, four,*
> *Five, six, seven, eight,*
> *All bad children*
> *Have to wait.*

I didn't have to have it pounded into my head twice. There was no getting at him—at least not with my hands. Sitting up, I looked at him. Then I saw he was an oldie—*real* oldie. His face was all wrinkled, and on his head there was only a fringe of white hair, he was bald on top. The rest of him was all covered up with those shining clothes. I had never seen such an oldie except on a tape—it was like seeing a story walking around.

"Where's Marsie?" If the oldie was an Up, maybe he could be startled into answering me. You can do that with Ups sometimes.

> *One color, two color,*
> *Three color, four,*
> *Five color, six color,*
> *Seven color more.*
> *What color is yours?*

He pointed to me. And he seemed to be expecting some answer. Did he mean the block I was sitting on? If he did— that was red, as he could see for himself. Unless he was on pills—then it sure could be any color as far as he was concerned.

"Red," I played along. Maybe I could keep him talking until the guys got here. Not that there was much chance in that; Sim had a good ways to go.

> *You're too tall,*
> *The door's too small.*

Again he was shaking his head as if he were really sorry for me for some reason.

"Listen," I tried to be patient, like with an Up you just *had* to learn something from, "Marsie was here. You pointed at her—she was gone. Now just where did she go?"

He took to singing again:

> *Build it up with stone so strong,*
> *Stone so strong, stone so strong.*
>
> *Hurrah, it will last ages long—*
> *Ages long, ages long—*

Somehow he impressed me that behind all his queer singing there was a meaning, if I could only find it. That bit about my being too tall now—

"Why am I too tall?" I asked.

> *A.B.C.D.*
> *Tell your age to me.*

Age? Marsie was a little—small, young. That fitted. He wanted littles. I was too big, too old.

"I don't know—maybe I'm about sixteen, I guess. But I want Marsie—"

He had been jiggling from one foot to the other as if he wanted to dance right out of the hall. But still he faced me and watched me with that queer I'm-sorry-for-you look of his.

> *Seeing's believing—no, no, no!*
> *Seeing's believing, you can't go!*
> *Believing, that is best,*
> *Believing's seeing, that's the test.*

Seeing's believing, believing's seeing—I tried to sort that out.

"You mean—the littles—they can believe in something,

even though they don't see it? But me, I can't believe unless I see?"

He was nodding now. There was an eager look about him. Like one of the littles playing some trick and waiting for you to be caught. Not a mean trick, a funny, surprise one.

"And I'm too old?"

He was watching me, his head a little on one side.

> *One, two, sky blue.*
> *All out but you.*

Sky blue—Outside! But the sky hadn't been blue for years—it was dirty, poisoned. The whole world Outside was poisoned. We'd heard the warnings from the speakers every time we got close to the old sealed gates. No blue sky—ever again. And if Marsie was Outside—dying—!

I pointed to him just as he had to the littles. I didn't know his game, but I could try to play it, if that was the only way of reaching Marsie now—I had to play it!

"I'm too big, maybe, and I'm too old, maybe. But I can try this believing-seeing thing. And I'm going to keep on trying until I make it work! Either that, or I turn into an oldie like you doing it. So—"

I turned my back on him and went right back to that line of blocks up which they had gone and I started along those with him watching, his head still a little to one side as if he were listening, but not to me. Under my feet those lights flashed. All the time he watched. I was determined to show him that I meant just what I said—I was going to keep on marching up and down there—maybe till I wore a hole through the floor.

Once I went up and nothing happened. So I just turned around, went back, ready to start again.

"This time," I told him, "you say it—loud and clear—you say it just like you did the other time—when the littles went."

At first he shook his head, backed away, making motions with his hands for me to go away. But I stood right there. I was most afraid he would go himself, that I would be left in that big bare hall with no one to open the gate for me. But so far he hadn't done that vanishing bit.

" 'Orrey,' " I prompted.

Finally, he shrugged. I could see he thought I was heading into trouble. Well, now it was up to me. Believing was seeing, was it? I had to keep thinking that this was going to work for me as well as it had for the littles. I walked up those flashing blocks.

The Rhyming Man pointed his finger at me.

"Erry, Orrey, Ickery Ann."

I closed my eyes. This was going to take me to Marsie; I had to believe that was true, I hung on to that—hard.

> *Fillisan, follison, Nicholas John.*
> *Queevy, quavey, English Navy*
> *One, two, three—*

This was it! Marsie—I'm coming!

"Out goes he!"

It was awful, a twisting and turning, not outside me, but in. I kept my eyes shut and thought of Marsie and that I must get to her. Then I fell, down flat. When I opened my eyes—this—this wasn't the city!

There was a *blue sky* over me and things I had seen in the T-casts—grass that was still green and not sere and brown like in the last recordings made before they sealed the city forever. There were flowers and a bird—a real live *bird*—flying overhead.

"Amazing!"

I was still on my knees, but I moved around to face him. The Rhyming Man stood there, but that glow which hung around him back in the hall was gone. He just looked like an ordinary oldie, a real tired oldie. But he smiled and waved his hand to me.

"You give me new hopes, boy. You're the first of your age and sex. Several girls have made it, but they were more imaginative by nature."

"Where are we? And where's Marsie?"

"You're Outside. Look over there."

He pointed and I looked. There was a big grey blot—ugly looking, spoiling the brightness of the grass, the blue of the sky. You didn't want to keep looking at it.

"There's your city, the last hope of mankind, they thought, those poor stubborn fools who had befouled their world. Silver and gold, iron and steel, mud and clay—cities they've been building and rebuilding for thousands of years. Their bridge cities broke and took them along in the destruction. As for Marsie, and those you call the littles, they'll know about real stone, how to really build. You'll find them over that hill."

"And where are you going?"

He sighed and looked even tireder. "Back to play some more games, to hunt for more builders."

"Listen here," I stood up. "Just let me see Marsie, and then I'll go back, too. They'll listen to me. Why, we can bring the whole crowd, Bart's too, out—"

But he'd started shaking his head even before I was through.

"Ibbity, bibbity, sibbity, Sam.

Ibbity, bibbity, as I am—" he repeated and then added, "No going back once you're out."

"You do."

He sighed. "I am programmed to do just that. And I can only bring those ready to believe in seeing—"

"You mean, Sim, Jak, the others can't get out here—ever?"

"Not unless they believe to see. That separates the builders, those ready to begin again, from the city blindmen."

Then he was gone, just like an old arc winking out for the last time.

I started walking, down over the hill. Marsie saw me coming. She had flowers stuck in her hair, and there was a soft furry thing in her arms. She put it down to hop away before she came running.

Now we wait for those the Rhyming Man brings. (Sam and Fanna came together two days ago.) I don't know who he is, or how he works his tricks. If we see him, he never stays long, and he won't answer questions. We call him Nicholas John, and we live in London Bridge, though it's not London, nor a bridge—just a beginning.

On Writing Fantasy

ONE of the first and most common questions put to any writer is: "Where do you get your ideas?" That is sometimes difficult to answer in particulars, but in general, the one source one must rely on is reading. In fact, the writer must read widely in many fields. For my own books (unless I am dealing with some specific period of history when research becomes highly concentrated) I read anthropology, folklore, history, travel, natural history, archeology, legends, studies in magic, and similiar material, taking notes throughout.

But the first requirement for writing heroic or sword and sorcery fantasy must be a deep interest in and a love for history itself. Not the history of dates, of sweeps and empires—but the kind of history which deals with daily life, the beliefs, and aspirations of people long since dust. (And it is amazing to find such telling parallels between a more ancient world and ours, as in the letter from the young Roman officer, quoted by Jack Lindsay in *The Romans Were Here*, who was writing home for money in much the same terms as might be used by a modern G.I.) While there are many things we can readily accept in these delvings into other times, there are others we must use imagination to translate.

There we can find aids in novels—the novels of those inspired writers who seem, by some touch of magic, to have actually visited a world of the past. There are flashes of brilliance in such novels, illuminating strange landscapes and ideas. To bring to life the firelit interior of a Pictish broch (about whose inhabitants even the most industrious of modern archeologists can tell us little) is, for example, a feat of real magic.

Read such books as Price's *Made In the Middle Ages*—then turn from her accounts of the great medieval fairs to the colorful description of the Thieves' Market in Van Arnan's *The Players of Hell*.

Renault's *The King Must Die:* here in Crete, and something within the reader is satisfied that this must be close to reality. Joan Grant's Egypt of *The Eyes of Horus* and *The Lord of The Horizon,* Mundy's *Tros of Samothrace* and the *Purple Pirate*—Rome at the height of its arrogant power but as seen by a non-Roman—the wharves of Alexandria in the torchlight of night, the great sea battles, a clash of arms loud enough to stir any reader.

Turn from those to the muted despair and dogged determination against odds in Rosemary Sutcliff's Britain after the withdrawal of the last legion—the beginning of the Dark Ages—as described in *The Lantern Bearers* and *Swords in the Sunset*. This lives, moves, involves the reader in emotion.

Davis's *Winter Serpent* presents the Viking coastal raids, makes very clear what it meant to live under the shadow of the "Winged Hats." And, a little later, the glories and the grim cruelties of the Middle Ages are a flaming tapestry of color in such novels as Barringer's *Gerfalcon* and its sequel, *Joris of the Rock;* Adam's *Desert Leopard* and Graham's *Vows of the Peacock* are also excellent.

There are "historical" novels, but their history is all sensuous color, heroic action raised to the point where the reader is thoroughly ensorcelled and involved.

So history is the base, and from there to imagination, rooted in fact, sun-warmed by inspired fiction, can flower into new patterns. And those can certainly be ingenious and exciting.

The very atmosphere of some portion of the past can be carried into fantasy in a telling fashion. Take Meade's *Sword of Morningstar*, which gathers in the telling validity from the author's interest and research into the history of the Robber Barons of Germany and the Black Forest region. Beam Piper's *Lord Kavin of Otherwhen* envisions a world in which the sweep of the migrating Aryan peoples—the People of the Axe—turned east instead of west, flowing through Asia, China, to eventually colonize this continent from the west instead of the east, with an entirely different affect on history.

Though historical novels can furnish impetus for story growth, the basic need is still history. General history can be mined at will, but there are various byways which are very rich in background material.

Herrmann's *Conquest of Man*, a fat volume to open new vistas as it discusses the far range of those Bronze Age traders who set out in their small ships hugging unknown coastlines in the Atlantic, or the North Seas, or went on foot with their trains of laden donkeys into new lands. Thus he presents a wealth of new knowledge barely touched upon by the usual history book.

Four Thousand Years Ago by Bibby—a world spread of history at a single date. What were the Chinese doing when Pharaohs held the throne of Egypt? And what then was going on in Peru, Central America?

Lewis Spense's careful studies of near forgotten legend and lore in his native British Isles, *Magic Arts in Celtic Britain* and the like, are very rich in nuggets to be used.

Rees gives us *Celtic Heritage*, Uden the beautifully illustrated *Dictionary of Chivalry*, Oakeshott's *Archeology of Weapons*—page after page of information on swords, shields, any other armament your hero needs.

Desire a new godling to squat in some shadowed temple? Try *Everyman's Dictionary of Non-Classical Mythology* and be straightway amazed at all the diverse gods the men of this world bowed head to down the ages.

For the layout of a castle, plus the numeration of a proper staff to man it, try Byfield's delightful *The Glass Harmonica* (which also goes into careful detail on such matters as trolls, ogres, and the training of sorcerers); it is indispensable. And Thompson's *The Folktale*, a careful listing of the basic plot of every known tale and its many variations, is a book to keep to hand.

The professional writer does have to build up his or her own library, though the rich shelves of the public libraries await. Unfortunately, many of the volumes one wishes the most for reference are also the most expensive. But there is an answer—the remainder houses which send out at monthly or six-weeks periods catalogues of their stock. For one half, one third of the original price one can pick up such volumes when dealing with Marboro or Publishers Central Bureau. And, in recent years, the paperback house of Dover has been reissuing long out of print works in folklore, history and natural history.

So, one has the material, one has the plot—now comes the

presentation. One must make come alive for the reader what one has created in one's mind.

Rider Haggard, who was the master of the romantic action adventure at its birth, stated firmly that those who write such books must themselves live in their creations, share every hope and care of their people. And this is the truth; you can not write fantasy unless you love it, unless you yourself can believe in what you are telling. (Unfortunately, as every writer learns, that which goes on paper, in spite of all one's struggles, is never the bright and shining vision which appeared in one's mind and led one to get to work. At times a scene, a page—if one is exceedingly lucky, a chapter—may draw close to the dream, but one is always left unsatisfied with the whole.)

The approach may be direct in the use of ancient saga or legendary material without much alteration. And this can result in excellence if done by a skillful craftsman who has steeped him or herself in the subject. In this category are such outstanding books as Walton's *Island of the Mighty,* those books by Thomas Swann based on classical myths, Garner's two stories and based on ancient legends of Britain: *Weirdstone of Brisinggamen* and *Moon of Gomrath.* While Poul Anderson drew first on Scandinavian sources for *The Broken Sword,* and then on the Charlemagne cycle for *Three Hearts and Three Lions,* Emil Petaja works from a classic lesser known to the general American public when he draws from the Finish Kalevala for a series of adventures. And Sprague de Camp has given us *The Incomplete Inchanter* with its roots in Spencer's *Faerie Queen: The Land of Unreason*—Oberon's kingdom plus the legend of Barbarossa; and *The Wall of Serpents,* another presentation from the Kalevala. Nicholas Gray has turned directly to fairy tales, writing the haunting and memorable *Seventh Swan* and the amusing *Stone Cage.* The former "what happened after" in the fairy tale of the Seven Swans wherein the hero, the seventh brother of that story, is forced to adjust to living with a swan's wing in place of his arm. While in the latter, he gives a new and sprightly version of Rapunzel.

From that background of general legend comes the work of masters who are so well read in such lore that they create their own gods and sagas, heroes and mysteries. Tolkien's Middle Earth is now so deeply embedded in our realm that his name need only be mentioned to provide a mountain-tall standard against which other works will be measured perhaps for generations to come.

Lord Dunsany is another of the masters. Eddison's *Worm Oroborous* is perhaps a little mannered in style for modern taste, but his descriptions are, like Merritt's, so overflowing in color and vivid beauty they flash across one's mind in sweeps of hues and forms one readily remembers.

To sample some of these earlier writers one can at present easily turn to the series of books under the editorship of Lin Carter—issued by Ballantine—where for the first time in many years some of the older, and to this generation perhaps even unknown, writers are introduced again. Such books as *Dragons, Elves and Heroes, The Young Magicians, Golden Cities, Far* provide small tastes. But this series also reprints in full length the works of William Morris, Dunsany, Cabell and kindred writers.

Those modern writers who create their own worlds stand well when measured to these pioneers, with some pruning of the dated flourishes of another day.

Hannes Bok, who was an artist with paint and brush, as well as with pen, produced *The Sorcerer's Ship*. Using the classic saga approach of the quest we have such treats as Van Arnan's *Players of Hell* and its sequel *Wizard of Storms*. David Mason gives us two excellent examples of the careful building of an entire world detailed to the full in *Kavin's World* and *The Sorcerer's Skull*. Ursula Le Guin has *Wizard of Earthsea*, an offering which not only presents a strange island-sea planet but makes clear the training of a would-be sorcerer, and the need for self-control in handling great forces. Jack Vance explores a far future in which our almost exhausted world turns to magic in its last days in his *Dying Earth*. And Katherine Kurtz with *Deryni Rising* pictures a dramatic meeting of alien forces in a strange setting loosely based on Welsh myths.

The common pattern of most sword and sorcery tales which incline to action-adventure is a super-man hero, generally a wandering mercenary (which is an excellent device for moving your hero about). Of this company Robert Howard's Conan is perhaps the best known—unless one may list Burroughs's John Carter thus. Howard's plots may have been stereotyped, but his descriptions of sinister ruins and sharp clash of action move the stories into leadership in the field. We now have John Jakes's Brak, a Viking type wanderer whose adventures tend to get better with each book. There is also Lin Carter's Thonger of Lemuria. And the unbeatable Grey Mouser and Ffahrd whom Fritz Leiber moves about an ancient world seeming to have some parts in common with our own middle east, but highly alien in others.

From the super-man we come to Moorcock's flawed heroes who tend to have massive faults as well as abilities, swinging sometimes to evil. The Elric of the demon-souled sword, and he of the four Runestaff stories are ambivalent.

There are moments of humor in the adventures of the Grey Mouser and his companion in arms, the great northern-er Ffahrd. But Sprague de Camp, almost alone of the writers of fantasy, can handle the humorous element as a continued and integrated part of the adventure itself. His teller of tales who is also a doughty fighting man, the hero of *The Goblin Tower*, is something quite different from the humorless Conan or the stormy men of Moorcock. Only the much put-upon magician of Bellairs's *Face in the Frost* can compare with him.

Brunner's *Traveller in Black* is still another type. A troubler of the status quo, he does not fight, merely uses his own form of magic to adjust the scales of alien gods in many lands. Wandering by the demands of some strange pattern he does not understand, on a timeless mission decreed by something beyond the human, he seems to drift, and yet his adventures have all the power of straight action.

These are the heroes, but what of the heroines? In the Conan tales there are generally beautiful slave girls, one pirate queen, one woman mercenary. Conan lusts, not loves, in the romantic sense, and moves on without remembering face or person. This is the pattern followed by the majority of the wandering heroes. Witches exist, so do queens (always in need of having their lost thrones regained or shored up by the hero), and a few come alive. As do de Camp's women, the thief-heroine of *Wizard of Storm*, the young girl in the Garner books, the Sorceress of *The Island of the Mighty*. But still they remain props of the hero.

Only C. L. Moore, almost a generation ago, produced a heroine who was as self-sufficient, as deadly with a sword, as dominate a character as any of the swordsmen she faced. In the series of stories recently published as *Jirel of Joiry* we meet the heroine in her own right, and not to be down-cried before any armed company.

When it came to write *Year of the Unicorn*, it was my wish to spin a story distantly based on the old tale of Beauty and the Beast. I had already experimented with some heroines who interested me, the Witch Jaelithe and Loyse of Verlane. But to write a full book from the feminine point of view was a departure. I found it fascinating to write, but the reception was oddly mixed. In the years now since it was first published I have had many letters from women readers who accepted Gillan with open arms, and I have had masculine readers who hotly resented her.

But I was encouraged enough to present a second heroine, the Sorceress Kaththea. And since then I have written several more shorter stories, both laid in Witch World and elsewhere, spun about a heroine instead of a hero. Perhaps now will come a shift in an old pattern; it will be most interesting to watch and see.

At any rate, there is no more imagination stretching form of writing, nor reading, than the world of fantasy. The heroes, heroines, colors, action, linger in one's mind long after the book is laid aside. And how wonderful it would be if world gates did exist and one could walk into Middle Earth, Kavin's World, the Land of Unreason, Atlantis, and all the other never-nevers! We have the windows to such worlds and must be content with those.

To offer a complete reference list would be a librarian's task and run for more pages than space allows. So the following bibliography is a restricted and personal one. In the non-fiction I list books which I found particularly rich in ideas for my own writing, and yet, I believe, would interest the browsing reader, too.

In the fiction you will find the fantasy books mentioned as good examples and worthy yardsticks to measure by.

BIBLIOGRAPHY

NON-FICTION REFERENCE BOOKS

Paul Herrmann, *Conquest by Man*, Harper & Row.

John Campbell, *Hero with 1000 Faces*, Meridian Books.

Peter Lum, *Fabulous Beasts*, Pantheon.

Basil Davidson, *Lost Cities of Africa*, Atlantic-Little Brown.

Geoffrey Bibby, *Four Thousand Years Ago*, Knopf.

Myles Dillan and Nora Chadwick, *The Celtic Realms*, New American Library.

E. A. Wallis Budge, *Amulets and Talismen*, University Books.

Stuart Piggott, *The Druids*, Thames Hudson.

Lewis Spence, *Fairy Traditions in Britain*, Rider.
Lewis Spence, *Magic Arts in Celtic Britain*, Rider.
Lewis Spence, *Minor Traditions of British Mythology*, Rider.
Alwyn Rees and Brisley Rees, *Celtic Heritage*, Grove Press.
Grant Uden, *Dictionary of Chivalry*, Longmans.
R. Ewart Oakeshott, *Archeology of Weapons*, Lutterworth.
Ed. by publisher, *Everyman's Dictionary of Non-Classical Mythology*, Dent-Dutton.
Ed. by publisher, *Crowell's Handbook for Readers and Writers*, Crowell.
Barbara Byfield, *The Glass Harmonica*, Macmillan.
Smith Thompson, *The Folktale*, Dryden Press.
L. Sprague de Camp, *Science-Fiction Handbook*, Hermitage.
L. Sprague de Camp, *Conan Swordbook*, Hermitage.
L. Sprague de Camp, *Conan Reader*, Hermitage.
Christine Price, *Made in the Middle Ages*, Bodley Head.
Isaac Asimov, *Dark Ages*, Houghton Mifflin.

FICTION

Elizabeth Walton, *Island of the Mighty*, Ballantine.
David Mason, *Kavin's World*, Lancer.
David Mason, *Sorcerer's Skull*, Lancer.
David Van Arnan, *Players of Hell*, Belmont.
David Van Arnan, *Wizard of Storm*, Belmont.
Michael Moorcock, *Swords of Dawn*, Lancer.
Michael Moorcock, *Jewel in the Skull*, Lancer.
Michael Moorcock, *Sorcerer's Amulet*, Lancer.
Michael Moorcock, *Secret of The Runestaff*, Lancer.
Michael Moorcock, *Stormbringer*, Lancer.
Michael Moorcock, *Stealer of Souls*, Lancer.
Fritz Leiber, *Swords of Lankhamar*, Ace.
Fritz Leiber, *Swords Against Death*, Ace.
Fritz Leiber, *Swords Against Deviltry*, Ace.
Fritz Leiber, *Swords in the Mist*, Ace.
Fritz Leiber, *Swords Against Wizardy*, Ace.
Richard Meade, *Sword of Morningstar*, Belmont.
L. Sprague de Camp, *Tritonian Ring*, Pyramid.
L. Sprague de Camp, *Incomplete Inchanter*, Pyramid.
L. Sprague de Camp, *Wall of Serpents*, Pyramid.
L. Sprague de Camp, *Land of Unreason*, Pyramid.
L. Sprague de Camp, *Castle of Iron*, Pyramid.
L. Sprague de Camp, *Goblin Tower*, Pyramid.
C. L. Moore, *Jirel of Joiry*, Paperback Library.
John Jakes, *Brak the Barbarian*, Avon.

John Jakes, *Brak and the Mark of Demons*, Paperback Library.

John Jakes, *Brak and the Sorceress*, Paperback Library.

John Brunner, *Traveler in Black*, Ace.

Robert Howard, *Conan series*, Lancer.

Robert Howard, *King Kull*, Lancer.

Alan Garner, *Weirdstone of Brisinggamen*, Ace.

Alan Garner, *Moon of Gomrath*, Ace.

Ursula Le Guin, *Wizard of Earthsea*, Ace.

John Bellairs, *Face in the Frost*, Macmillan.

Poul Anderson, *Broken Sword*.

Poul Anderson, *Three Hearts and Three Lions*, Avon.

Nicholas Stuart Grey, *Stone Cage*, Dobson.

Nicholas Stuart Grey, *Seventh Swan*, Dobson.

Lin Carter, ed., *Golden Cities, Far*, Ballantine.

Lin Carter, ed., *Dragons, Elves and Heroes*, Ballantine.

Lin Carter, ed., *Young Magicians*, Ballantine.

Mousetrap

REMEMBER that old adage about the man who built a better mouse trap and then could hardly cope with the business which beat a state highway to his door? I saw that happen once—on Mars.

Sam Levatts was politely introduced—for local color—by the tourist guides as a "desert spider." "Drunken bum" would have been the more exact term. He prospected over and through the dry lands out of Terraport and brought in Star Stones, Gormel ore, and like knickknacks to keep him sodden and mostly content. In his highly scented stupors he dreamed dreams and saw visions. At least his muttered description of the "lovely lady" was taken to be a vision, since there are no ladies in the Terraport dives he frequented and the females met there are far from lovely.

But Sam continued a peaceful dreamer until he met Len Collins and Operation Mousetrap began.

Every dumb tourist who steps into a scenic sandmobile at Terraport has heard of the "sand monsters." Those which still remain intact are now all the property of the tourist bureaus. And, brother, they're guarded as if they were a part of that cache of Martian royal jewels Black Spragg stumbled on twenty years ago. Because the monsters, which can withstand the dust storms, the extremes of desert cold and heat, crumble away if so much as a human finger tip is poked into their ribs.

Nowadays you are allowed to get within about twenty feet of the "Spider Man" or the "Armed Frog" and that's all. Try to edge a little closer and you'll get a shock that'll lay you flat on your back with your toes pointing Earthwards.

80

And, ever since the first monster went drifting off as a puff of dust under someone's hands, the museums back home have been adding to the cash award waiting for the fellow who can cement them for transportation. By the time Len Collins met Sam that award could be quoted in stellar figures.

Of course, all the bright boys in the glue, spray and plastic business had been taking a crack at the problem for years. The frustrating answer being that when they stepped out of the rocket over here, all steamed up about the stickability of their new product, they had nothing to prove it on. Not one of the known monsters was available for testing purposes. Every one is insured, guarded, and under the personal protection of the Space Marines.

But Len Collins had no intention of trying to reach one of these treasures. Instead he drifted into Sam's favorite lapping ground and set them up for Levatts—three times in succession. At the end of half an hour Sam thought he had discovered the buddy of his heart. And on the fifth round he spilled his wild tale about the lovely lady who lived in the shelter of two red rocks—far away—a vague wave of the hand suggesting the general direction.

Len straightway became a lover of beauty panting to behold this supreme treat. And he stuck to Sam that night closer than a Moonman to his oxy-supply. The next morning they both disappeared from Terraport in a private sandmobile hired by Len.

Two weeks later Collins slunk into town again and booked passage back to New York. He clung to the port hotel, never sticking his head out of the door until it was time to scuttle to the rocket.

Sam showed up in the Flame Bird four nights later. He had a nasty sand burn down his jaw and he could hardly keep his feet for lack of sleep. He was also—for the first time in Martian history—cold and deadly sober. And he sat there all evening drinking nothing stronger than Sparkling Canal Water. Thereby shocking some kindred souls half out of their wits.

What TV guy doesn't smell a story in a quick change like that? I'd be running the dives every night for a week—trying to pick up some local color for our 6 o'clock casting. And the most exciting and promising thing I had come across so far was Sam's sudden change of beverage. Strictly off the record—we cater to the family and tourist public mostly—I started to do a little picking and prying. Sam answered most of my feelers with grunts.

Then I hit pay dirt with the casual mention that the Three Planets Travel crowd had picked up another shocked cement dealer near their pet monster, "The Ant King." Sam rolled a mouthful of the Sparkling Water around his tongue, swallowed with a face to frighten all monsters, and asked a question of his own.

"Where do these here science guys think all the monsters come from?"

I shrugged. "No explanation that holds water. They can't examine them closely without destroying them. That's one reason for the big award awaiting any guy who can glue them together so they'll stand handling."

Sam pulled something from under the pocket flap of his spacealls. It was a picture, snapped in none too good a light, but clear enough.

Two large rocks curved toward each other to form an almost perfect archway and in their protection stood a woman. At least her slender body had the distinctly graceful curves we have come to associate with the stronger half of the race. But she also had wings, outspread in a grand sweep as if she stood on tiptoe almost ready to take off. There were only the hints of features—that gave away the secret of what she really was—because none of the sand monsters ever showed clear features.

"Where—?" I began.

Sam spat. "Nowhere now." He was grim, and his features had tightened up. He looked about ten years younger and a darn sight tougher.

"I found her two years ago. And I kept going back just to look at her. She wasn't a monster like the rest of 'em. She was perfect. Then that—" Sam lapsed into some of the finest space-searing language I have ever been privileged to hear— "that Collins got me drunk enough to show him where she was. He knocked me out, sprayed her with his goo, and tried to load her into the back of the 'mobile. It didn't work. She held together for about five minutes and then—" He snapped his fingers. "Dust just like 'em all!"

I found myself studying the picture for a second time. And I was beginning to wish I had Collins alone for about three minutes or so. Most of the sand images I had seen I could cheerfully do without—they were all nightmare material. But, as Sam had pointed out, this was no monster. And it was the only one of its type I had ever seen or heard about. Maybe there might just be another somewhere—the desert dry lands haven't been one quarter explored.

Sam nodded as if he had caught that thought of mine right out of the smoky air.

"Won't do any harm to look. I've noticed one thing about all of the monsters—they are found only near the rocks. Red rocks like these," he tapped the snapshot, "that have a sort of blue-green moss growin' on 'em." His eyes focused on the wall but I had an idea that he was seeing beyond it, beyond all the sand barrier walls in Terraport, out into the dry lands. And I guessed that he wasn't telling all he knew—or suspected.

I couldn't forget that picture. The next night I was back at the Flame Bird. But Sam didn't show. Instead rumor had it that he had loaded up with about two months' supplies and had gone back to the desert. And that was the last I heard of him for weeks. Only, his winged woman had crept into my dreams and I hated Collins. The picture was something—but I would have given a month's credits—interstellar at that—to have seen the original.

During the next year Sam made three long trips out, keeping quiet about his discoveries, if any. He stopped drinking and he was doing better financially. Actually brought in two green Star Stones, the sale of which covered most of his expenses for the year. And he continued to take an interest in the monsters and the eternal quest for the fixative. Two of the rocket pilots told me that he was sending to Earth regularly for everything published on the subject.

Gossip had already labeled him "sand happy." I almost believed that after I met him going out of town one dawn. He was in his prospector's crawler and strapped up in plain sight on top of his water tanks was one of the damnedest contraptions I'd ever seen—a great big wire cage!

I did a double take at the thing when he slowed down to say good-by. He saw my bug-eyes and answered their protrusion with a grin, a wicked one.

"Gonna bring me back a sand mouse, fella. A smart man can learn a lot from just watchin' a sand mouse, he sure can!"

Martian sand mice may live in the sand—popularly they're supposed to eat and drink the stuff, too—but they are nowhere near like their Terran namesakes. And nobody with any brains meddles with a sand mouse. I almost dismissed

Sam as hopeless then and there and wondered what form the final crack-up would take. But when he came back into town a couple of weeks later—minus the cage—he was still grinning. If Sam had held any grudge against me, I wouldn't have cared for that grin—not one bit!

Then Len Collins came back. And he started in right away at his old tricks—hanging around the dives listening to prospectors' talk. Sam had stayed in town and I caught up with them both at the Flame Bird, as thick as thieves over one table, Sam lapping up imported rye as if it were Canal Water and Len giving him cat at the mouse hole attention.

To my surprise Sam hailed me and pulled out a third stool at the table, insisting that I join them—much to Collins' annoyance. But I'm thick-skinned when I think I'm on the track of a story and I stuck. Stuck to hear Sam spill his big secret. He had discovered a new monster, one which so far surpassed the winged woman that they couldn't be compared. And Collins sat there licking his chops and almost drooling. I tried to shut Sam up—but I might as well have tried to can a dust storm. And in the end he insisted that I come along on their expedition to view this fabulous wonder. Well, I did.

We took a wind plane instead of a sandmobile. Collins was evidently in the chips and wanted speed. Sam piloted us. I noticed then, if Collins didn't, that Sam was a lot less drunk than he had been when he spilled his guts in the Flame Bird. And, noting that, I relaxed some—feeling a bit happier about the whole affair.

The red rocks we were hunting stood out like fangs—a whole row of them—rather nasty looking. From the air there was no sign of any image, but then those were mostly found in the shadow of such rocks and might not be visible from above. Sam landed the plane and we slipped and slid through the shin-deep sand.

Sam was skidding around more than was necessary and he was muttering. Once he sang—in a rather true baritone—just playing the souse again. However, we followed along without question.

Collins dragged with him a small tank which had a hose attachment. And he was so eager that he fairly crowded on Sam's heels all the way. When at last Sam stopped short he slid right into him. But Sam apparently didn't even notice the bump. He was pointing ahead and grinning fatuously.

I looked along the line indicated by his finger, eager to see another winged woman or something as good. But there wa nothing even faintly resembling a monster—unless you could count a lump of greenish stuff puffed up out of the sand a foot or so.

"Well, where is it?" Collins had fallen to one knee and had to put down his spray gun while he got up.

"Right there." Sam was still pointing to that greenish lump.

Collins' face had been wind-burned to a tomato red but now it darkened to a dusky purple as he stared at that repulsive hump.

"You fool!" Only he didn't say "fool." He lurched forward and kicked that lump, kicked it good and hard.

At the same time Sam threw himself flat on the ground and, having planted one of his oversize paws between my shoulders, took me with him. I bit into a mouthful of grit and sand and struggled wildly. But Sam's hand held me pinned tightly to the earth—as if I were a laboratory bug on a slide.

There was a sort of muffled exclamation, followed by an odd choking sound, from over by the rocks. But, in spite of my squirming, Sam continued to keep me more or less blindfolded. When he at last released me I was burning mad and came up with my fists ready. Only Sam wasn't there to land on. He was standing over by the rocks, his hands on his hips, surveying something with an open and proud satisfaction.

Because now there *was* a monster in evidence, a featureless anthropoidic figure of reddish stuff. Not as horrible as some I'd seen, but strange enough.

"Now—let's see if his goo does work this time!"

Sam took up the can briskly, pointed the hose tip at the monster, and let fly with a thin stream of pale bluish vapor, washing it all over that half-crouched thing.

"But—" I was still spitting sand between my teeth and only beginning to realize what must have happened. "Is that—that *thing*—"

"Collins? Yeah. He shouldn't have shown his temper that way. He kicked just once too often. That's what he did to her when she started to crumple, so I counted on him doing it again. Only, disturb one of those puff balls and get the stuff that's inside them on you and—presto—a monster! I got on to it when I was being chased by a sand mouse a couple of months back. The bugger got too close to one of those things—thinking more about dinner than danger, I guess—and whamoo! Hunted me up another mouse and another puff ball—just to be on the safe side. Same thing again. So—here we are! Say, Jim, I think this *is* going to work!" He had drawn one finger along the monster's outstretched arm and nothing happened. It still stood solid.

"Then all those monsters must once have been alive!" I shivered a little, remembering a few of them.

Sam nodded. "Maybe they weren't all natives of Mars—too many different kinds have been found. Terra was probably not the first to land a rocket here. Certainly the antmen and that big frog never lived together. Some day I'm going to get me a stellar ship and go out to look for the world my lady came from. This thin air could never have supported her wings.

"Now, Jim, if you'll just give me a hand, we'll get this work of art back to Terraport. How many million credits are the science guys offering if one is brought back in one piece?"

He was so businesslike about it that I simply did as he asked. And he collected from the scientists all right—collected enough to buy his stellar ship. He's out there now, prospecting along the Milky Way, hunting his winged lady. And the unique monster is in the Interplanetary Museum to be gaped at by all the tourists. Me—I avoid red rocks, green puff balls, and never, never kick at objects of my displeasure—it's healthier that way.

All Cats Are Gray

STEENA of the Spaceways—that sounds just like a corny title for one of the Stellar-Vedo spreads. I ought to know, I've tried my hand at writing enough of them. Only this Steena was no glamorous babe. She was as colorless as a lunar planet—even the hair netted down to her skull had a sort of grayish cast, and I never saw her but once draped in anything but a shapeless and baggy gray spaceall.

Steena was strictly background stuff, and that is where she mostly spent her free hours—in the smelly, smoky, background corners of any stellar-port dive frequented by free spacers. If you really looked for her you could spot her—just sitting there listening to the talk—listening and remembering. She didn't open her own mouth often. But when she did, spacers had learned to listen. And the lucky few who heard her rare spoken words—these will never forget Steena.

She drifted from port to port. Being an expert operator on the big calculators, she found jobs wherever she cared to stay for a time. And she came to be something like the master-minded machines she tended—smooth, gray, without much personality of their own.

But it was Steena who told Bub Nelson about the Jovan moon rites—and her warning saved Bub's life six months later. It was Steena who identified the piece of stone Keene Clark was passing around a table one night, rightly calling it unworked Slitite. That started a rush which made ten fortunes overnight for men who were down to their last jets. And, last of all, she cracked the case of the *Empress of Mars*.

All the boys who had profited by her queer store of knowl-

87

edge and her photographic memory tried at one time or another to balance the scales. But she wouldn't take so much as a cup of canal water at their expense, let alone the credits they tried to push on her. Bub Nelson was the only one who got around her refusal. It was he who brought her Bat.

About a year after the Jovan affair, he walked into the Free Fall one night and dumped Bat down on her table. Bat looked at Steena and growled. She looked calmly back at him and nodded once. From then on they traveled together—the thin gray woman and the big gray tomcat. Bat learned to know the inside of more stellar bars than even most spacers visit in their lifetimes. He developed a liking for Vernal juice, drank it neat and quick, right out of the glass. And he was always at home on any table where Stenna elected to drop him.

This is really the story of Steena, Bat, Cliff Moran, and the *Empress of Mars,* a story which is already a legend of the spaceways. And it's a damn good story, too. I ought to know, having framed the first version of it myself.

For I was there, right in the Rigel Royal, when it all began on the night that Cliff Moran blew in, looking lower than an antman's belly and twice as nasty. He'd had a spell of luck foul enough to twist a man into a slug snake, and we all knew that there was an attachment out for his ship. Cliff had fought his way up from the back courts of Venaport. Lose his ship and he'd slip back there—to rot. He was at the snarling stage that night when he picked out a table for himself and set out to drink away his troubles.

However, just as the first bottle arrived, so did a visitor. Steena came out of her corner, Bat curled around her shoulders stolewise, his favorite mode of travel. She crossed over and dropped down, without invitation, at Cliff's side. That shook him out of his sulks. Because Steena never chose company when she could be alone. If one of the man-stones on Ganymede had come stumping in, it wouldn't have made more of us look out of the corners of our eyes.

She stretched out one long-fingered hand, set aside the bottle he had ordered, and said only one thing. "It's about time for the *Empress of Mars* to appear."

Cliff scowled and bit his lip. He was tough, tough as jet lining—you have to be granite inside and out to struggle up from Venaport to a ship command. But we could guess what was running through his mind at that moment. The *Empress of Mars* was just about the biggest prize a spacer could aim for. But in the fifty years she had been following her queer derelict orbit through space, many men had tried to bring her in—and none had succeeded.

A pleasure ship carrying untold wealth, she had been mysteriously abandoned in space by passengers and crew, none of whom had ever been seen or heard of again. At intervals thereafter she had been sighted, even boarded. Those who ventured into her either vanished or returned swiftly without any believable explanation of what they had seen—wanting only to get away from her as quickly as possible. But the man who could bring her in—or even strip her clean in space —that man would win the jackpot.

"All right!" Cliff slammed his fist on the table. "I'll try even that!"

Steena looked at him, much as she must have looked at Bat that day Bub Nelson brought him to her, and nodded. That was all I saw. The rest of the story came to me in pieces, months later and in another port half the system away.

Cliff took off that night. He was afraid to risk waiting— with a writ out that could pull the ship from under him. And it wasn't until he was in space that he discovered his passengers—Steena and Bat. We'll never know what happened then. I'm betting Steena made no explanation at all. She wouldn't.

It was the first time she had decided to cash in on her own tip and she was there—that was all. Maybe that point weighed with Cliff, maybe he just didn't care. Anyway, the three were together when they sighted the *Empress* riding, her deadlights gleaming, a ghost ship in night space.

She must have been an eerie sight because her other lights were on too, in addition to the red warnings at her nose. She seemed alive, a Flying Dutchman of space. Cliff worked his ship skillfully alongside and had no trouble in snapping magnetic lines to her lock. Some minutes later the three of them passed into her. There was still air in her cabins and corridors, air that bore a faint corrupt taint which set Bat to sniffing greedily and could be picked up even by the less sensitive human nostrils.

Cliff headed straight for the control cabin, but Steena and Bat went prowling. Closed doors were a challenge to both of them and Steena opened each as she passed, taking a quick look at what lay within. The fifth door opened on a room which no woman could leave without further investigation.

I don't know what had been housed there when the *Em-*

press left port on her last lengthy cruise. Anyone really curious can check back on the old photo-reg cards. But there was
a lavish display of silk trailing out of two travel kits on the
floor, a dressing table crowded with crystal and jeweled containers, along with other lures for the female which drew
Steena in. She was standing in front of the dressing table
when she glanced into the mirror—glanced into it and froze.

Over her right shoulder she could see the spider-silk cover
on the bed. Right in the middle of that sheer, gossamer ex-
panse was a sparkling heap of gems, the dumped contents of
some jewel case. Bat had jumped to the foot of the bed and
flattened out as cats will, watching those gems, watching
them and—something else!

Steena put out her hand blindly and caught up the nearest
bottle. As she unstoppered it, she watched the mirrored bed.
A gemmed bracelet rose from the pile, rose in the air and
tinkled its siren song. It was as if an idle hand played. . . . Bat
spat almost noiselessly. But he did not retreat. Bat had not
yet decided his course.

She put down the bottle. Then she did something which
perhaps few of the men she had listened to through the years
could have done. She moved without hurry or sign of disturbance on a tour about the room. And, although she approached the bed, she did not touch the jewels. She could not
force herself to do that. It took her five minutes to play out
her innocence and unconcern. Then it was Bat who decided
the issue.

He leaped from the bed and escorted something to the
door, remaining a careful distance behind. Then he mewed
loudly twice. Steena followed him and opened the door
wider.

Bat went straight on down the corridor, as intent as a
hound on the warmest of scents. Steena strolled behind him,
holding her pace to the unhurried gait of an explorer. What
sped before them was invisible to her, but Bat was never baffled by it.

They must have gone into the control cabin almost on the
heels of the unseen—if the unseen had heels, which there was
good reason to doubt—for Bat crouched just within the doorway and refused to move on. Steena looked down the length
of the instrument panels and officers' station seats to where
Cliff Moran worked. Her boots made no sound on the heavy
carpet, and he did not glance up but sat humming through

set teeth, as he tested the tardy and reluctant responses to buttons which had not been pushed in years.

To human eyes they were alone in the cabin. But Bat still followed a moving something, which he had at last made up his mind to distrust and dislike. For now he took a step or two forward and spat—his loathing made plain by every raised hair along his spine. And in that same moment Steena saw a flicker—a flicker of vague outline against Cliff's hunched shoulders, as if the invisible one had crossed the space between them.

But why had it been revealed against Cliff and not against the back of one of the seats or against the panels, the walls of the corridor or the cover of the bed where it had reclined and played with its loot? What could Bat see?

The storehouse memory that had served Steena so well through the years clicked open a half-forgotten door. With one swift motion, she tore loose her spaceall and flung the baggy garment across the back of the nearest seat.

Bat was snarling now, emitting the throaty rising cry that was his hunting song. But he was edging back, back toward Steena's feet, shrinking from something he could not fight but which he faced defiantly. If he could draw it after him, past that dangling spaceall. . . . He had to—it was their only chance!

"What the . . ." Cliff had come out of his seat and was staring at them.

What he saw must have been weird enough: Steena, barearmed and bareshouldered, her usually stiffly netted hair falling wildly down her back; Steena watching empty space with narrowed eyes and set mouth, calculating a single wild chance. Bat, crouched on his belly, was retreating from thin air step by step and wailing like a demon.

"Toss me your blaster." Steena gave the order calmly—as if they were still at their table in the Rigel Royal.

And as quietly, Cliff obeyed. She caught the small weapon out of the air with a steady hand—caught and leveled it.

"Stay where you are!" she warned. "Back, Bat, bring it back."

With a last throat-spitting screech of rage and hate, Bat twisted to safety between her boots. She pressed with thumb and forefinger, firing at the spaceall. The material turned to powdery flakes of ash—except for certain bits which still flapped from the scorched seat—as if something had protected them from the force of the blast. Bat sprang straight up in the air with a screech that tore their ears.

"What . . . ?" began Cliff again.

Steena made a warning motion with her left hand. *"Wait!"*

She was still tense, still watching Bat. The cat dashed madly around the cabin twice, running crazily with white-ringed eyes and flecks of foam on his muzzle. Then he stopped abruptly in the doorway, stopped and looked back over his shoulder for a long, silent moment. He sniffed delicately.

Steena and Cliff could smell it too now, a thick oily stench which was not the usual odor left by an exploding blaster shell.

Bat came back, treading daintily across the carpet, almost on the tips of his paws. He raised his head as he passed Steena, and then he went confidently beyond to sniff, to sniff and spit twice at the unburned strips of the spaceall. Having thus paid his respects to the late enemy, he sat down calmly and set to washing his fur with deliberation. Steena sighed once and dropped into the navigator's seat.

"Maybe now you'll tell me what in the hell's happened?" Cliff exploded as he took the blaster out of her hand.

"Gray," she said dazedly, "it must have been gray—or I couldn't have seen it like that. I'm color-blind, you see. I can see only shades of gray—my whole world is gray. Like Bat's—his world is gray, too—all gray. But he's been compensated, for he can see above and below our range of color vibrations, and apparently so can I!"

Her voice quavered, and she raised her chin with a new air Cliff had never seen before—a sort of proud acceptance. She pushed back her wandering hair, but she made no move to imprison it under the heavy net again.

"That is why I saw the thing when it crossed between us. Against your spaceall it was another shade of gray—an outline. So I put out mine and waited for it to show against that—it was our only chance, Cliff.

"It was curious at first, I think, and it knew we couldn't see it—which is why it waited to attack. But when Bat's actions gave it away, it moved. So I waited to see that flicker against the spaceall, and then I let him have it. It's really very simple. . . ."

Cliff laughed a bit shakily. "But what *was* this gray thing. I don't get it."

"I think it was what made the *Empress* a derelict. Something out of space, maybe, or from another world some-where." She waved her hands. "It's invisible because it's a color beyond our range of sight. It must have stayed in here all these years. And it kills—it must—when its curiosity is satisfied." Swiftly she described the scene, the scene in the cabin, and the strange behavior of the gem pile which had betrayed the creature to her.

Cliff did not return his blaster to its holder. "Any more of them aboard, d'you think?" He didn't look pleased at the prospect.

Steena turned to Bat. He was paying particular attention to the space between two front toes in the process of a com-plete bath. "I don't think so. But Bat will tell us if there are. He can see them clearly, I believe."

But there weren't any more and two weeks later, Cliff, Steena and Bat brought the *Empress* into the lunar quaran-tine station. And that is the end of Steena's story because, as we have been told, happy marriages need no chronicles. Steena had found someone who knew of her gray world and did not find it too hard to share with her—someone besides Bat. It turned out to be a real love match.

The last time I saw her, she was wrapped in a flame-red cloak from the looms of Rigel and wore a fortune in Jovan rubies blazing on her wrists. Cliff was flipping a three-figured credit bill to a waiter. And Bat had a row of Vernal juice glasses set up before him. Just a little family party out on the town.

The Long Night
Of Waiting

"WHAT—what are we going to do?" Lesley squeezed her hands so tightly together they hurt. She really wanted to run, as far and as fast as she could.

Rick was not running. He stood there, still holding to Alex's belt, just as he had grabbed his brother to keep him from following Matt. Following him where?

"We won't do anything," Rick answered slowly.

"But people'll ask—all kinds of questions. You only have to look at that—" Lesley pointed with her chin to what was now before them.

Alex still struggled for freedom. "Want Matt!" he yelled at the top of his voice. He wriggled around to beat at Rick with his fists.

"Let me go! Let me go—with Matt!"

Rick shook him. "Now listen here, shrimp. Matt's gone. You can't get to him now. Use some sense—look there. Do you see Matt? Well, do you?"

Lesley wondered how Rick could be so calm—accepting all of this just as if it happened every day—like going to school, or watching a tel-cast, or the regular, safe things. How could he just stand there and talk to Alex as if he were grown up and Alex was just being pesty as he was sometimes? She watched Rick wonderingly, and tried not to think of what had just happened.

"Matt?" Alex had stopped fighting. His voice sounded as if he were going to start bawling in a minute or two. And when

94

Alex cried—! He would keep on and on, and they would have questions to answer. If they told the real truth—Lesley drew a deep breath and shivered.

No one, no one in the whole world would ever believe them! Not even if they saw what was right out here in this field now. No one would believe—they would say that she, Lesley, and Rick, and Alex were all mixed up in their minds. And they might even be sent away to a hospital or something! No, they could never tell the truth! But Alex, he would blurt out the whole thing if anyone asked a question about Matt. What could they do about Alex?

Her eyes questioned Rick over Alex's head. He was still holding their young brother, but Alex had turned, was gripping Rick's waist, looking up at him demandingly, waiting, Lesley knew, for Rick to explain as he had successfully most times in Alex's life. And if Rick couldn't explain this time?

Rick hunkered down on the ground, his hands now on Alex's shoulders.

"Listen, shrimp, Matt's gone. Lesley goes, I go, to school—"

Alex sniffed. "But the bus comes then, and you get on while I watch—then you come home again—" His small face cleared. "Then Matt—he'll come back? He's gone to school? But this is Saturday! You an' Lesley don't go on Saturday. How come Matt does? An' where's the bus? There's nothin' but that mean old dozer that's chewin' up things. An' now all these vines and stuff—and the dozer tipped right over an'—" He screwed around a little in Rick's grip to stare over his brother's hunched shoulder at the disaster area beyond.

"No," Rick was firm. "Matt's not gone to school. He's gone home—to his own place. You remember back at Christmas time, Alex, when Peter came with Aunt Fran and Uncle Porter? He came for a visit. Matt came with Lizzy for a visit—how he's gone back home—just like Peter did."

"But Matt said—he said *this* was his home!" countered Alex. "He didn't live in Cleveland like Peter."

"It was his home once," Rick continued still in that grown-up way. "Just like Jimmy Rice used to live down the street in the red house. When Jimmy's Dad got moved by his company, Jimmy went clear out to St. Louis to live."

"But Matt was sure! He said *this* was his home!" Alex frowned. "He said it over and over, that he had come home again."

"At first he did," Rick agreed. "But later, you know that

Matt was not so sure, was he now? You think about that, shrimp."

Alex was still frowning. At least he was not screaming as Lesley feared he would be. Rick, she was suddenly very proud and a little in awe of Rick. How had he known how to keep Alex from going into one of his tantrums?

"Matt—he did say funny things. An' he was afraid of cars. Why was he afraid of cars, Rick?"

"Because where he lives they don't have cars."

Alex's surprise was open. "Then how do they go to the store? An' to Sunday School, an' school, an' every place?"

"They have other ways, Alex. Yes, Matt was afraid of a lot of things, he knew that this was not his home, that he had to go back."

"But—I want him—he—" Alex began to cry, not with the loud screaming Lesley had feared, but in a way now which made her hurt a little inside as she watched him butt his head against Rick's shoulder, making no effort to smear away the tears as they wet his dirty cheeks.

"Sure you want him," Rick answered. "But Matt—he was afraid, he was not very happy here, now was he, shrimp?"

"With me, he was. We had a lot of fun, we did!"

"But Matt wouldn't go in the house, remember? Remember what happened when the lights went on?"

"Matt ran an' hid. An' Lizzy, she kept telling him an' telling him they had to go back. Maybe if Lizzy hadn't all the time told him that—"

Lesley thought about Lizzy. Matt was little—he was not more than Alex's age—not really, in spite of what the stone said. But Lizzy had been older and quicker to understand. It had been Lizzy who had had asked most of the questions and then been sick (truly sick to her stomach) when Lesley and Rick answered them. Lizzy had been sure of what had happened then—just like she was sure about the other—that the stone must never be moved, nor that place covered over to trap anybody else. So that nobody would fall through—

Fall through into what? Lesley tried to remember all the bits and pieces Lizzy and Matt had told about where they had been for a hundred and ten years—a *hundred* and *ten* just like the stone said.

She and Rick had found the stone when Alex had run away. They had often had to hunt Alex like that. Ever since he learned to open the Safe-tee gate he would go off about once a week or so. It was about two months after they moved here, before all the new houses had been built and the big apartments at the end of the street. This was all more like real country then. Now it was different, spoiled—just this one open place left and that (unless Lizzy was right in thinking she'd stopped it all) would not be open long. The men had started to clear it off with the bulldozer the day before yesterday. All the ground on that side was raw and cut up, the trees and bushes had been smashed and dug out.

There had been part of an old orchard there, and a big old lilac bush. Last spring it had been so pretty. Of course, the apples were all little and hard, and had worms in them. But it had been pretty and a swell place to play. Rick and Jim Bowers had a house up in the biggest tree. Their sign said "No girls allowed," but Lesley had sneaked up once when they were playing Little League ball and had seen it all.

Then there was the stone. That was kind of scarey. Yet they had kept going to look at it every once in a while, just to wonder.

Alex had found it first that day he ran away. There were a lot of bushes hiding it and tall grass. Lesley felt her eyes drawn in that direction now. It *was* still there. Though you have to mostly guess about that, only one teeny bit of it showed through all those leaves and things.

And when they had found Alex he had been working with a piece of stick, scratching at the words carved there which were all filled up with moss and dirt. He had been so busy and excited he had not tried to dodge them as he usually did, instead he wanted to know if those were real words, and then demanded that Rick read them to him.

Now Lesley's lips silently shaped what was carved there.

> *A long night of waiting.*
> *To the Memory of our dear children,*
> *Lizzy and Matthew Mendal,*
> *Who disappeared on this spot*
> *June 23, 1861.*
> *May the Good Lord return them*
> *to their loving parents and this*
> *world in His Own reckoned time.*
> *Erected to mark our years of watching,*
> *June 23, 1900.*

It had sounded so queer. At first Lesley had thought it was a grave and had been a little frightened. But Rick had pointed out that the words did not read like those on the stones in the cemetery where they went on Memorial Day with flowers for Grandma and Grandpa Targ. It was different because it never said "dead" but "disappeared."

Rick had been excited, said it sounded like a mystery. He had begun to ask around, but none of the neighbors knew anything—except this had all once been a farm. Almost all the houses on the street were built on that land. They had the oldest house of all. Dad said it had once been the farm house, only people had changed it and added parts like bathrooms.

Lizzy and Matt—

Rick had gone to the library and asked questions, too. Miss Adams, she got interested when Rick kept on wanting to know what this was like a hundred years ago (though of course he did not mention the stone, that was their own secret, somehow from the first they knew they must keep quiet about that). Miss Adams had shown Rick how they kept the old newspapers on film tapes. And when he did his big project for social studies, he had chosen the farm's history, which gave him a good chance to use those films to look things up.

That was how he learned all there was to know about Lizzy and Matt. There had been a lot in the old paper about them. Lizzy Mendal, Matthew Mendal, aged eleven and five—Lesley could almost repeat it word for word she had read Rick's copied notes so often. They had been walking across this field, carrying lunch to their father who was ploughing. He had been standing by a fence talking to Doctor Levi Morris who was driving by. They had both looked up to see Lizzy and Matthew coming and had waved to them. Lizzy waved back and then—she and Matthew—they were just gone! Right out of the middle of an open field they were gone!

Mr. Mendal and the Doctor, they had been so surprised they couldn't believe their eyes, but they had hunted and hunted. And the men from other farms had come to hunt too. But no one ever saw the children again.

Only about a year later, Mrs. Mendal (she had kept coming to stand here in the field, always hoping, Lesley guessed, they might come back as they had gone) came running home all excited to say she heard Matt's voice, and he had been calling "Ma! Ma!".

She got Mr. Mendal to go back with her. And he heard it,

too, when he listened, but it was very faint. Just like someone a long way off calling "Ma!". Then it was gone and they never heard it again.

It was all in the papers Rick found, the story of how they hunted for the children and later on about Mrs. Mendal hearing Matt. But nobody ever was able to explain what had happened.

So all that was left was the stone and a big mystery. Rick started hunting around in the library, even after he finished his report, and found a book with other stories about people who disappeared. It was written by a man named Charles Fort. Some of it had been hard reading. But Rick and Lesley had both found the parts which were like what happened to Lizzy and Matt. And in all those other disappearances there had been no answers to what had happened, and nobody came back.

Until Lizzy and Matt. But suppose she and Rick and Alex told people now, would any believe them? And what good would it do, anyway? Unless Lizzy was right and people should know so they would not be caught. Suppose someone built a house right over where the stone stood, and suppose some day a little boy like Alex, or a girl like Lesley, or even a mom or dad, disappeared? She and Rick, maybe they ought to talk and keep on talking until someone believed them, believed them enough to make sure such a house was never going to be built, and this place was made safe.

"Matt—he kept sayin' he wanted his mom," Alex's voice cut through her thoughts. "Rick, where was his mom that she lost him that way?"

Rick, for the first time, looked helpless. How could you make Alex understand?

Lesley stood up. She still felt quite shaky and a little sick from the left-over part of her fright. But the worst was past now, she had to be as tough as Rick or he'd say that was just like a girl.

"Alex," she was able to say that quite naturally, and her voice did not sound too queer, "Matt, maybe he'll find his mom now, he was just looking in the wrong place. She's not here any more. You remember last Christmas when you went with Mom to see Santy Claus at the store and you got lost? You were hunting mom and she was hunting you, and at first you were looking in the wrong places. But you did find each other. Well, Matt's mom will find him all right."

She thought that Alex wanted to believe her. He had not

pushed away from Rick entirely, but he looked as if he were listening carefully to every word she said.

"You're sure?" he asked doubtfully. "Matt—he was scared he'd never find his mom. He said he kept calling an' calling an' she never came."

"She'll come, moms always do." Lesley tried to make that sound true. "And Lizzy will help. Lizzy," Lesley hesitated, trying to choose the right words, "Lizzy's very good at getting things done."

She looked beyond to the evidence of Lizzy's getting things done and her wonder grew. At first, just after it had happened, she had been so shocked and afraid, she had not really understood what Lizzy had done before she and Matt had gone again. What—what *had* Lizzy learned during that time when she had been in the other place? And how had she learned it? She had never answered all their questions as if she was not able to tell them what lay on the other side of that door, or whatever it was which was between *here* and *there*.

Lizzy's work was hard to believe, even when you saw it right before your eyes.

The bulldozer and the other machines which had been parked there to begin work again Monday morning—Well, the bulldozer was lying over on its side, just as if it were a toy Alex had picked up and thrown as he did sometimes when he got over-tired and cross. And the other machines— they were all pushed over, some even broken! Then there were the growing things. Lizzy had rammed her hands into the pockets of her dress-like apron and brought them out with seeds trickling between her fingers. And she had just thrown those seeds here and there, all over the place.

It took a long time for plants to grow—weeks—Lesley knew. But look—these were growing right while you watched. They had already made a thick mat over every piece of the machinery they had reached, like they had to cover it from sight quickly. And there were flowers opening—and butterflies—Lesley had never seen so many butterflies as were gathering about those flowers, arriving right out of nowhere.

"Rick—how—?" She could not put her wonder into a full question, she could only gesture toward what was happening there.

Her brother shrugged. It was as if he did not want to look

at what was happening. Instead he spoke to both of them sharply.

"Listen, shrimp, Les, it's getting late. Mom and Dad will be home soon. We'd better get there before they do. Remember, we left all the things Matt and Lizzy used out in the summer house. Dad's going to work on the lawn this afternoon. He'll want to get the mower out of there. If he sees what we left there he'll ask questions for sure and we might have to talk. Not that it would do any good."

Rick was right. Lesley looked around her regretfully now. She was not frightened any more—she, well, she would like to just stay awhile and watch. But she reached for Alex's sticky hand. To her surprise he did not object or jerk away, he was still hiccuping a little as he did after he cried. She was thankful Rick had been able to manage him so well.

They scraped through their own private hole in the fence into the backyard, heading to the summer house which Rick and Dad had fixed up into a rainy day place to play and a storage for the outside tools. The camping bags were there, even the plates and cups. Those were still smeared with jelly and peanut butter. Just think, Matt had never tasted jelly and peanut butter before, he said. But he had liked it a lot. Lesley had better sneak those in and give them a good washing. And the milk—Lizzy could not understand how you got milk from a bottle a man brought to your house and not straight from a cow. She seemed almost afraid to drink it. And she had not liked Coke at all—said it tasted funny.

"I wish Matt was here." Alex stood looking down at the sleeping bag, his face clouding up again. "Matt was fun—"

"Sure he was. Here, shrimp, you catch ahold of that and help me carry this back. We've got to get it into the camper before Dad comes."

"Why?"

Oh, dear, was Alex going to have one of his stubborn question-everything times? Lesley had put the plates and cups back into the big paper bag in which she had smuggled the food from the kitchen this morning, and was folding up the extra cover from Matt's bed.

"You just come along and I'll tell you, shrimp." She heard Rick say. Rick was just *wonderful* today. Though Mom always said that Rick could manage Alex better than anyone else in the whole family when he wanted to make the effort.

There, she gave a searching look around as the boys left (one of the bags between them) this was cleared. They

would take the other bag, and she would do the dishes. Then
Dad could walk right in and never know that Lizzy and Matt
had been here for two nights and a day.

Two nights and a day—Lizzy had kept herself and Matt
out of sight yesterday when Lesley and Rick had been at
school. She would not go near the house, nor let Matt later
when Alex wanted him to go and see the train Dad and Rick
has set up in the family room. All she had wanted were
newspapers. Lesley had taken those to her and some of the
magazines Mom had collected for the Salvation Army. She
must have read a lot, because when they met her after
school, she had a million questions to ask.

It was then that she said she and Matt had to go away,
back to where they had come from, that they could not stay
in this mixed up horrible world which was not the right one
at all! Rick told her about the words on the stones and how
long it had been. First she called him a liar and said that was
not true. So after dark he had taken a flashlight and went
back to show her the stone and the words.

She had been the one to cry then. But she did not for long.
She got to asking what was going to happen in the field,
looking at the machines. When Rick told her, Lizzy had said
quick and hot, no, they mustn't do that, it was dangerous—a
lot of others might go through. And *they*, those in the other
world, didn't want people who did bad things to spoil everything.

When Rick brought her back she was mad, not at him, but
at everything else. She made him walk her down to the place
from which you could see the inter-city thru-way, with all the
cars going whizz. Rick said he was sure she was scared. She
was shaking, and she held onto his hand so hard it hurt. But
she made herself watch. Then, when they came back, she
said Matt and she—they had to go. And she offered to take
Alex, Lesley, and Rick with them. She said they couldn't
want to go on living *here*.

That was the only time she talked much of what it was
like *there*. Birds and flowers, no noise or cars rushing about,
nor bulldozers tearing the ground up, everything pretty. It
was Lesley who had asked then:

"If it was all that wonderful, why did you want to come
back?"

Then she was sorry she had asked because Lizzy's face
looked like she was hurting inside when she answered:

"There was Ma and Pa. Matt, he's little, he misses Ma bad

at times. Those *others*, they got their own way of life, and it ain't much like ours. So, we've kept a-tryin' to get back. I brought somethin'—just for Ma." She showed them two bags of big silvery leaves pinned together with long thorns. Inside each were seeds, all mixed up big and little together.

"Things grow *there*," she nodded toward the field, "they grow strange-like. Faster than seeds hereabouts. You put one of these," she ran her finger tip in among the seeds, shifting them back and forth, "in the ground, and you can *see* it grow. Honest-Injun-cross-my-heart-an'-hope-to-die if that ain't so. Ma, she hankers for flowers, loves 'em truly. So I brought her some. Only, Ma, she ain't here. Funny thing—*those* over *there*, they have a feelin' about these here flowers and plants. *They* tell you right out that as long as *they* have these growin' 'round *they*'re safe."

"Safe from what?" Rick wanted to know.

"I dunno—safe from somethin' as *they* think may change 'em. See, we ain't the onlyest ones gittin' through to *there*. There's others, we've met a couple. Susan—she's older 'n me and she dresses funny, like one of the real old time ladies in a book picture. And there's Jim—he spends most of his time off in the woods, don't see him much. Susan's real nice. She took us to stay with her when we got *there*. But she's married to one of *them*, so we didn't feel comfortable most of the time. Anyway *they* had some rules—they asked us right away did we have anything made of iron. Iron is bad for *them*, *they* can't hold it, it burns *them* bad. And *they* told us right out that if we stayed long we'd change. We ate *their* food and drank *their* drink stuff—that's like cider and it tastes good. That changes people from here. So after awhile anyone who comes through is like *them*. Susan mostly is by now, I guess. When you're changed you don't want to come back."

"But you didn't change," Lesley pointed out. "You came back."

"And how come you didn't change?" Rick wanted to know. "You were there long enough—a hundred and ten years!"

"But," Lizzy had beat with her fists on the floor of the summer house then as if she were pounding a drum. "It weren't that long, it couldn't be! Me, I counted every day! It's only been ten of 'em, with us hunting the place to come through on every one of 'em, calling for Ma and Pa to come and get us. It weren't no hundred and ten years—"

And she had cried again in such a way as to make Lesley's

throat ache. A moment later she had been bawling right along with Lizzy. For once Rick did not look at her as if he were disgusted, but instead as if he were sorry, for Lizzy, not Lesley, of course.

"It's got to be that time's different in that place," he said thoughtfully. "A lot different. But, Lizzy, it's true, you know—this is 1971, not 1861. We can prove it."

Lizzy wiped her eyes on the hem of her long apron. "Yes, I got to believe. 'Cause what you showed me ain't my world at all. All those cars shootin' along so fast, lights what go on and off when you press a button on the wall—all these houses built over Pa's good farmin' land—what I read today. Yes, I gotta believe it—but it's hard to do that, right hard!

"And Matt 'n' me, we don't belong here no more, not with all this clatter an' noise an' nasty smelling air like we sniffed down there by that big road. I guess we gotta go back *there*. Leastwise, we know what's there now."

"How can you get back?" Rick wanted to know.

For the first time Lizzy showed a watery smile. "I ain't no dunce, Rick. *They* got rules, like I said. You carry something outta that place and hold on to it, an' it pulls you back, lets you in again. I brought them there seeds for Ma. But I thought maybe Matt an' me—we might want to go visitin' *there*. Susan's been powerful good to us. Well, anyway, I got these too."

She had burrowed deeper in her pocket, under the packets of seeds and brought out two chains of woven grass, tightly braided. Fastened to each was a small arrowhead, a very tiny one, no bigger than Lesley's little fingernail.

Rick held out his hand. "Let's see."

But Lizzy kept them out of his reach.

"Them's no Injun arrowheads, Rick. Them's what *they* use for *their* own doin's. Susan, she calls them 'elf-shots.' Anyway, these here can take us back if we wear 'em. And we will tomorrow, that's when we'll go."

They had tried to find out more about *there*, but Lizzy would not answer most of their questions. Lesley thought she could not for some reason. But she remained firm in her decision that she and Matt would be better off *there* than *here*. Then she had seemed sorry for Lesley and Rick and Alex that they had to stay in such a world, and made the suggestion that they link hands and go through together.

Rick shook his head. "Sorry—no. Mom and Dad—well, we belong here."

Lizzy nodded. "Thought you would say that. But—it's so ugly now, I can't see as how you want to." She cupped the tiny arrowheads in her hand, held them close. "Over *there* it's so pretty. What are you goin' to do here when all the ground is covered up with houses and the air's full of bad smells, an' those cars go rush-rush all day and night too? Looky here—" She reached for one of the magazines. "I'm the best reader in the school house. Miss Jane, she has me up to read out loud when the school board comes visitin'." She did not say that boastfully, but as if it were a truth everyone would know. "An' I've been readin' pieces in here. They've said a lot about how bad things are gittin' for you all—bad air, bad water— too many people—everything like that. Seems like there's no end but bad here. Ain't that so now?"

"We've been studying about it in school," Lesley agreed, "Rick and me, we're on the pick-up can drive next week. Sure we know."

"Well, this ain't happening over *there*, you can bet you! *They* won't let it."

"How do they stop it?" Rick wanted to know.

But once more Lizzy did not answer. She just shook her head and said *they* had their ways. And then she had gone on:

"Me an' Matt, we have to go back. We don't belong here now, and back *there* we do, sorta. At least it's more like what we're used to. We have to go at the same hour as before—noon time—"

"How do you know?" Rick asked.

"There's rules. We were caught at noon then, we go at noon now. Sure you don't want to come with us?"

"Only as far as the field," Rick had answered for them. "It's Saturday, we can work it easy. Mom has a hair appointment in the morning, Dad is going to drive her 'cause he's seeing Mr. Chambers, and they'll do the shopping before they come home. We're supposed to have a picnic in the field, like we always do. Being Saturday the men won't be working there either."

"If you have to go back at noon," Lesley was trying to work something out, "how come you didn't get here at noon? It must have been close to five when we saw you. The school bus had let us off at the corner and Alex had come to meet us—then we saw you—"

"We hid out," Lizzy had said then. "Took a chance on you 'cause you were like us—"

Lesley thought she would never forget that first meeting, seeing the fair haired girl a little taller than she, her hair in two long braids, but such a queer dress on—like a "granny" one, yet different, and over it a big coarse-looking checked apron. Beside her Matt, in a check shirt and funny looking pants, both of them barefooted. They had looked so unhappy and lost. Alex had broken away from Lesley and Rick and had run right over to them to say "Hi" in the friendly way he always did.

Lizzy had been turning her head from side to side as if hunting for something which should be right there before her. And when they had come up she had spoken almost as if she were angry (but Lesley guessed she was really frightened) asking them where the Mendal house was.

If it had not been for the stone and Rick doing all that hunting down of the story behind it, they would not have known what she meant. But Rick had caught on quickly. He had said that they lived in the old Mendal house now, and they had brought Lizzy and Matt along with them. But before they got there they had guessed who Lizzy and Matt were, impossible as it seemed.

Now they were gone again. But Lizzy, what had she done just after she had looped those grass strings around her neck and Matt's and taken his hand? First she had thrown out all those seeds on the ground. And then she had pointed her finger at the bulldozer, and the other machines which were tearing up the rest of the farm she had known.

Lesley, remembering, blinked and shivered. She had expected Lizzy and Matt to disappear, somehow she had never doubted that they would. But she had not foreseen that the bulldozer would flop over at Lizzy's pointing, the other things fly around as if they were being thrown, some of them breaking apart. Then the seeds sprouting, vines and grass, and flowers, and small trees shooting up—just like the time on TV when they speeded up the camera somehow so you actually saw a flower opening up. What had Lizzy learned *there* that she was able to do all that?

Still trying to remember it all, Lesley wiped the dishes. Rick and Alex came in.

"Everything's put away," Rick reported. "And Alex, he understands about not talking about Matt."

"I sure hope so, Rick. But—how did Lizzy do that—make the machines move by just pointing at them? And how can plants grow so quickly?"

"How do I know?" he demanded impatiently. "I didn't see any more than you did. We've only one thing to remember, we keep our mouths shut tight. And we've got to be just as surprised as anyone else when somebody sees what happened there—"

"Maybe they won't see it—maybe not until the men come on Monday," she said hopefully. Monday was a school day, and the bus would take them early. Then she remembered.

"Rick, Alex won't be going to school with us. He'll be here with Mom. What if somebody says something and he talks?"

Rick was frowning. "Yeah, I see what you mean. So—we'll have to discover it ourselves—tomorrow morning. If we're here when people get all excited we can keep Alex quiet. One of us will have to stay with him all the time."

But in the end Alex made his own plans. The light was only grey in Lesley's window when she awoke to find Rick shaking her shoulder.

"What—what's the matter?"

"Keep it low!" He ordered almost fiercely. "Listen, Alex's gone—"

"Gone where?"

"Where do you think? Get some clothes on and come on!"

Gone to *there*? Lesley was cold with fear as she pulled on jeans and a sweat shirt, thrust her feet into shoes. But how could Alex—? Just as Matt and Lizzy had gone the first time. They should not have been afraid of being disbelieved, they should have told Dad and Mom all about it. Now maybe Alex would be gone for a hundred years. No—not Alex!

She scrambled down stairs. Rick stood at the back door waving her on. Together they raced across the backyard, struggled through the fence gap and—

The raw scars left by the bulldozer were gone. Rich foliage rustled in the early morning breeze. And the birds—! Lesley had never seen so many different kinds of birds in her whole life. They seemed so tame, too, swinging on branches, hopping along the ground, pecking a fruit. Not the sour old apples but golden fruit. It hung from bushes, squashed on the ground from its own ripeness.

And there were flowers—and—

"Alex!" Rick almost shouted.

There he was. Not gone, sucked into *there* where they could never find him again. No he was sitting under a bush where white flowers bloomed. His face was smeared with juice as he ate one of the fruit. And he was patting a bunny!

A real live bunny was in his lap. Now and then he held the fruit for the bunny to take a bite too. His face, under the smear of juice, was one big smile. Alex's happy face which he had not worn since Matt left.

"It's real good," he told them.

Scrambling to his feet he would have made for the fruit bush but Lesley swooped to catch him in a big hug.

"You're safe, Alex!"

"Silly!" He squirmed in her hold. "Silly Les. This is a good place now. See, the bunny came 'cause he knows that. An' all the birds. This is a *good* place. Here—" he struggled out of her arms, went to the bush and pulled off two of the fruit. "You eat—you'll like them."

"He shouldn't be eating those. How do we know it's good for him?" Rick pushed by to take the fruit from his brother.

Alex readily gave him one, thrust the other at Lesley.

"Eat it! It's better'n anything!"

As if she had to obey him, Lesley raised the smooth yellow fruit to her mouth. It smelled—it smelled good—like everything she liked. She bit into it.

And the taste—it did not have the sweetness of an orange, nor was it like an apple or a plum. It wasn't like anything she had eaten before. But Alex was right, it was good. And she, saw that Rick was eating, too.

When he had finished her elder brother turned to the bush and picked one, two, three, four—

"You *are* hungry," Lesley commented. She herself had taken a second. She broke it in two, dropped half to the ground for two birds. Their being there, right by her feet, did not seem in the least strange. Of course one shared. It did not matter if life wore feathers, fur, or plain skin, one shared.

"For Mom and Dad," Rick said. Then he looked around.

They could not see the whole of the field, the growth was too thick. And it was reaching out to the boundaries. Even as Lesley looked up a vine fell like a hand on their own fence, caught fast, and she was sure that was only the beginning.

"I was thinking Les," Rick said slowly. "Do you remember what Lizzy said about the fruit from *there* changing people. Do you feel any different?"

"Why no." She held out her finger. A bird fluttered up to perch there, watching her with shining beads of eyes. She laughed. "No, I don't feel any different."

Rick looked puzzled. "I never saw a bird that tame before.

Well, I wonder—Come on, let's take these to Mom and Dad."

They started for the fence where two green runners now clung. Lesley looked at the house, down the street to where the apartment made a monstrous outline against the morning sky.

"Rick, why do people want to live in such ugly places. And it smells bad—"

He nodded. "But all that's going to change. You know it, don't you?"

She gave a sigh of relief. Of course she knew it. The change was beginning and it would go on and on until *here* was like *there* and the rule of iron was broken for all time.

The rule of iron? Lesley shook her head as if to shake away a puzzling thought. But, of course, she must have always known this. Why did she have one small memory that this was strange? The rule of iron was gone, the long night of waiting over now.

The Gifts Of Asti

EVEN here, on the black terrace before the forgotten mountain retreat of Asti, it was possible to smell the dank stench of burning Memphir, to imagine that the dawn wind bore upward from the pillaged city the faint tortured cries of those whom the barbarians of Klem hunted to their prolonged death. Indeed it was time to leave.

Varta, last of the virgin Maidens of Asti, shivered. The scaled and wattled creature who crouched beside her thigh turned his reptilian head so that golden eyes met the aquamarine ones set slantingly at a faintly provocative angle in her smooth ivory face.

"We go—?"

She nodded in answer to that unvoiced question Lur had sent into her brain, and turned toward the dark cavern which was the mouth of Asti's last dwelling place. Once, more than a thousand years before when the walls of Memphir were young, Asti had lived among men below. But in the richness and softness which was trading Memphir, empire of empires, Asti found no place. So He and those who served Him had withdrawn to this mountain outcrop. And she, Varta, was the last, the very last to bow knee at Asti's shrine and raise her voice in the dawn hymn—for Lur, as were all his race, was mute.

Even the loot of Memphir would not sate the shaggy headed warriors who had stormed her gates this day. The stairway to Asti's Temple was plain enough to see and there would be those to essay the steep climb hoping to find a treasure which did not exist. For Asti was an austere God, delighting in plain walls and bare altars. His last priest had lain in the grave niches these three years, there would be none to hold that gate against intruders.

Varta passed between tall, uncarved pillars, Lur padding beside her, his spine mane erect, the talons on his forefeet clicking on the stone in steady rhythm. So they came into the innermost shrine of Asti and there Varta made graceful obeisance to the great cowled and robed figure which sat enthroned, its hidden eyes focused upon its own outstretched hand.

And above the flattened palm of that wide hand hung suspended in space the round orange-red sun ball which was twin to the sun that lighted Erb. Around the miniature sun swung in their orbits the four worlds of the system, each obeying the laws of space, even as did the planets they represented.

"Memphir has fallen," Varta's voice sounded rusty in her own ears. She had spoken so seldom during the last lonely months. "Evil has risen to overwhelm our world, even as it was prophesied in Your Revelations, O, Ruler of Worlds and Maker of Destiny. Therefore, obeying the order given of old, I would depart from this, Thy house. Suffer me now to fulfill the Law—"

Three times she prostrated her slim body on the stones at the foot of Asti's judgment chair. Then she arose and, with the confidence of a child in its father, she laid her hand palm upward upon the outstretched hand of Asti. Beneath her flesh the stone was not cold and hard, but seemed to have an inner heat, even as might a human hand. For a long moment she stood so and then she raised her hand slowly, carefully, as if within its slight hollow she cupped something precious.

And, as she drew her hand away from the grasp of Asti, the tiny sun and its planets followed, spinning now above her palm as they had above the statue's. But out of the cowled figure some virtue had departed with the going of the miniature solar system, it was now but a carving of stone. And Varta did not look at it again as she passed behind its bulk to seek a certain place in the temple wall, known to her from much reading of the old records.

Having found the stone she sought, she moved her hand in a certain pattern before it so that the faint radiance streaming from the tiny sun, gleamed on the grayness of the wall.

There was a grating, as from metal long unused, and a block fell back, opening a narrow door to them.

Before she stepped within, the priestess lifted her hand above her head and when she withdrew it, the sun and planets remained to form a diadem just above the intricate braiding of her dull red hair. As she moved into the secret way, the five orbs swung with her, and in the darkness there the sun glowed richly, sending out a light to guide their feet.

They were at the top of a stairway and the hollow clang of the stone as it moved back into place behind them echoed through a gulf which seemed endless. But that too was as the chronicles had said and Varta knew no fear.

How long they journeyed down into the maw of the mountain and, beyond that, into the womb of Erb itself, Varta never knew. But, when feet were weary and she knew the bite of real hunger, they came into a passageway which ended in a room hollowed of solid rock. And there, preserved in the chest in which men born in the youth of Memphir had laid them, Varta found that which would keep her safe on the path she must take. She put aside the fine silks, the jeweled cincture, which had been the badge of Asti's service and drew on over her naked body a suit of scaled skin, gemmed and glistening in the rays of the small sun. There was a hood to cover the entire head, taloned gloves for the hands, webbed, clawed coverings for the feet—as of the skin of a giant, man-like lizard had been tanned and fashioned into this suit. And Varta suspected that that might be so—the world of Erb had not always been held by the human-kind alone.

There were supplies here too, lying untouched in ageless containers within a lizard-skin pouch. Varta touched her tongue without fear to a powdered restorative, sharing it with Lur, whose own mailed skin would protect him through the dangers to come.

She folded the regalia she had stripped off and laid it in the chest, smoothing it regretfully before she dropped the lid upon its shimmering color. Never again would Asti's servant wear the soft stuff of His Livery. But she was resolute enough when she picked up the food pouch and strode forward, passing out of the robing chamber into a narrow way which was a natural fault in the rock unsmoothed by the tools of man.

But when this rocky road ended upon the lip of a gorge, Varta hesitated, plucking at the throat latch of her hood-like helmet. Through the unclouded crystal of its eye-holes she could see the sprouts of yellow vapor which puffed from crannies in the rock wall down which she must climb. If the records of the Temple spoke true, these curls of gas were death to all lunged creatures of the upper world. She could only trust that the cunning of the scaled hood would not fail her.

The long talons fitted to the finger tips of the gloves, the claws of the webbed foot coverings clamped fast to every hand and foot hold, but the way down was long and she caught a message of weariness from Lur before they reached the piled rocks at the foot of the cliff. The puffs of steamy gas had become a fog through which they groped their way slowly, following a trace of path along the base of the cliff.

Time did not exist in the underworld of Erb. Varta did not know whether it was still today, or whether she had passed into tomorrow when they came to a cross roads. She felt Lur press against her, forcing her back against a rock.

"There is a thing coming—" his message was clear.

And in a moment she too saw a dark hulk nosing through the vapor. It moved slowly, seeming to balance at each step as if travel was a painful act. But it bore steadily to the meeting of the two paths.

"It is no enemy—" But she did not need that reassurance from Lur. Unearthly as the thing looked it had no menace.

With a last twist of ungainly body the creature squatted on a rock and clawed the clumsy covering it wore about its bone-thin shoulders and domed-skull head. The visage it revealed was long and gray, with dark pits for eyes and a gaping, fang-studded, lipless mouth.

"Who are you who dare to tread the forgotten ways and rouse from slumber the Guardian of the Chasms?"

The question was a shrill whine in her brain, her hands half arose to cover her ears.

"I am Varta, Maiden of Asti. Memphir has fallen to the barbarians of the Outer Lands and now I go, as Asti once ordered—"

The Guardian considered her answer gravely. In one skeleton claw it fumbled a rod and with this it now traced certain symbols in the dust before Varta's webbed feet. When it had done, the girl stooped and altered two of the lines with a swift stroke from one of her talons. The creature of the Chasms nodded its misshapen head.

"Asti does not rule here. But long, and long, and long ago there was a pact made with us in His Name. Pass free from us, woman of the Light. There are two paths before you—"

The Guardian paused for so long that Varta dared to prompt it.

"Where do they lead, Guardian of the Dark?"

"This will take you down into my country," it jerked the rod to the right. "And that way is death for creatures from the surface world. The other—in our old legends it is said to bring a traveler out into the upper world. Of the truth of that I have no proof."

"But that one I must take," she made slight obeisance to the huddle of bones and dank cloak on the rock and it inclined its head in grave courtesy.

With Lur pushing a little ahead, she took the road which ran straight into the flume-veiled darkness. Nor did she turn to look again at the Thing from the Chasm world.

They began to climb again, across the slimed rock where there were evil trails of other things which lived in this haunted darkness. But the sun of Asti lighted their way and perhaps some virtue in the rays from it kept away the makers of such trails.

When they pulled themselves up onto a wide ledge the talons on Varta's gloves were worn to splintered stubs and there was a bright girdle of pain about her aching body. Lur lay panting beside her, his red-forked tongue protruding from his foam ringed mouth.

"We walk again the ways of men," Lur was the first to note the tool marks on the stone where they lay. "By the Will of Asti, we may win out of this maze after all."

Since there were no signs of the deadly steam Varta dared to push off her hood and share with her companion the sustaining power she carried in her pouch. There was a freshness to the air they breathed, damp and cold though it was, which hinted of the upper world.

The ledge sloped upwards, at a steep angle at first, and then more gently. Lur slipped past her and thrust head and shoulders through a break in the rock. Grasping his neck spines she allowed him to pull her through that narrow slit into the soft blackness of a surface night. They tumbled down together, Varta's head pillowed on Lur's smooth side, and so slept as the sun and worlds of Asti whirled protectingly above them.

A whir of wings in the air above her head awakened Varta. One of the small, jewel bright flying lizard creatures of the deep jungle poised and dipped to investigate more closely the worlds of Asti. But at Varta's upflung arm it uttered a rasping cry and planed down into the mass of vegetation below. By the glint of sunlight on the stone around them the day was already well advanced. Varta tugged at Lur's mane until he roused.

There was a regularity to the rocks piled about their sleeping place which hinted that they had lain among the ruins left by man. But of this side of the mountains both were ignorant, for Memphir's rule had not run here.

"Many dead things in times past," Lur's scarlet nostril pits were extended to their widest. "But that was long ago. This land is no longer held by men."

Varta laughed cheerfully. "If here there are no men, then there will rise no barbarian hordes to dispute over rule. Asti has led us to safety. Let us see more of the land He gives us."

There was a road leading down from the ruins, a road still to be followed in spite of the lash of landslip and the crack of time. And it brought them into a cup of green fertility where the lavishness of Asti's sowing was unchecked by man. Varta seized eagerly upon globes of blood red fruit which she recognized as delicacies which had been cultivated in the Temple gardens, while Lur went hunting into the fringes of the jungle, there dining on prey so easily caught as to be judged devoid of fear.

The jungle-choked highway curved and they were suddenly fronted by a desert of sere desolation, a desert floored by glassy slag which sent back the sun beams in a furnace glare. Varta shaded her eyes and tried to see the end of this, but, if there was a distant rim of green beyond, the heat distortions in the air concealed it.

Lur put out a front paw to test the slag but withdrew it instantly.

"It cooks the flesh, we can not walk here," was his verdict.

Varta pointed with her chin to the left where, some distance away, the mountain wall paralleled their course.

"Then let us keep to the jungle over there and see if it does not bring around to the far side. But what made this—?" She leaned out over the glassy stuff, not daring to touch the slick surface.

"War." Lur's tongue shot out to impale a questing beetle. "These forgotten people fought with fearsome weapons."

"But what weapon could do this? Memphir knew not such—"

"Memphir was old. But mayhap there were those who raised cities on Erb before the first hut of Memphir squatted on tidal mud. Men forget knowledge in time. Even in Memphir the lords of the last days forgot the wisdom of their earlier sages—they fell before the barbarians easily enough."

"If ever men had wisdom to produce this—it was not of Asti's giving," she edged away from the glare. "Let us go."

But now they had to fight their way through jungle and it was hard—until they reached a ridge of rock running out from the mountain as a tongue thrust into the blasted valley. And along this they picked their slow way.

"There is water near—" Lur's thought answered the girl's desire. She licked her dry lips longingly. "This way—" her companion's sudden turn was to the left and Varta was quick to follow him down a slide of rock.

Lur's instinct was right, as it ever was. There was water before them, a small lake of it. But even as he dipped his fanged muzzle toward that inviting surface, Lur's spined head jerked erect again. Varta snatched back the hand she had put out, staring at Lur's strange actions. His nostrils expanded to their widest, his long neck outstretched, he was swinging his head back and forth across the limpid shallows.

"What is it—?"

"This is no water such as we know," the scaled one answered flatly. "It has life within it."

Varta laughed. "Fish, water snakes, your own distant kin, Lur. It is the scent of them which you catch—"

"No. It is the water itself which lives—and yet does not live—" His thought trailed away from her as he struggled with some problem. No human brain could follow his unless he willed it so.

Varta squatted back on her heels and began to look at the water and then at the banks with more care. For the first time she noted the odd patches of brilliant color which floated just below the surface of the liquid. Blue, green, yellow, crimson, they drifted slowly with the tiny waves which lapped the shore. But they were not alive, she was almost sure of that, they appeared more a part of the water itself.

Watching the voyage of one patch of green she caught sight of the branch. It was a drooping shoot of the turbi, the same tree vine which produced the fruit she had relished less than an hour before. Above the water dangled a cluster of the fruit, dead ripe with the sweet pulp stretching its skin. But below the surface of the water. . . .

Varta's breath hissed between her teeth and Lur's head snapped around as he caught her thought.

The branch below the water bore a perfect circle of green flowers close to its tip, the flowers which the turbi had born naturally seven months before and which should long ago have turned into just such sweetness as hung above.

With Lur at her heels the girl edged around to pull cautiously at the branch. It yielded at once to her touch, swinging its tip out of the lake. She sniffed—there was a languid perfume in the air, the perfume of the blooming turbi. She examined the flowers closely, to all appearances they were perfect and natural.

"It preserves," Lur settled back on his haunches and waved one front paw at the quiet water. "What goes into it remains as it was just at the moment of entrance."

"But if this is seven months old—"

"It may be seven years old," corrected Lur. "How can you tell when that branch first dipped into the lake? Yet the flowers do not fade even when withdrawn from the water. This indeed is a mystery!"

"Of which I would know more!" Varta dropped the turbi and started on around the edge of the lake.

Twice more they found similar evidence of preservation in flower or leaf, wherever it was covered by the opaline water.

The lake itself was a long and narrow slash with one end cutting into the desert of glass while the other wet the foot of the mountain. And it was there on the slope of the mountain that they found the greatest wonder of all, Lur scenting it before they sighted the remains among the stones.

"Man made," he cautioned, "but very, very old."

And truly the wreckage they came upon must have been old, perhaps even older than Memphir. For the part which rested above the water was almost gone, rusty red stains on the rocks outlining where it had lain. But under water was a smooth silver hull, shining and untouched by the years.

Varta laid her hand upon a ruddy scrap between two rocks and it became a drift of powdery dust. And yet—there a few feet below was strong metal!

Lur padded along the scrap of shore surveying the thing.

"It was a machine in which men traveled," his thoughts arose to her. "But they were not as the men of Memphir. Perhaps not even as the son of Erb—"

"Not as the sons of Erb!" her astonishment broke into open speech.

Lur's neck twisted as he looked up at her. "Did the men of Erb, even in the old chronicles fight with weapons such as would make a desert of glass? There are other worlds than Erb, mayhap this strange thing was a sky ship from such a world. All things are possible by the Will of Asti."

Varta nodded. "All things are possible by the Will of Asti," she repeated. "But, Lur," her eyes were round with wonder, "perhaps it is Asti's Will which brought us here to find this marvel! Perhaps He has some use for us and it!"

"At least we may discover what lies within it." Lur had his own share of curiosity.

"How? The two of us can not draw that out of the water!"

"No, but we can enter into it!"

Varta fingered the folds of the hood on her shoulders. She knew what Lur meant, the suit which had protected her in the underworld was impervious to everything outside its surface—or to every substance its makers knew—just as Lur's own hide made his flesh impenetrable. But the fashioners of her suit had probably never known of the living lake and what if she had no defense against the strange properties of the water?

She leaned back against a rock. Overhead the worlds and sun of Asti still traveled their appointed paths. The worlds of Asti! If it was His Will which had brought them here, then Asti's power would wrap her round with safety. By His Will she had come out of Memphir over ways no human of Erb had ever trod before. Could she doubt that His Protection was with her now?

It took only a moment to make secure the webbed shoes, to pull on and fasten the hood, to tighten the buckles of her gloves. Then she crept forward, shuddering as the water rose about her ankles. But Lur pushed on before her, his head disappearing fearlessly under the surface as he crawled through the jagged opening in the ship below.

Smashed engines which had no meaning in her eyes occupied most of the broken section of the wreck. None of the metal showed any deterioration beyond that which had occurred at the time of the crash. Under her exploring hands it was firm and whole.

Lur was pulling at a small door half hidden by a mass of twisted wires and plates and, just as Varta crawled around this obstacle to join him, the barrier gave way allowing them to squeeze through into what had once been the living quarters of the ship.

Varta recognized seats, a table, and other bits of strictly utilitarian furniture. But of those who had once been at home there, there remained no trace. Lur, having given one glance to the furnishings, was prowling about the far end of the cabin uncertainly, and now he voiced his uneasiness.

"There is something beyond, something which once had life—"

Varta crowded up to him. To her eyes the wall seemed without line of an opening, and yet Lur was running his broad front paws over it carefully, now and then throwing his weight against the smooth surface.

"There is no door—" she pointed out doubtfully.

"No door—ah—here—" Lur unsheathed formidable fighting claws to their full length for perhaps the first time in his temple-sheltered life, and endeavored to work them into a small crevice. The muscles of his forelegs and quarters stood out in sharp relief under his scales, his fangs were bare as his lips snapped back with effort.

Something gave, a thin black line appeared to mark the edges of a door. Then time, or Lur's strength, broke the ancient locking mechanism. The door gave so suddenly that they were both sent hurtling backward and Lur's breath burst from him in a huge bubble.

The sealed compartment was hardly more than a cupboard but it was full. Spread-eagled against the wall was a four-limbed creature whose form was so smothered in a bulky suit that Varta could only guess that it was akin in shape to her own. Hoops of metal locked it firmly to the wall, but the head had fallen forward so that the face plate in the helmet was hidden.

Slowly the girl breasted the water which filled the cabin and reached her hands toward the bowed helmet of the prisoner. Gingerly, her blunted talons scraping across metal, she pulled it up to her eye level.

The eyes of that which stood within the suit were closed, as if in sleep, but there was a warm, healthy tint to the bronze skin, so different in shade to her own pallid coloring. For the rest, the prisoner had the two eyes, the centered nose, the properly shaped mouth which were common to the men of Erb. Hair grew on his head, black and thick and there was a faint shadow of beard on his jaw line.

"This is a man—" her thought reached Lur.

"Why not? Did you expect a serpent? It is a pity he is dead—"

Varta felt a rich warm tide rising in her throat to answer that teasing half question. There were times when Lur's thought reading was annoying. He had risen to his hind legs so that he too could look into the shell which held their find.

"Yes, a pity," he repeated. "But—"

A vision of the turbi flowers swept through her mind. Had Lur suggested it, or had that wild thought been hers alone? Only this ship was so old—so very old!

Lur's red tongue flicked. "It can do no harm to try—" he suggested slyly and set his claws into the hoop holding the captive's right wrist, testing its strength.

"But the metal on the shore, it crumpled into powder at my touch—" she protested. "What if we carry him out only to have—to have—" Her mind shuddered away from the picture which followed.

"Did the turbi blossom fade when pulled out?" countered Lur. "There is a secret to these fastenings—" He pulled and pried impatiently.

Varta tried to help but even their united strength was useless against the force which held the loops in place. Breathless the girl slumped back against the wall of the cabin while Lur settled down on his haunches. One of the odd patches of color drifted by, its vivid scarlet like a jewel spiraling lazily upward. Varta's eyes followed its drift and so were guided to what she had forgotten, the worlds of Asti.

"Asti!"

Lur was looking up too.

"The power of Asti!"

Varta's hand went up, rested for a long moment under the sun and then drew it down, carefully, slowly, as she had in Memphir's temple. Then she stepped toward the captive. Within her hood a beaded line of moisture outlined her lips, a pulse thundered on her temple. This was a fearsome thing to try.

She held the sun on a line with one of the wrist bonds. She must avoid the flesh it imprisoned, for Asti's power could kill.

From the sun there shot an orange-red beam to strike full upon the metal. A thin line of red crept across the smooth hoop, crept and widened. Varta raised her hand, sending the sun spinning up and Lur's claws pulled on the metal. It broke like rotten wood in his grasp.

The girl gave a little gasp of half-terrified delight. Then the old legends were true! As Asti's priestess she controlled powers too great to guess. Swiftly she loosed the other hoops and restored the sun and worlds to their place over her head as the captive slumped across the threshold of his cell.

Tugging and straining they brought him out of the broken ship into the sunlight of Erb. Varta threw back her hood and breathed deeply of the air which was not manufactured by the wizardry of the lizard skin and Lur sat panting, his nostril flaps open. It was he who spied the spring on the mountain side above, a spring of water uncontaminated by the strange life of the lake. They both dragged themselves there to drink deeply.

Varta returned to the lake shore reluctantly. Within her heart she believed that the man they had brought from the ship was truly dead. Lur might hold out the promise of the flowers, but this was a man and he had lain in the water for countless ages.

So she went with lagging steps, to find Lur busy. He had solved the mystery of the space suit and had stripped it from the unknown. Now his clawed paw rested lightly on the bared chest and he turned to Varta eagerly.

"There is life—"

Hardly daring to believe that, she dropped down beside Lur and touched their prize. Lur was right, the flesh was warm and she had caught the faint rhythm of shallow breath. Half remembering old tales, she put her hands on the arch of the lower ribs and began to aid that rhythm. The breaths were deeper.

Then the man half turned, his arm moved. Varta and Lur drew back.

For the first time the girl probed gently the sleeping mind before her—even as she had read the minds of those few of Memphir who had ascended to the temple precincts in the last days.

Much of what she read now was confused or so alien to Erb that it had no meaning for her. But she saw a great city plunged into flaming death in an instant and felt the horror and remorse of the man at her feet because of his own part in that act, the horror and remorse which had led him to open rebellion and so to his imprisonment. There was a last dark and frightening memory of a door closing on light and hope.

The space man moaned softly and hunched his shoulders as if he struggled vainly to tear loose from bonds.

"He thinks that he is still prisoner," observed Lur. "For

him life begins at the very point it ended—even as it did for the turbi flowers. See—now he awakens."

The eyelids rose slowly, as if the man hated to see what he must look upon. Then, as he sighted Varta and Lur, his eyes went wide. He pulled himself up and looked dazedly around, striking out wildly with his fists. Catching sight of the clumsy suit Lur had taken from him he pulled at it, looking at the two before him as if he feared some attack.

Varta turned to Lur for help. She might read minds and use the wordless speech of Lur. But his people knew the art of such communication long before the first priest of Asti had stumbled upon their secret. Let Lur now quiet this outlander.

Delicately Lur sought a way into the other's mind, twisting down paths of thought strange to him. Even Varta could not follow the subtle waves sent forth in the quick examination and reconnoitering, nor could she understand all of the conversation which resulted. For the man from the ancient ship answered in speech aloud, sharp harsh sounds of no meaning. It was only after repeated instruction from Lur that he began to frame his messages in his mind, clumsily and disconnectedly.

Pictures of another world, another solar system, began to grow more clear as the space man became more at home in the new way of communication. He was one of a race who had come to Erb from beyond the stars and discovered it a world without human life. So they had established colonies and built great cities—far different from Memphir—and had lived in peace for centuries of their own time.

Then on the faraway planet of their birth there had begun a great war, which brought flaming death to all that world. The survivors of a last battle in outer space had fled to the colonies on Erb. But among this handful were men driven mad by the death of their world, and these had blasted the cities of Erb, saying that their kind must be wiped out.

The man they had rescued had turned against one such maddened leader and had been imprisoned just before an attack upon the largest of the colony's cities. After that he remembered nothing.

Varta stopped trying to follow the conversation—Lur was only explaining now how they had found the space man and brought him out of the wrecked ship. No human on Erb, this one had said, and yet were there not her own people, the ones who had built Memphir? And what of the barbarians, who, ruthless and cruel as they seemed by the standards of Memphir, were indeed men? Whence had they come then, the men of Memphir and the ancestors of the barbarian hordes? Her hands touched the scaled skin of the suit she still wore and then rubbed across her own smooth flesh. Could one have come from the other, was she of the blood and heritage of Lur?

"Not so!" Lur's mind, as quick as his flickering tongue, had caught that panic-born thought. "You are of the blood of this space wanderer. Men from the riven colonies must have escaped to safety. Look at this man, is he not like the men of Memphir—as they were in the olden days of the city's greatness?"

The stranger was tall, taller than the men of Memphir and there was a certain hardness about him which those city dwellers in ease had never displayed. But Lur must be right, this was a man of her race. She smiled in sudden relief and he answered that smile. Lur's soft laughter rang in both their heads.

"Asti in His Infinite Wisdom can see through Centuries. Memphir has fallen because of its softness and the evildoing of its people and the barbarians will now have their way with the lands of the north. But to me it appears that Asti is not yet done with the pattern He was weaving there. To each of you He granted a second life. Do not disdain the Gifts of Asti, Daughter of Erb!"

Again Varta felt the warm tide of blood rise in her cheeks. But she no longer smiled. Instead she regarded the outlander speculatively.

Not even a Maiden of the Temple could withstand the commands of the All Highest. Gifts from the Hand of Asti dared not be thrown away.

Above the puzzlement of the stranger she heard the chuckling of Lur.

Long Live Lord Kor!

When in 3450 (old Terran reckoning) El Zim made the momentous breakthrough that allowed time travel, the long-discussed threat of fatal meddling in the past became real. Strong measures were quickly taken to ensure no indiscriminate exploration, though Zim and his assistants had already promised great caution.

By 3465 the controls had hardened into a bureaucratic system of monitorial services with trained and screened operatives. Meddling was allowed, even authorized, if done "by the book" and not on planets included in the home systems of the existing in-power groups.

For example, on some planets discovered by the ever-widening space search of Survey, history had taken grim turns. Such worlds were declared open "for the good of all" to the newly organized Bureau of Time Exploration and Manipulation.

Several dazzling successes in bringing, as it were, the dead back to life were enough to entrench the Bureau. And the benefits, so widely advertised, could not be denied by even the most cautious and conservative. Of course, there were failures, too. But most of those were mentioned only in obscure reports carefully swallowed by the headquarters computer under a do-not-divulge code.

By 3500 the whole operation had been refined sufficiently to run more or less smoothly under data supplied by ZAT, a master computer whose limitations had yet to be discovered.

But men are not machines. Occasionally crises arose. The answer was a second elite corps trained to snatch victory from defeat if such were possible.

I

Creed Trapnell snorted, "What's the alibi this time—computer error? Of course, anyone with a grain of imagination might think that's been a little bit overworked. Let's see—that leaves that other bit of blame-shuffling, the one about insufficient native data obtained by survey crew."

Controller Goddard, Field Force Five, had never been known to display emotion. There was a legend sometimes accepted by cadets as truth, that he was only a humanoid body housing an extension of ZAT's computer brain. Now he did not raise his eyes from the TV screen implanted in his desk.

Goddard had no easirests in his office. He carefully cultivated the art of making visitors uncomfortable so that they would not linger and use up his valuable time. But Trapnell sprawled as much as his stiff chair allowed, his booted feet leaving faint smudges on the neutral green of the carpet.

Creed Trapnell was far from being in uniform. The boots were scuffed, the breeches above them bagged and stained. His shirt, tucked into a wide belt studded with metal bosses, had once had sleeves as a ragged fringe about the arm-holes testified. Now his deeply tanned arms were bare. He looked the ragged wanderer, which gave him pleasure. He had no reason to want to please Goddard.

"Insufficient native data," he repeated lazily. "That must be it. They haven't used it for—" He held out his hands, reckoning time by turning down fingers, "For at least four calls now: And," he added, "I am on certified leave." Such a reminder might do him no good but at least it would register on the tape Goddard kept running.

Goddard looked up, eyes blank. When he spoke his voice held enough metallic twang to carry out the robot illusion.

"The excuse is falsified work reports."

Trapnell sat up as if jerked.

"I don't believe it!" He slapped his knee and dust flew from the breeches. "It isn't possible they would ever admit that."

"They had no choice." Had there, or had there not been a flicker of feeling in Goddard's eyes? This he should relish that the arrogant Fore Office, which always expected Goddard's

men to pick up the pieces without open recognition of their services and only grudging acceptance of their existence, had to admit an error of its own.

Trapnell was excited, a little. This was more than he had expected when Goddard had recalled him from a well-earned leave. It must be N hot, if the front office admitted a mistake.

Goddard flashed on the wall screen and said twangily, "Vallek." The word meant nothing to Trapnell, but the screen filled with a picture. They could be looking out of a window at a brilliantly hued landscape. In the foreground stretched a city: walled, towered, enveloped by fields of vegetation not a true green, having a golden sheen. And the architecture of the city was alien.

Swiftly Trapnell's trained mind evaluated and filed the scene.

Then the city disappeared into a new panorama. Desert country. The sky was a golden sheet deepening into orange, the ground underneath was umber. No vegetation at all—yet the soil was broken here and there by ridges of rock, buttes. And against the horizon loomed a chain of mountains.

Now the desert picture gave way to a close-up of one of the mountains. One slope was broken by a cliff carved and embellished, the patterns inlaid with metal and gems, so that it glittered under the yellow sky.

"Orm Temple," Goddard indentified.

There were other scenes, some within that cleft where rock-walled ways bore murals. As they scanned this spot or that, Goddard supplied brief explanation.

Finally the Controller snapped off the viewer. "The position is this. Vallek lies today in Point Six Sector—but it is a radioactive cinder."

"N War? I don't get it. That view was of a feudal level civilization."

"You saw a time of split," Goddard returned. "From there the future is in doubt. Shortly thereafter a Holy War was proclaimed by the priests of the Worm—their oracle made a prophecy which helped defeat the Kor-King of the city— Lanascol. Then their theocracy fell apart ten years later, making way for a conqueror from the south. He established a line, which some two hundred years later, developed a technology that within five hundred years more blew Vallek into a cinder. The priests of the worm must not start that war—if we can help it."

"How do we work—through the oracle?"

"Just so. You'll have briefing—but the situation is this—their oracle is always an imbecile. And he never lives very long. When he dies the priests set out on a quest which reaches out all over Vallek. They must find an idiot baby, male, born at the very moment of the previous oracle's passing. The child is always completely empty-minded."

"Then he must mouth what some priest tells him—"

"You would think so," Goddard agreed. "Only, as far as the spy rays have discovered, that isn't true. When they want a prophecy he is taken to a seat overlooking a so-called 'worm walk' and left there for the night. When they bring him out he repeats, in perfectly intelligible language—though normally he only mouths sounds—an answer. The entrance to the Walk is guarded closely. So far we cannot detect any manner of fraud. But ZAT says it is more than meddling by some priest. And this time he must not give any war prophecy."

"How can you be so sure that your southern conqueror won't eventually take over anyway?"

"ZAT says no. If Lanascol continues to exist as a strong power the development of a higher civilization will follow another road altogether. Now—you perceive the advantage of the idiot oracle?"

"You mean he is the one to be occupied? Sounds simple enough. What went wrong?"

"That is what you must find out. ZAT says wrong data was fed in and our man never arrived."

"But—" Trapnell was startled.

"Yes—but! This was not discovered until the official weekly summary was supplied by ZAT. There was an alarm—we found the falsified tapes."

"It should be easy to discover who had access—"

"The falsification was done in the spy records—on the other side. So ZAT reports."

"Wow! We have a resident agent there?"

"Naturally. ZAT gives clearance in that direction. It's plain someone else meddled."

"But that's impossible!" Trapnell felt as if the green carpet under his dusty boots had opened a mouth. Facts he had accepted as solid all his life. . . .

"We have pushed ZAT for an answer. The reply was insufficient data. But no denial. So we are faced with two possibilities. One, we have a traitor in our service. Two, we are not the only ones operating along this line. After all the galaxy is too large for any one empire, confederation or species to know. There may well be another Service in business. That we have not come across it before is a perfectly reasonable chance."

"But why a falsified report?"

"One can think of several reasons. We may be under observation. We wish to save Vallek—the others might not want that. Or they may be throwing up an obstacle to test us."

"A nice dish you've put on my table," Trapnell commented sourly. "So I play the oracle and, at the same time, try to discover who doesn't want me there. By the way, does the front office have any trace of what happened to their man?"

"Not as yet. The resident agent has been alerted. Look, this is a rush job. They are waiting for you in briefing. You've only a few planet days before you're supposed to prophesy. And this must go through—it's AA priority."

Trapnell stood up. "Aren't they always when we get them?"

"We don't get them until they hit the hot line. Remember, this time the job's double."

"As if I can forget," Trapnell said as he went out.

Lying in the send-sling, a briefing helm clamped on his head, watching the techs make ready, Trapnell wondered why he stayed in the Service. He was tired. Gone was the bounce he had once known. He had lived how many other lives? He couldn't even reckon them. And most had been dangerous ones. Twice he had even been killed and the techs had had to pull him back in a hurry to save him in time. To say nothing of the occasions he had lived through torture, maiming and other ills in his borrowed bodies. There was always the one fact, too, he could be planted only in a mindless, near-zero-idiot body, which meant complications from the start. That was why the resident agents went through in another technique to receive and sustain the action man. They never had any hope of return. At least he did not have to face permanent exile in that manner.

He suffered through that last moment of rebellion, as usual—the desire to throw off the helm and shout out a refusal to go. Then the tech threw the switch.

Wakening from the send was always to be dreaded. There was a period of disorientation miserable for the victim. And

Trapnell always hated to open his eyes to the new surroundings, to inspect his new body. But delay offered nothing and
he nerved himself to open his eyes.

He stared straight up into the folds of a tent or canopy. It
was not of the vivid colors he associated with this world but
of a pearl shade with a shimmering rainbow overcast. Turning his head gave him sight of a window with the yellow sky
beyond. Over that opening stretched a finely barred netting.
And on either side hung drapes of the same pearl luster as
the canopy.

His hands slid over a silky surface. It was apparent he lay
in a richly provided bed. Now he dared to brace himself up
on his elbows. He saw that set in the footposts of the bed
were rings of metal from which ran chains disappearing under the coverings. He threw those aside. His ankles were fitted with silver bands to which the chains were fastened. A
prisoner!

Perhaps this oracle was not so much of an idiot as to lead
a vegetable existence. Perhaps this oracle, rather, was mobile,
apt to wander off if not restrained. The grill at the window
could be a further barrier. He had a role to play which
would automatically be triggered as soon as he sighted his
keepers. The briefing would have seen to that.

Now he tried to judge the length of the chains and when
he moved they clashed with a faintly musical ring. For the
first time he examined his body. Somehow he had thought to
find it small and puny or else of a bloated, unhealthy aspect.
But his legs, the rest of him, were lean, well muscled, the
skin a tan-red in color. There was a puckered scar down the
outside of one thigh, long healed yet still the reminder of a
wound.

He ran his fingertips over his face, found a second scar-
pucker above his left eye and running up into the line of his
hair. And that was tender. Odd—if he were the idiot oracle
kept by the priests since childhood, how had his body, in such
fit condition, acquired those scars?

His movements again set the chains to ringing. A man
came around the canopy curtains. He was not wearing the
red robes the briefing had said were a priest's. Nor did the
sight of him trigger the response Trapnell expected.

Though it was hard to judge Trapnell in another race, the newcomer might be on the verge of middle years. He wore high
boots, above them skin-tight leggings, and a high-collared,
long-sleeved, wide-skirted tunic without visible fastenings.

That was of a dull blue shade and on the breast was embroidered an elaborate symbol in silver, parts of the design glinting with tiny gems.

He had a belt of silver links which supported the holster of a rodlike weapon. And he gave the appearance of a competent fighting man. His skin was red-brown, his hair seemingly black until he walked into the full window light to prove it a dark red.

Staring at the newcomer, Trapnell was disturbed by his lack of other reaction. This was the first time a send-briefing had ever failed to fit him at once into his assumed role. He simply had no background to fit here. Unless this were another case of a send gone wrong and he was in a place not meant ... He would have to be careful until either his briefing knowledge would be triggered to life or he could discover what had happened.

The man voiced an exclamation as he studied Trapnell.

"My Lord Kor!" His voice was sharp, excited. "Your mind—it is back from the dark!"

My Lord Kor—the Kor-King? But that was in Lanascol, not in Orm Temple! It was clear he was neither where he was supposed to be nor whom. He put his hand to his head without realizing he made that gesture.

"Your wound, Lord Kor—does it still pain you? It was indeed a grievous slash, dealing a hard blow—"

A head wound. And an exchange of bodies could never be made with a sentient subject. So had he arrived in a body where a head wound had made the victim an imbecile? If so—well, he perhaps had a chance. Certainly it was a logical explanation, though if he had not reached the oracle—why?

"It pains—a little—" he mumbled. "I—I cannot remember—" Give them that explanation and use it for the only cloak he had.

"It like to split your skull, Lord Kor," the other men assured him. "You have wandered in the dark for many days, not knowing the Kor-King, your father, nor the Lady Yarakoma, those nearest to you. Food had to be put in your mouth, and you tended like a babe of tender years. And then—when the ravings came upon you—" He shook his head. "You would have harmed yourself had we not—"

"Had we not what, Girant?" A second man moved out to stand beside the first. He bore no symbol on the front of his green tunic. And he had a sleeveless cloak, his arms thrust through the open slits. The garment was of white with strange red symbols bordering its hem.

For the first time Trapnell's briefing worked. The newcomer was a medico, or the closest to one of that training Vallek knew. The man shouldered Girant aside, proceeded to grip Trapnell's wrist, peer searchingly into his eyes.

"Well enough," he said after a long moment. Then he felt gently along the seal of the healing scar.

"Better than we hoped, Lord Kor," was his brisk opinion. "Tell me—what do you remember?"

Trapnell shook his head. "Nothing—I do not even know your name—or his." He pointed to the man in blue.

The latter started to talk but the medico waved his hand for quiet.

"Some difficulty is to be expected. Praise be that you have at least come to your senses. For the rest, it may be that your memory shall return, if raggedly. And there are enough here to tell you of the past—some who will enjoy it." He looked sober, as if he had some subtle meaning for that last remark.

"You are," he pointed to Trapnell, "the Lord Kor Kenric, second son to Kor-King Hernaut. Until three months ago you were Warden of the South, in command of the Border Guard. There was an attack by the Kawyn, after which you were found nigh to dead. Girant here managed to keep you breathing until he could get you back to Lanascol. You had a hole in your skull wide enough for your brains to leak through, and for a goodly while your actions have been such that we thought they had."

His words held little deference. If the Lord Kor was his superior in rank, this medico was no subservient courtier. And Trapnell-Kenric, he must begin to think of himself as Kenric—found the fellow's brusqueness bracing.

"And you are?"

"Atticus, Body Healer. You'll see much of me—as you have not before, having had a body which served you well, Lord Kor." He turned to Girant. "Best inform the Kor-King of this recovery."

"Of course." The other hurried away. Atticus seemed to be listening until there came the sound of a closing door. Then he looked to his patient once again.

"It is perhaps not meet to trouble a man with a broken head over possible danger," he said quickly. "But it is well you be warned. There are those who will take it ill that you have your wits clear again."

Now what have I gotten into, thought Trapnell. It sounded like a tangle here also. But any help he could get from Atticus he needed.

"Those being?" he prompted.

"Namely the Lady Yarakoma." Atticus paused, watching closely. Seeing no sign that his patient recognized the name, he frowned. "If you cannot remember her, you are indeed set adrift, Lord Kor."

"But I cannot. So tell me."

"She is bedfellow-in-chief to your brother Folkward, eldest son to your father. She desired to follow the old custom to secure the lineage by entering your bed also, but you would have none of her. Thus she fears lest you take a concubine and so imperil the heritage of her lord. Were you lack-witted, she need no longer hold that fear. And there are those who would stand high if she were the sole mate to the princes. So she is chief within these walls to wish you ill—"

"And outside the walls?"

The medico shrugged. "As Border Warden, one who has turned his face against any alliance with Kawyn, you have many who wish you anything but the blessing of health."

"So there are troubles to conquer," Trapnell said.

"That is so, Lord Kor. We live in troubled times. Though it is also true that all times are troubled for some who live through them. Kawyn moves in the south, her eyes ever upon Lanascol which she wishes to sweep from her path. And they say that the worm priests blat much of some dire prophecy. They expect it from that drooling voice they cherish to pronounce weighty dooms on men and nations."

Trapnell seized on that. "A new prophecy? When do they say it will be delivered?"

"Within five days. They have sent a messenger to the Kor-King, bidding him come to listen. Though he is in two minds about answering their invitation. Invitation—I would say their order. They grow more and more puffed up with their own importance since the Rovers of Dupt have winged in to pay them homage and tribute. Though were I a worm priest I would look well at any largesse offered by a Rover lest blood drip from it to stain my hands. Also I would ask myself why such would suddenly want to make one with the Worms. The Rovers have no piety in their crooked bodies. Just another worry for the Kor-King."

Trapnell nodded, not knowing what else to do.

"It is well, Lord Kor," said the medico, "that the son upon whom he can depend the most is able once more to stand at his back. You could not have regained your senses more opportunely. The Kor-King must not be allowed to enter the worm burrows."

"You are very plain of speech, Atticus."

The medico smiled grimly. "Be you glad I am, Lord Kor. I have proved my right to plain speaking, and I shall continue to exercise it."

The sound of a door, then, and Girant stepped into sight.

"The Kor-King," he announced. "And the Lady Yarakoma."

II

The night was lighted by three moons; Lord Kor Kenric gripped the balcony rail and stared down into the city. At least this much he had retained of his failed briefing: in that maze was help. The permanent agent had headquarters there. The problem was to reach him. Being the Lord Kor, newly recovered from a hurt all had believed unhealable, Trapnell did not believe he would be suffered to go about alone.

He feared such as Atticus would be on watch—for Lord Kor's good. Yet he could not waste time. He knew that within five days the oracle would signal the uprising that would finish all lying below him now.

So he had to make a move now, tonight. And he was ignorant of the passages of this keep. It would be only too easy to lose his way and alert some guard. Which meant that for egress he had to use the outside of the building rather than the inside, and now he was studying that way.

The balcony on which he stood was one of three on the same level. The one to his left overhung an arch two stories high, one story carved deeply and offering hand-holes.

He had already plundered the Lord Kor's wardrobe, donning the most inconspicuous garments he had found there. The boots he carried slung on a cord around his neck.

The tricky bit was reaching the next balcony. Setting his teeth hard upon his lower lip, he took the leap, his hands reaching for the other rail. He caught it, scrambled to firm footing. Not only his past training served him now, but the fact that he wore the body of a man who had kept in good condition.

The rest was easy. The carvings on the arch served excellently as a ladder. Once on the cobbled pavement he looked up and back. There was a dim glow in the third balconied window, but his own and that immediately above the arch were dark.

He did not have to fear sentries here. He vaulted over a bolted ceremony gate protected by solemn curses, not men. And he slipped along a blind-walled road—since it was *lese majeste'* to have a window looking out upon that way.

Reaching a main avenue, Trapnell—now thinking completely of himself as Kenric, calling himself Kenric—suited his pace to those around him. Again local custom favored him in the hooded cloaks of night wear. His impatience was good enough to have sent him running had he not held tight rein upon it. So little time! He must discover what had gone wrong. And there was a thin chance that if he could reach the oracle, he might complete the sending after all. There had been one or two cases in the past when the subject to be possessed had been in such circumstances that an intermediary had had to be used to reach him. Of course, on those occasions the action had been programed by ZAT. He put aside speculation and hurried toward his immediate goal.

At this hour there were few abroad. Twice he dodged into dark doorways and stood waiting for the night watch to pass. Then he reached a side alley and a part of his briefing went into action. Two doors down—under a shadowed overhang.

He reached the place quickly, ran fingertips over the surface. There were no street torches near and he was in the dark. His forefinger found a promising groove, followed it to a stud that he pressed three times. Then his head jerked aound. That faint sound! He flattened himself against the door.

Someone was coming down the lane as noiselessly as possible. Another agent? Someone hunting him?

As if he saw her now standing in a small slash of moonlight across the alley, Kernic suddenly recalled the woman who had come with the Kor-King to his chamber earlier. She had been soft of voice, perilously sweet of countenance—and as deadly as a falcon in swoop. He had known her type on many worlds. The women who used their bodies as weapons. Atticus had been right—the Lady Yarakoma was to be feared. Yet she had played her part well, probably hoping to win the newly recovered and memory-less Lord Kor to her wishes. If she had set a watch on him—and that could well be. . . .

His hand was on the rod in his belt holster. He did not know the nature of that weapon yet, but he did know the button that released whatever form of attack it delivered.

The faint sound which had alerted him was not repeated. He could see nothing other than a few more arched doors along the lane. The signal—why had no one answered? He felt behind him with his left hand, his right now holding the weapon. Perhaps he must press again—

The door at that instant opened soundlessly.

"Seven-nine-two."

"Eight-ten-three," came at him out of the darkness. Fingers closed about his wrist and he was drawn in. The door closed.

The hand on him tugged and he followed, not yet holstering his weapon. He felt fabric flap about. Soon they were in a dim light and he saw a small room. Its walls were hung with lengths of cloth masking any entrance, cloth night-black in color but worked with silver runes. The light came from a ball mounted on a stand in the exact center of the chamber. Two stools of a black wood faced each other across the light.

All this matched his briefing, and he instantly recognized the woman who had led him here. She was tall and rather spare, young, her face oval with well-marked features. Her skin was the red-brown of Lanascol's people, just as her hair, which she wore loose, was of a darker red.

Her robe of black bore the same silver stitching of occult designs as did the curtains. Her hands were covered by black gloves, to the fingertips of which were sewn talonlike silver nails.

He spoke first. "Niccolae."

"True." Her voice was a quiet contralto. "But who are you, wearing the guise of Lord Kor Kenric? Were you not one I should harbor you could not have passed the door warn. But of your coming I have not been advised."

He unbuckled the throat latch of his cloak.

"Something happened. I was sent to replace the oracle at Orm Temple. I awoke in this body instead."

Her eyes were long, slanting upward a little toward her temples. She studied him.

"I must believe you, since there is that here which checks your story and it has not denied you. But never before has a sending ended so."

"There was another agent—from the First Service. We have had no further word from him."

"True. Nor can I tell you aught either. I could not trace him within the temple. It is closed to all women and the priests have safeguards more formidable than this primitive world suggests. I must work in devious ways—mainly through that—" She gestured at the globe. "I have learned only this much. There are many strangers gathering at the temple now. Even the Rovers of Dupt. He whom I contacted by mind-see—though he thought he dreamed only—no longer answers. The wife of the steward for Orm Temple here in Lanascol comes to me for foreseeing. She is a good subject for sleep search but knows little. I know, however, that the priests have friends at court ready for an overturn in rule. Their first target is the man whose body you wear, their second is the Kor-King himself. I have sifted rumor and used sleep search where I could. And I believe that Lord Kor Kenric was not the victim of any Kawyn sword but of a traitor stroke."

"I have been warned by the medico Atticus of the Lady Yarakoma. But this tangle of intrigue has nothing to do with my reaching the oracle—"

She had moved to rest her strangely gloved hands on the globe, half veiling it. "You think that if you face him you may transfer?"

"Such has been known to happen. But I have an idea that if I go openly to Orm Temple, I'll have little chance of seeing the oracle—though they have sent for the Kor-King. If I am too late, that plan will no longer be of use."

She nodded. "And Orm Temple has its safeguards. Your task will be hard."

"There are only a few days left, Niccolae."

"We—"

What she would say Kenric was never to hear. He reeled back, clutching at the wall hangings for support. The material tore loose and he fell. And he saw her also crumple where she stood. His last meaningful thought was that they had been attacked by some mind thrust, and then the darkness closed in.

Consciousness returned slowly. It was like being shaken out of a deep sleep and required to solve, while still dazed, an obtuse problem. Stirring deep within him was an alarm. He felt pain then, his bruised body shifting back and forth on an unsteady surface which rose and fell. While in his ears there was a creaking.

When he tried to move, he discovered his wrists were bound together, as were his ankles, the two bonds linked by yet another cord to fetter him securely. There was a bag over his head acting as both blindfold and gag.

Kenric forced himself to think back. He had been with the agent Niccolae—then they had both been struck down. Almost as if a stunner turned on mind beam had . . . A stunner! But such a weapon was unknown here, existing far ahead in the future.

A personality could be sent back; the Service had been doing that for many years now. But such a transfer was an intricate operation. Spy rays were relatively simple compared to it. And to send weapons—impossible! Unless Goddard's suggestion of some parallel force of men could be true . . . a competing Service.

But if such were able to transport arms they must be far in advance of ZAT. Kenric chewed on that and found the thought more than a little daunting.

Niccolae had mentioned an in-gathering of strangers at Orm Temple. Among them were there other time and space travelers? Perhaps they had in some manner detected Kenric's arrival. It was never wise to underrate the enemy. Was Yarakoma a part of some intrigue they fostered? She could even be a plant for them, as Niccolae was for the Service. The possibilities were endless and unpleasant.

But speculation was of no help now. He struggled, trying to gauge the efficiency of his ties. They were tight and strong. No trick he remembered could free him.

The bag over his head was to a degree translucent. By the light filtering through he judged this to be day. He felt, too, that they were in the open. He was hot, as if he lay under the full rays of a sun. He longed for water.

Now the surface under him tilted. He slid forward, winding up against a hard wall. He could hear muffled cries. From the jolting that followed he gathered the vehicle carrying him was out of control.

His struggles suddenly brought him against something softer than the bruising surfaces, something that wriggled frantically as if trying to escape the weight of his body. Then, with a crash which slammed them together, the carrier came to an abrupt halt.

A low moan sounded close to his ear. There was a feeble pushing against him. Niccolae? He tried to roll away and did lift some of his weight from that close contact. Then a punishing grip closed on his shoulders. He was jerked across an uneven surface that left splinters in his hands, then thrown to the ground. Only the bag saved his face from grinding into rough gravel. And the fall knocked the breath out of him.

He lay gasping until hands hooked in his armpits, drew him along on his back bumping over rocks, and slammed him finally against a stone that supported him in a half-sitting position, his legs drawn into a cramping curve by the bonds. The stone behind him was hot. Fingers fumbled about his throat and in a moment the bag was off, he was near blinded by sun glare.

Squinting as his sight adjusted, he observed three men in rough clothing. And this must be the desert with its rusty sands. Though there was the shimmer of heat resembling those Goddard had shown him on the viewing screen.

One of the three put fingers to his lips and whistled shrilly. He was answered in a like manner from not too far away. In the meantime Kenric worked his head around to see Niccolae's black robe, now creased and torn, making a dark blot at a neighboring rock. She rested also in a cramped position, her head fallen forward so her hair screened her face. He could not tell whether she were conscious or not.

"We have delivered—" So the whistler spoke.

He stood with his hand out in demand, but there was an air of uneasiness about him. His two companions closed in as if all three were ready to take to their heels as soon as their transaction were completed.

"We have delivered," the man repeated. "Now you pay!" Even if he were uneasy, he appeared determined to get his full due. A rock stood as a screen so that Kenric could not see whom he addressed.

Then a purse was tossed and a man grabbed it, weighed it for a moment in his hand as if he could reckon its contents by heft alone. He stowed it in his tunic, turned on his heel and departed, his followers with him. But he who had paid made no move into the captives' sight.

Kenric half closed his eyes against the sun. Lying here was like being trussed in an oven. He wondered if this were the end, to be left tied in this sere wilderness.

Then—he was touched. He nearly cried out, for being what it was, that touch surely shocked him. Someone was using a mind probe! As that weapon which had led to their capture, such was totally foreign. This was not esper probing, he knew. No, this had a mechanical origin. And alien—so alien that it nicked his own mental band only at intervals like a kind of remote pecking.

He was mind-shielded, of course. No agent was sent without that protection. And Niccolae must be also. Any invasion of their thoughts could read only their assumed identities. But this probe worked so unevenly, surely it was not working at all. And whoever used it apparently could not adjust to the proper band.

Though he continued to try. Kenric could imagine the unseen wrestling with exasperation to center his probe. Then at last the pecking stopped. Confrontation should follow. Kenric tensed, waiting for the appearance of whoever had paid off the kidnappers. But the stifling hot minutes dragged by and nothing showed. Nor could he hear the least sound.

Niccolae stirred, and he could see a thin cheek.

"He is gone." Her words were hoarse, as if her mouth were dry and had difficulty uttering them.

She seemed so sure, Kenric relaxed a little. But if they had been deserted in this condition. . . .

"Yes." She might be reading his mind as the probe had tried to do. "They could well have left us. If so, we shall be dead before night—the sun slays speedily here."

"How—" he began.

"Wait! There may be an answer—yonder—" She pointed with her chin.

Closer to him than to her was a break in the ground, the shadow of a standing rock giving it shade. It was a circular opening about the size of his thumb, and around it mounded loose bits of gravel and sand. As he looked a reddish ball appeared from the hole. It was the head of a segmented creature that now crawled out, arose on jointed, plated legs. The head had three eyes set well to the fore, and not far below those a fringe of tentacles straggled, not unlike a stiff beard. Down its back extended a rough growth of black hairlike fibers.

"Fire worm," Niccolae identified. Her voice came weaker, more slowly. "It craves salt above all else. Look to your bonds."

His bonds? Kenric looked down. Those ties were of fabric. And they were wet with his sweat. Sweat. Salt. . . .

Fire worms had not been included in his briefing. But Niccolae seemed to know. He pushed then with his feet and, wriggling away from his support, thudded to the ground. He wriggled his way to the holes down which the fire worm had whipped at his first movement.

Finally he could move no more, his one cheek rasping against gravel, the sun strong enough to fry him. He fought against panic, hoping against hope that Niccolae's suggestion would work.

III

Though his hands were numb a prick of pain hit. And he guessed a fire worm was finding salt on more than his bonds. He steeled himself not to jerk away. The pain grew worse, and his imagination pictured a feeding on his tormented flesh.

It was hard to lie still, the more so when he was not sure but that he was providing a useless feast. But he endured, and the end came as a sharper pain did make him jerk. His hands fell apart. The strain on the cord between them and his ankles was gone. He could straighten out.

He rolled out of the shadow of the rock, scrabbling in the gravel with his numb and bleeding hands to pull himself away. Somehow he reached one of the taller boulders, rested against it.

There was a milling around the fire-worm hole he had left. Several of the creatures scuttled back and forth, their heads erect as if they sought by sight or scent their vanished prey.

Kenric tore at his ankle ties. Now for the first time he could see Niccolae clearly. She had slumped so that only the rock at her back kept her from the ground. He crawled to her side, pulled her around to get at the strips which held her. She did not stir as he worried them, life returning painfully to his numb fingers as he worked.

Somehow he loosed her, steadied her body against his shoulder while he swept back her hair. Her eyes were closed, her cracked lips open. Shallow breath whistled between them.

"Niccolae!" He shook her gently. He patted her cheek, his gnawed hand leaving a smear of blood.

She gasped. Her eyes came half-open. Encouraged, he began to pull her with him back into what poor shade the standing stones offered, away from the fire-worm nest from which more and more inhabitants were issuing. No longer aids, they were now a menace.

"What—!" The girl in his arms turned her head.

"It's all right. We are free."

She opened her eyes fully with a visible effort, raised her arms to look at her puffed and swollen hands.

"Did the fire worms—?"

"Yes. But they liked the taste they had too well. They want more."

"We—" Her voice was the faintest of whispers as she ran her tongue over seared lips. "We had better move—"

He put out new effort, managed to attain his feet. The stones around him stood like tree boles in a wood, but the leaves and branches which would have been sun shelter were missing. He could not see far in any direction. He began to fear that although they were no longer captives they might still die in this furnace.

Niccolae struggled to pull herself up. He stooped to help her. She leaned against him, lifted her hands clumsily to sweep back her hair.

"Come on!" His arm supporting her, they sidled around one of the stones and then the next.

Suddenly she cried out, pointing with a puffed finger.

He had not thought the stones around them were any more than a freak of nature. But here was a find that argued differently. Protruding from the hard, sun-cracked soil was an unmistakable arch, though its supporting pillars were so buried that the shadowed space it enclosed was no higher than what they could crawl into. Yet even that was a promise for survival. Kenric lurched toward it, bearing the girl with him.

At the edge of that much eroded stone he went to his knees, carrying her along. Together they crept into the hollow. If they might so last out the day, they would have a chance after the coming of night.

He crawled in blindly, for the transition from the glare to this dark was more than his eyes could immediately adjust to. But without warning the surface under them gave way. They slid down, engulfed in clay dust, gravel, debris enough to set them coughing and choking, until they lay half buried in the stuff.

"Niccolae?" Kenric felt about, trying to find her. Then his fingers tangled in the mass of her hair. "Niccolae!" he cried again, only to hear his rumble of voice answered by a rattle as more of the loose stuff slid down. He set about frantically to dig out, afraid a second slide might completely bury them.

Having broken free, he used the hair as a guide to uncover the girl. His questing hand found a reassuring heartbeat. He pulled her well away from the debris before he set out to explore the pit into which they had fallen.

Only it was not a pit. The opening above gave some light and by that and his sweeping hands he discovered they had landed in a passage. The arch must have been a doorway, plugged with earth and stone at some remote date.

At least it was much cooler here. He remembered that natural caves lowered in temperature as one drew farther from their entrances. Perhaps a similar principle operated here. His next discovery was more serious. For when he tried to reclimb the slope, it continued to give way under him. The whole surface was so fluid that the least touch sent it slipping.

"Where—?" Her whisper heartened him and he closed his arms about her in thankful relief.

"We've fallen into a passage of some kind."

"Dark—cool—" she said wonderingly. "But how do we get out?"

"We can't climb back," he told her frankly. "We can only go the other way."

But would air last? And the dark—dared they face that?

He could feel her moving against him. Suddenly there was a subdued glow coming from a small sphere she held, and she gave a small and shaky laugh.

"As a sorceress, consulted by the good people of Lanascol—" her voice was stronger and steadier— "I have my own tricks, friend. What served me in mind-sleep, can do even more good here. Now let us see truly where we stand."

Though the light from the sphere was limited, there seemed to be an answer to it—coming from points on the walls. Kenric heard her exclaim, and she lurched forward, he quickly supporting her, to one of those gleaming patches. She advanced her sphere closer to it.

As the lights drew together, so did both grow sharper and brighter.

She answered his questioning glance. "Like works upon like. This sphere, one of the secrets of those who follow my calling, is radiant at my touch. But it would seem that those who fashioned this place had unlimited supplies of orm ore to place in their walls. I do not believe we shall have to fear the dark much."

They advanced at a pace suiting their battered bodies. Those patches on the walls did ignite, letting them see more.

While at first the studding of orm ore followed no pattern,

that altered as the corridor continued, sloping a little down. Now there were carvings, and the patches of radiance formed eyes, coated fangs, swords and spears of warriors struggling in titantic battle. Here are shown fire worms, too, but these were no two-inch wrigglers. Rather the lost artist had pictured them as formidable monsters, on the hairy backs of which rode men—or humanoid creatures resembling men. And this weird cavalry fought not only other men, but was harrassed by large flying reptiles.

Niccolae pointed to one such leather-winged, snake-necked thing.

"A Dupt fanger! Those might be the Rovers of Dupt! They live and ride today—"

"And these fire worms—look at their size. Did they, or a species like them, ever exist to your knowledge?"

"No. But as I have said, the Orm priests guard secrets. They take their oracle down into what they call the worm ways—so it might be that once the fire worms did have larger kin. This place must be very old. And if the Dupt fangers are still known in our day—"

"Perhaps the monster fire worms exist also? Let us trust not here. . . ."

The air had continued breathable—to his surprise—but he thought it must have been ages since anyone had come this way. The battle scenes continued to cover the walls until they became monotonous viewing. The slight coolness gradually became a definite chill.

How far they had come, there was no way of telling. Their best pace was slow and they had to stop and rest now and then to favor their aching bodies. And their torment of thirst grew ever stronger.

It was during one of the rest pauses that Kenric made his first hopeful finding. He had put his hand to the wall; now he snatched it back. In one of the hollows of a fire worm's leg his fingers had found damp. Swiftly he ran his hands over the pitted mass of carving, calling to Niccolae to hold the light closer.

So they discovered moisture, enough to be licked from the gritty stone. Then Kenric hurried them ahead; perhaps the deeper they went the more chance there was for water. They came to a stairs dropping into a dark well unlit by any orm ore.

That descent seemed endless. But they hurried, for the air

was dank. When they did reach the end of the stairway the sphere awoke a glitter from the surface of a pool.

This was no freak of nature but a round artificial basin holding water into which they avidly plunged their hands to drink from cupped palms. The water flowed in from the mouth of a grotesque head. Niccolae sighed, sat back, water dripping from her chin until she scrubbed it away with the edge of her torn, earth-encrusted robe.

"Having given us water, do you think that the Over Fates might also give food?" She asked as one who might expect any miracle from this time forth.

Her question triggered Kenric's own hunger. It was a long time since he had shared that meal with the Kor-King in the palace of Lanascol. He got to his feet, then stooped to pick up the sphere from where Niccolae had left it on the floor. The dark here was so thick that this small gleam hardly battled it. He could see the bottom steps of the stairs and a part of a wall—the rest was hidden. But now that his raging thirst was satisfied, he was aware of something else. An acrid odor. Not born from damp, but separate, coming in strong whiffs as if blown by some breeze.

He hated to leave the water. They could not be sure they would find more in this burrow. And they must now be far under the surface of the desert—but whether headed north, east, south or west, he could not say.

When he spoke his thoughts aloud, the girl nodded. She had been ripping at the torn hem of her robe, balling up the tattered strips into a coil. She knotted it around her waist, pulling her skirts up through it to shorten them.

"We have no choice," she commented. "These ways must have been made for some purpose. Therefore ahead must lie another door or arch or exit or something."

Her composure was that of their first meeting, as if she once more had full confidence in herself and their future. Kenric wished he could feel as she did. She held out her hand and he gave her the sphere. With the left wall for a guide they went on.

There was no slope here. The floor ran straight. Nor were the walls carved, though they bore marks as if something passing here many times had rubbed the stone, leaving well-smoothed ribbons halfway between floor and roof.

No girl or dust drifted on the floor. Then, as another wall loomed to their right and they seemed to be entering another passage, Kenric was heartened by something more. Along the base of that wall, cut into the rock, was a runnel in which water ran, perhaps the overflow of the pool from which they had drunk.

Niccolae flashed her light at the ditch and he heard her laugh. "The Over Fates favor us. We have water—at least for now."

But they had something else, too. A strong gust of that acrid air in their faces. Kenric caught her hand, bringing her to a stop as he listened intently. On his wrists and across the backs of his hands the wounds left by the fire worms smarted. He thought of the carvings in the upper passage—of fire worms large enough to carry riders.

No sound—only that scent ever heavier. They went on warily. There was an opening in the wall to their left from which came another stench he knew of old—death and decay waited there. He drew Niccolae closer, as far as he could from that sinister doorway. Then the girl gave an exclamation and broke his grip, reaching for something lying on the floor.

It was a trail of vine, as thick as his forearm, bearing fruit of a paler green, two of which had been crushed to show white pulp. But the other four were intact, if bruised.

Niccolae had the vine. "Salas!" Her voice was as jubilant as if she had stumbled across the fabled treasure of Xotal. "These are food!"

They plucked the fruit, each as big as Kenric's fist. As he bit into a glore, he was wondering how vines came to be here. Niccolae, having thrust a second fruit into the front of her robe, was chewing on the other. She slipped from his side to stand in the doorway of that stinking place.

Kenric charged after her, only to halt in astonishment as her light revealed what lay beyond. For what little he could see of the area was crammed with wilting and decaying vegetation. More fruited vines were entangled with other material, looking as if they had been continually pressed down by new additions. He could not guess the purpose of such a noisome collection.

"Come!" Niccolae sat the sphere on the floor, plucked at the buckles fastening her outer robe on her shoulders, twitching loose the belt of tatters she had adjusted only a short time before. In a moment the folds of her robe fell about her feet, leaving her standing in a white undergarment.

Hastily she smoothed out the discarded robe and began to plunder the edge of the pile nearest the door, picking out fruit and also what looked like a type of grain, choosing and discarding any too ripe, too bruised. Kenric followed her lead. In the end they had a pack of foodstuffs to be bundled and fastened by her rag cord. Thankfully they withdrew to the clearer air of the passage.

"How do you suppose that got there?" Kenric made the bundle into a carrying pack with a rag sling for his shoulder.

"It's the storage place of a fire worm," she told him. "Their nature is to fill a place underground with vegetation, leaving it to decay and ferment before they eat it. But—"

"The size of this—yes!" He had already noted the significance of that.

None of the small desert worms could have hauled such large vines underground or raised that vast dump. He nursed his hands and knew that they must accept it as almost certain that the worms in these burrows were giant ones. Men had ridden the ones in the carvings, but the carvings were very old. The partnership of man and worm must have ended long ago, since Niccolae had never heard of it. Unless—

"Could we possible be close to Orm Temple?" he demanded.

"I have been wondering that also. Yet I do not believe we were kidnapped by worm priests. The mind probe—that does not belong to them. They have their own magic."

"They plan to launch a war, according to ZAT. Suppose they produce an army mounted on fire worms—what could Lanascol's men then do? And if the Rovers join with them—"

"Such could overset any force the Kor-King might put in the field," she said, "But with all that at their command, why do they need the prophecy?"

"Perhaps because they believe in it themselves. Tell me, what do you know of the Orm priests?"

"Only what I learned through a planted spy ray feeding data to ZAT. Anything else I have heard reached me second hand. I understand that for generations their hierarchy has not stirred from the temple, only the lowest class of the order venturing abroad. Even those hold themselves aloof from the common people, dealing solely with the Kor-King and his high officers. From time to time the priests send messages summoning some noble—or the king—to the temple to be informed of a new prophecy. The Kor-Kings have usually gone. There are tales of two who refused and were thereafter maltreated by fortune. But any connnection between the priests themselves and the subsequent disasters could not be proven. They have never before summoned the present king. I have heard that even what ZAT has learned is little more—"

"You said they have secrets and protections—"

"Yes. One of the Kor-Kings who defied them disappeared after he took a force to storm the temple. Only a few stragglers of his rear guard returned, all in a state of shock. That story is two hundred planet years old—but there are elements in it which suggest that perhaps the priests did have the giant fire worms then."

"So after that, strict response was made to any summons from the priests," Kenric commented. "Yes, such an object lesson would have an effect. However, here we have proof of one thing. A lot of this vegetation is fresh. So the one who stored it here has access to the outer world, and not a desert one either."

"The sooner we find that access the better." She was kilting up the skirt of her underdress. "Let us go."

The promise of a way out, plus food, heartened them so that they kept to a faster pace. They passed a second door in the wall, this one with a worse stench than the first, suggesting greater rot within. Then the tunnel split in two. Since both ways looked alike and appeared to run in the same general direction, there was little choice between them.

They took the left way, counting paces as went, planning to return if, at the end of two hundred, they saw no suggestion of an exit. Kenric was ridden by the need for haste. He kept remembering that trail or vine and thought that the harvester might return with another burden. To meet one of the giant worms here might mean quick disaster.

The walls ran smooth. There was no encouraging upward curve. But in the light of the sphere, another doorway loomed. And no stench emerged from it.

With caution they crept through into a dim glow of light from far above their heads. Above them towered a ledge, and on it sat a high-backed armed chair cut from a solid block of stone. On the arms, light glinted. There were metal bands and another band on the back.

Before them, below the ledge, stretched an open space. Equidistant around it were openings of tunnels like the one through which they had come. But they heard no sound, saw no sign that anything moved in those ways.

Seeing that chair ready and waiting for an enforced occupant, Kenric's briefing awoke. This was the place where the oracle was left, manacled to the chair above, while he received the prophecy.

IV

"Kenric!"

Hands trying to hold him prisoner. This was like waking from a dream. He was at the wall, trying to climb to the waiting chair, while the girl clung stubbornly to anchor him below. He kicked out to break her hold. Then the power of the briefing broke. He loosed his clutch on the projecting hand holds and fell, taking her with him.

"I should be up there!" He was afraid to look up again lest the chair once more pull him.

"No." Her clutch was fierce. "You are not the oracle. You are Lord Kor Kenric—that you must remember!"

"But the briefing—"

"Yes." Her whisper had the power of a shout. "I know. You are conditioned to sit above. However, the sending failed. You must play out the game as another piece altogether. But this much is true—we are no longer lost under the desert. We're in Orm Temple. Maybe we can find a way of escape."

She was right, and she had pulled him out of the mental haze now. He was not the oracle. Also it was true that they seemed to have reached a defined point of compass.

He heard a cracked laugh from the girl.

"Escape—yes—if fire worms can fly! This is the most secret part of Orm Temple, best guarded of all. Suppose we do go aloft into ways known to your briefing, and come upon the oracle himself. What chances then?"

"Transfer for me, maybe." By some amazing stroke of fortune he had come within a handsbreadth of where he should have been at the beginning of this send. And if he could transfer, then the mission was not an abort. The thought of that gave him new energy and once more he studied the wall.

"Very well." Her voice was as low and harsh as it had been in the desert. "But until you do find him, you must take care to remain fully Kenric. Otherwise you will be easy meat for any guard."

His arm caught about her waist and he drew her with him to one of the tunnel mouths. He had heard something moving toward them. They flattened back to wait.

She had put away the sphere, leaving them in the dark.

But the faint gray light of the place was enough to make visible the creature padding out into the open.

Fire worm indeed, but a giant—just as they had speculated! The small desert worms had been merely grotesque; this was a monster. Yet according to the wall carvings, men had ridden such.

Niccolae's nails cut into his flesh in her excitement but she was silent, caution curbing her. On the back of the thing was strapped a wide seat or saddle, too roomy for a single rider, Kenric judged. Fastened to one of the peaked fore-ends of that seat were reins, the other ends of which disappeared into the creature's beard of tentacles, those working as if trying to rid themselves of the reins' restraint.

The worm came entirely out of the tunnel, halted in the open space. Its three eyes glowed dully. If it sighted the two fugitives it gave no sign of interest. Rather it stood as if in meditation, only the working tentacles, from which spun threads of slime, showing that it was alive.

As it remained so quiescent, Kenric moved out, trying to see its accouterments the better. There was a scabbard fastened to the fore of the saddle where it would swing close to hand for a rider. A scabbard that carried a burden.

Kenric drew a sharp breath. For what he saw could not possibly exist in this time and place. Identities could be exchanged *via* sendings. Back at HQ now his body—or rather Creed Trapnell's—was encased in a protective device to keep it living against his return. But here he was the man who wore—if one could term it that—another's covering of flesh and bone.

Yet in that scabbard was a weapon known in his own time—a blazer. Objects could not be transported. But neither could a blazer be made here. To manufacture such required a series of highly technical operations. They could not have set up such a factory, which would require transportation of a whole crew of techs.

The mind probe had been alien—at least on an unknown band. Suppose another Service were operating here—one that had developed parallel to his own but had made the breakthrough for transporting without the need for substitution? The test might be whether that blazer were exactly like the weapon he knew. He wanted to get his hands on it to make sure.

This fire worm had been ridden—but dare he approach it? He had hesitated too long. In his head a pain, he clapped his hands over his ears instinctively though he had heard no sound.

The fire worm raised its head, turned to face the tunnel from which it had come. Then it padded back into that opening.

"Did you see what was in that scabbard?" Niccolae demanded.

"It looked like a blazer—"

"Except none could be sent. And neither can such be made by any smith of Vallek. Perhaps we are wrong in thinking only of sending—what if that was brought by an off-world ship? Four thousand-five thousand years—" He was going to add "ago," except that he was in the past now himself.

"Our kind did not pioneer deep space," Niccolae reminded him. "There are many traces of those before us. We are very young as species are reckoned among the stars."

That was true—but a blazer! He must find out if it had come from parallel technology. A breakthrough for a direct send—that information would be worth more to the Service than anything else he could learn on Vallek. He had to get his hands on that weapon. Niccolae's thoughts must have run with his as she said:

"The beast was summoned by an ultra-sonic call—one we could feel if not hear. We can follow—"

He nodded. "I felt it."

Again she laughed. "Do you know what the worm priests do to any female found in their domain? If not, bring your worst imaginings to the fore of your mind and study them. I would far rather die by my own choice than live for the priests, I assure you. And we may already have triggered a protective device leading their guards here."

"I thought they dared not come to the oracle's seat."

"That's only legend. The worm priests put about what they wish outsiders to know. Who is it teaches the oracle here what he must intone as prophecy? A fire worm? No, the priests know these ways well."

So they went together after the fire worm. The part of Creed Trapnell that was Kenric walked softly, his hands opening and closing, longing for the feel of a weapon. As a trained fighting man he felt naked lacking that. And his nose told him that trouble lay ahead, for the acrid odor of the worms was thick.

Under their feet the floor began to climb on easy grades and far ahead showed what could only be daylight. So they were again approaching the surface of the ground. They walked slowly, close to the wall, listening—

The chill of the underways receded also. At last they came to the end of the tunnel to look out.

Into empty space. And they had to stare down before they saw the trap that way ended in—for truly it was a trap. Projecting from the walls, both on their side of the narrow valley and the opposite one, were stakes supporting a metal mesh. This ran completely around an earth-walled pocket into which opened a number of the tunnels—and it was plainly intended to keep fire worms from climbing out.

At the far end of the pocket was a platform on which lay a tangled mass of vegetation that might have been tossed from the top of the cliff. Several of the fire worms were busied there, collecting loads with their mouth tentacles, carrying the stuff back into tunnels.

Apart from these were other worms, larger, wearing a thicker growth of black hair. And each wore a saddle; so Kenric could not be sure which one they had trailed here.

"Below—" Niccolae whispered in his ear.

She was right. Immediately below them was one of the riding monsters. It had squatted low, its plated belly resting on the ground. Whether it was the right one, Kenric could not be sure. But it did carry a weapon at saddle bow.

He slipped the sling of the food bag from his shoulder. The creature's head was low, its tentacles curled in a tight knot. Even as he watched, the big head slipped lower. Maybe the thing slept.

The stone was rough here, deeply pitted with holes which perhaps the worms used—deep enough to make a rude stairway for human feet and hands. Kenric had to face the cliff during that descent and for all he knew the sleeping worm had roused, could be reaching up for him. He was sweating from more than the exertion of his descent when his boots met the gravel at the cliff foot.

Now he edged around, half expecting to face the worm, wondering if he would have time to catch up a handful of sand to hurl into its three eyes. But the creature lay still. He could see the slow reaction and expansion of its sides as it breathed. With it lying flat like that, he ought to be able to reach the scabbard and ease the blazer out.

But he could hardly believe his good fortune when he did have it free. It was strangely light of weight, unlike familiar weapons. He thrust it in the back of his belt to leave his

hands free for the return climb. He joined Niccolae aloft
with all the speed he could summon.

In general shape the weapon was indeed like a blazer. It
had a barrel, a stock, two hand grips with one well to the
fore, a sighting mechanism. When he tested that he found it
to be telescopic to an extent inherent in no arm with which
he was familiar.

The material, he decided, must be some lightweight alloy.
And very hard. He could not scratch it with the edge of his
belt buckle or dent it with a stone. Could it have come from
a starship—one roving the galaxy long before his own race
had raised eyes speculatively to the moon companying their
own world?

"It was made for humanoid use," Niccolae commented.

True. The grip and balance had been designed for one of
his own body structure. But that was only a small discovery.
He dared not try to fire it, lest he give an alarm. However,
with it he now had an answer to one part of his problem.

"Have you ever handled a blazer?"

"Before my sending?" She smiled. "No. I was drilled in
some weapons, such as a stunner. But I had no need for the
heavier arms. Since I was to be a permanent agent my
studies were to fit me as a sorceress. In that calling I do not
resort to material weapons. I am supposed to rely on other
methods."

"Why," he asked, "did you choose a permanent assignment?—not many women do."

"Didn't they ever warn you that is a question never asked?
I have chosen, and until this particular action things have
gone well for me." She shrugged. "There are compensations
for life on less sophisticated levels. Surely you have had at
least one sending where you would have opted to remain
when your recall came. That is why they now have a built-in
compel-to-end. Before they took that precaution there were
exiles by choice. The life of a sorceress in Lanascol is quite
enough to satisfy me. Our master, ZAT—though a machine—is careful as to waste. Now—this is no time for such
a discussion. You have something in mind?"

"Whether you have had training or not," he returned, a little chilled, "this is a simple weapon. The one button apparently controls the firing of whatever ray is loaded. And the
sighting is foolproof sighting. Armed with this you can be
safe—"

"While you go hunting the oracle?"

"Do I have a choice?"

"Perhaps not, in your own form. But you are dwelling in the form of a man noted for good sense and leadership, and especially for the winning of battles."

"He didn't seem to have much luck in his last one."

"Luck and treachery do not march hand in hand. The Lady Yarakoma knows more about that than is fit—and one could learn a lot if words could be shaken out of her crooked mouth."

Niccolae's vehemence surprised Kenric. She must have read that in his face for she continued:

"I have heard many things of the Lady Yarakoma. And of those I cannot count one good. She is an evil, rotting out the heart of Lanascol—as much a source of trouble for Vallek as the Orm priests, and not so open a one. But now—so you give me this," she gripped the weapon butt, "while you go exploring. Well, this time I shall not deny you. I shall hide near the chair chamber and wait."

They ate again before he left her to climb the wall.

"Do you have an idea as to how to go?" she asked as he made ready for the assent.

"I know the chair. Perhaps the briefing will lead me farther. The spy ray they planted was exact enough—before it faded."

"What if the overlay of briefing clouds your wits when you need them?"

"I don't know. But it is all the guide I have. I must try to find the oracle. And if the Kor-King is enticed here, there may be some treachery also—"

"Against which one man can serve as guard? Do not forget that earlier King and his vanished army." She seemed occupied by her own gloomy prophecy. There was that in her voice—perhaps because her work was reading the future for clients—which did impress. But Kenric refused to be influenced. With the blazer she could defend herself, and his duty urged him on.

He climbed to the chair ledge. Nor did he look back from that point, for he must put her out of his mind, be singlethoughted from now on. His assignment came first.

The chair was just as his briefing had told him it must be, those metal hoops on arms and back ready to hold a witless creature in place after the priests left him to spend the night here. But the prey did receive a message from somewhere, so potent a one that it could remain in a brain unable to com-

mand a body, could make that body drool understandable
words. How was it done? Surely the most careful drilling
could not bring a connected phrase, let alone rhetorical
prophesies, out of an idiot. What was the trick or secret?
Suppose he could find out and be able to defeat it from that
direction—if he could not play the oracle?

Cautiously Kenric seated himself in the chair. It was chill
wherever it touched his skin. He could not lean back against
it nor lay his arms along the arms since the metal hoops were
in the way. Were those fastened, the occupant would be
caught in a vice, unable to move or turn.

But when he put his head back against the rise of stone
Kenric felt a sensation not far removed from that which had
struck with the mind probe. He squirmed around, ran his fingertips over the seat back. Thus he was able to trace a
square of some substance not visible to the eye. And from it
arose a tingling warmth to run up his fingers, his arms, as if
he had touched a source of energy. He jerked away—there
was something disquieting about that flow.

A man secured as the oracle was must remain, until once
more freed, with the back of his head resting firmly against
that plate. Was that how it was done? Some form of briefing,
potent enough to be imprinted on an idiot's mind. Unless—
that was the very point—only the blank mind of an idiot could
receive it at all. Just as a sending had to use such to imprint
the identity of an agent.

But this oracle had operated for centuries—it was no new
arrangement. It could not be the result of a Service traitor's
meddling or something from off-world. For if Vallek had
been visited by starmen over any length of time some hint of
that would exist if only as a rumor. The Service briefing experts had fed all data into ZAT and the computer would
speedily have isolated such a momentous bit of information.

Yet there was some form of energy in the chair. Kenric
walked around to the back, which was so tall it formed a
wall of sorts. Once more he explored the stone. But on this
side there was nothing to be felt at all except its natural cold.

At any rate, he had discovered how the prophecies might
be set up—but not by whom. And that was the important
question. Beyond him now was a doorway, and he knew
from his briefing that this was where they entered with the
oracle. There was no road now but this. He took it.

The passage beyond was unlit and narrow, the walls
smooth. He felt his way through a thickening dusk. Soon he

would come to a stair—he slipped each foot ahead a step at a time to feel for the riser. His boot toe rapped and he began to climb, counting as he went—such knowledge was a help in the dark.

He had counted off twenty when the hand he held out before him struck solid surface. He explored it, finding heavy metal bands across a door. Finally his fingers tightened on a kind of latch common enough on Vallek.

Quietly Kenric bore down on the bar. If the door were locked, he was defeated. But the bar moved. He might be the greatest fool in the world, but he had no choice. He pushed open the door and walked into danger.

V

The light came from small insets of the orm ore but they were not parts of pictures. And the plain passage was like any of the lower tunnels.

He had expected a guard. None was visible. Kenric closed his eyes. He had known the oracle's seat at once; could he trace the path from here? But if his briefing had once laid out a path it had not survived his imperfect sending. He would have to depend upon any hunch or faint suggestion. So he padded down that dusty way, alert to any sound.

The light was so dim that when he glanced back he could see only the outline of the door. And just before him the corridor angled right to give upon a stairway. Climbing was promising for he knew that the main portion of the temple still lay well overhead.

Soon the ore patches were gone and again he had to depend more on touch than sight. Another door, this one banded also with metal—as if both this and the other had been intended for defensive measures. But for all his fumbling he could find here no latch.

Baffled, Kenric leaned one shoulder to the wall. It would seem this portal opened only from the other side, bottling him in. But he was not ready for defeat. Once more he felt across its surface, beginning systematically at the top. The metal bands were close set and the edges of some serrated, deeply gashed in places—as if torn by fangs. The worms!

Niccolae down there—but she had the blazer. . . .

No hint of any latch or handhold—not until he reached studs on the fourth bar. One of those moved a fraction. For want of any other encouragement, he caught it with his nails and turned. There was a distinct click. There was answering movement.

What he had so unlatched was not the whole of the door but only a narrow panel. So narrow that he had difficulty wriggling through. On the other side, as it thudded back into place, he found indications that in the past the whole door had been sealed.

. Ahead was the foot of another staircase. Orm ore lights appeared again, small and far apart, as the stairs narrowed. His shoulders brushed the walls on either side. Now he heard a murmur as of voices, which seemed to come out of the stone on his right. There was a dark patch there and he stopped to examine it more closely, finding it to be a circle of metal that slipped to one side to reveal a peephole.

Kenric looked through. Some distance below was the pavement of a long hall, its roof supported by a series of pillars carven and painted to resemble rearing fire worms. They were not entirely lifelike, having certain horrific embellishments to make them even more vicious looking.

But they were much worn, legs broken off here and there, missing tentacles, cracks across their painted armor plates— giving them the seeming of great age. Among them men moved—priests. Kenric's briefing named the red robes with their wide collars of clawlike ornaments that resembled either dried worn tentacles or excellent representations of such. Most of the men wore their cowls up about their heads so he could not see their faces. But two almost directly below the peephole did not. Their shaven heads glistened in the light and they had the countenances of young men.

Kawyn? There could be no mistaking the tribal tattoos on their cheeks. The part of Kenric in this borrowed body responded to that marking. He heard his breath hiss, realized his hand fumbled at his belt for a weapon he did not wear.

Talking with the Kawyn was another man, much shorter, almost dwarfish. He wore no robe. Instead, his squat body was only half-clothed in a lower garment which was boots and breeches in one. It was made of a leathery stuff which gave off prismatic gleams as he moved, as if that leather or skin was overlaid with opaline scales. His wide shoulders and barrel chest carried a shag of coarse black hair, and another long tuft of it hung in a single strand from the point of his chin though the rest of his face was clean. The growth on his head had been trained and hardened with some substance into the semblance of a comb, beginning above his forehead and extending to the nape of his neck. Half buried in his furry body hair was a wealth of jewel-set metal.

A Rover? Then it was true—the men of Dupt came into Orm. If one needed any further proof of the dire disaster for Lanascol brewed here, the sight of that party of three supplied it amply.

Their voices reached Kenric only as a murmur, strain as he did to hear. And there was no use lingering at this peephole with the goal of his quest still ahead. He started on, but he was thinking of the significance of what he had seen.

To find Rovers in any kind of alliance was startling. From what he knew of Vallek, the Rovers lived enemies to all others. The reason for their exile from the human race was lost in the midsts of unremembered time. But by now they were so alien to others that they might be considered of another species. Their very territory was a secret, for all their raids were carried out by air and no tracker on the ground had ever been able to follow them. Since technology on Vallek had not yet advanced to the invention of sky travel, the raiders were invulnerable.

Their form of travel was to ride giant flying reptiles, not too unlike very ancient creatures of Kenric's home world, predating the evolution of mankind. The things in themselves were terrifying opponents in any battle. Ridden by rapacious men, they were doubly fearsome.

It was thought that the numbers of both Rovers and their mounts were small, since never more than ten or so made up a raid squad. But few as they might number, they were formidable. So far they had harried only farming communities, fishing villages along the coast, caravans of traders stupid enough to venture far into the wastes for a quicker journey.

Kenric judged he must now be well above the hall. His hand rested on a second spy-hole, this time to the left. And he made use of it.

He saw not a hall but a small chamber. It held a massive table with a top of lustrous kiffa stone mounted on thick pillar legs. At its head, almost directly below, was a chair with a tall carved back. Along the sides of the table ran benches. At the far end stood a second chair. The walls were hung, save about the peephole, with strips of dark red cloth, giving the unpleasant impression of drawing about the table to entrap and stifle those sitting there. Yet the four men who did so appeared at their ease.

No one occupied the chair, but on the benches, facing each

other across the smooth surface in pairs, sat the four. And they were very different. One was a red-robed priest, his garments so much the color of the wall draperies behind him that at times he seemed to disappear. The more so because he wore his cowl up and only the movements of his hands were noticeable.

At his side sat another of the Rovers, as much like the one Kenric had sighted before as to be his twin. He played with something as he listened—a band of metal, which, fitting over his hand below the knuckles, provided him with a set of vicious claws into which he slipped his fingers as he might wear a glove.

To Kenric's right were the other two. One wore the clothing of a courtier of Lanascol and the device worked on the breast of his tunic. Kenric's hand rose mechanically to touch his own, grimed as it was. The royal arms! But—was the Kor-King already here! Though that any of his men would sit companionably with a Rover was not believable.

There was only one answer—the Lady Yarakoma. In her burning ambition she might have taken the final step to ally herself with the Kor-King's enemies, sent some spokesman here. He wished at that moment he had Kenric's own memory to draw upon.

The fourth man wore clothing which might be that of any lower class citizen of Lanascol. Yet he sat at ease with the noble, and both the priest and the Rover were listening to what he said in a voice so low that only the rise and fall of tone reached Kenric.

That fourth man now brought out a writing stick and began to draw swift lines on the table top. But he was never to finish what he was trying to picture. The drapes on the left wall were twitched aside and looped back for the coming of another priest, who then stood deferentially aside to allow the passage of a smaller figure, much muffled in a robe which appeared too large for his meager body.

The robe was banded at shoulder level with a crossing of rust-orange, and the necklace or collar was more elaborate than those of the others. The men at the table looked up and the courtier, the priest, and the stranger, who had been drawing, all arose. However the Rover only grinned, remaining seated. He made it plain that he would make no polite gesture.

Then the priest who had entered first offered his small companion the support of his arm—only to have that shoved away petulantly. But the progress of his superior toward the chair at the head of the table was a wavering one and the priest pressed close, ready to steady the other if need be.

Once seated in the chair, the small man raised two hands as claw-like as the metal glove with which the Rover still played. These shook with a constant tremor as he swept back his cowl.

"You have asked for speech——" The ancient priest's voice was shrill and high-pitched. "You have your chance—speak! This is a time wherein there is much to be done, much to be done. If you trouble the Ceremonies for a thing of little import, then there shall be a reckoning."

It was the man with the writing stick who answered, this time raising his voice so Kenric could hear him.

"The Mightiness of Orm would certainly not be troubled during his preparations for the great day without need. It is thus—our brother-in-heart-and-hope, the Swordmaster Suward, has brought news. It seems that the thrice-cursed Kenric and the seeing woman are not where they were left. Yet they were well bound. When his men passed by the Place of Ancient Stones—they were gone! Even the Rovers have taken to the sky to spy them out, but without result."

"Fools," sputtered the mummy in the chair. Suward shrank back as if the ancient priest had spewed forth poison instead of a word. "The Place of Ancient Stones is accursed, as all know," the old one continued. "If Orm has seen fit to take them to himself, of course you would find no sign of them. Is this your great news?"

"O High Priest of Orm, suppose Orm in his infinite wisdom is not responsible for their disappearance? Suppose they have managed to escape? Should they reach Lanascol with their tale——"

The Rover laughed with harsh contempt. He spoke sourly, his words so accented and twisted Kenric could hardly understand him. "They will not. Our riders will make sure. The desert is easy to search from aloft."

"True." The writer nodded. "But if the Kor-King comes—and Suward has brought us assurance that he will—there is a chance, is there not, that our fugitives might meet with some scout of his?"

The High Priest screwed around to look directly at the courtier.

"Why would the Kor-King march with scouts? What know you of this? He was sent the High Word of Orm. One does not bring an army against Orm." He paused to emit a high tittering sound, sickening to hear. "Does he not remember that once a Kor-King came to Orm weapons in hand, though he did not go hence again? No, no." His tittering grew stronger, shaking his whole shrunken body. And his attendant pressed closer, put out one hand hesitatingly. But his master controlled that evil shadow of mirth. He leaned back in the chair, smeared his sleeve of his robe across his pale, wrinkled lips. "Now," his voice became firmer. "Answer me—does the Kor-King march with scouts—and why?"

"Because of the Lord Kor Kenric," Suward answered. "Somehow the King's Eyes were able to trace him to the witch-bag's house. The Eyes are many and the King has some not even his heir can put name to. What they found there suggested struggle. Also the roll keeper of the gate mentioned a late-moving cart, outward bound. Before it reached my Lady's ears it was a story already past her changing. She did hasten to muddy it where she could with suggestions concerning Kenric and the witch, and the unnatural longings of evil men. But that slime does not stick well on Kenric. He has walked too warily and many remember why she hates him— may the Thousand Teeth of Namur gnaw the flesh from his bones!"

For the first time the priest sitting at the table spoke.

"Mightiness, remember what you yourself have said. To have a female mixed with such high matters is not only an abomination to Orm, but also great folly—"

Perhaps it was his taunting tone rather than the words uttered that aroused the courier.

"Speak so of the Lady, and—"

"Silence to this yapping!" The High Priest's voice again held the ghostly timbre of what once must have been a resonant tone. "The female has served us in her own fashion. She has given us an ear to many secret matters, though this taking of the Lord Kor was a badly done affair. It is of prime importance that the Kor-King obey the Word. But he seems to be doing it more as an enemy than a servant. And servant he is, as he shall learn! Orm has long hinted of a new day when he shall make plain his words—and those shall be the law not only of Orm Temple but of all Vallek! Long, long has been the waiting in the night. Now comes the dawn. For even Kor-King, when he hears the true words of Orm from the oracle, cannot nay-say them. And if he does play the fool and tries, there are enough true believers among his people to make his end. So—a few days more and we shall be the fingers and the hands of Orm reaching forth to hold the world!"

There were small flecks of spittle on his lips and he scrubbed at them with his sleeve. The two other priests had bowed their heads, Suward likewise, and even the lay stranger nodded. Only the Rover sat grinning, giving no more respect to Orm than he did to Orm's followers.

"Much to be done." The firmer note was gone from the High Priest's voice. He was querulous again. "Do not disturb us again—too much to be done. The oracle must be prepared—"

He struggled to get to his feet and the two priests had to move in to raise him. This time he did not push them away but shuffled out between them. The other men watched them go in silence.

When the door latch clicked, the Rover laughed.

"Strange—he still has wits enough, that old one. Much has he planned and planned well, that I will say for him." He paused, his eyes narrowed. He looked first to Suward, then to the stranger. "Or is he the planner? Not that it means much at this time. But that one, he also believes in his own god tales—that this Orm will come riding on a giant fire worm to conquer the world. Such a tale is for the thick-headed. Now this is what the All-Mother of Dupt would have me learn—" He tapped his claws on the table directly before the stranger. "What gain you from this? The Kawyns—all know what they want. And this Yarakoma would see her husband Kor-King with no rival such as Kenric, who is a good fighter and well liked by your maggot city-dwellers. And the priests yell of Orm and prophecy spouted out of the mouth of a drooling madman that Orm comes to rule the world. Three reasons for swearing partnership—at least for the span of putting down the Kor-King. But you—you have given no reason your suggested help. This I will say of you, stranger, you speak well when you talk of war and manners of outwitting the enemy." He spat, and the splatter of moisture lay in a drop on the board. He put a claw to it and drew a small wet line that crossed the one made with the writing stick. "We have been promised loot—which is well enough—and a chance to try our wings south. Now, what is your portion? I have heard strange tales of you—that you are not of this world, that you brought the unusual weapons given to some of our men. To what end do you this? The All-Mother would like to know!"

"Fair enough. You have seen some of the weapons and what they can do. There are to be more and greater ones in the future. As for my gain—it is a simple thing, Rover, one meaning little to the rest of you. I want orm ore. You are right—I am not of this world, and orm ore is of Vallek only. We cannot buy it from the temple for they deem it Orm's sweat. But if we help the High Priest achieve his purposes, then Orm will smile on us and we shall be granted favors."

"Or take them—when this fire-worm hill is in such ferment none can be spared to say you nay."

Suward started, shot a quick glance at the stranger. But the latter did not seem disturbed.

"Or take it," he agreed. "Does that disgust you, or would it trouble your All-Mother?"

"Not so. It is such a play as we could relish. As for Orm ore—what matters it? City man—" he stared at Suward now—"get your wench her throne if you can. Though whether she will thereafter sit steady on it, is another matter. It is enough we understand each other—for this time."

He slid off the bench, turning his back on the two without farewell to tramp out of the chamber. Suward ran his hands nervously back and forth on the edge of the table. "I distrust all Rovers."

The other man shrugged. "As who does not? It is a pity that they must be used. But they have what we need most at the moment—a path through the sky. Also they are potent in battle. Have you not had proof of that in the past?"

"Yes. But they hold to no oaths—"

"You forget. This one does speak boldly as do his fellows. But we have that which will finish them in the end."

"Not we—you," Suward returned. "You have shown us that picture of your fashioning which makes it seem that you have found their foul nest. You have assured us that certain of your men with their flame weapons have it under control but that these here know nothing of it."

"Do doubt the truth of that. The Rovers will serve us just as long as they are needed. When the moment is passed, they will be treated—so—"

He snapped the writing stick in two.

"Now, as His Mightiness says, the hour grows late—"

"Will his oracle perform as he thinks, I wonder?" Suward

made no move to rise. He appeared wanting assurance, or so it seemed to Kenric.

"Has it not always been so in the past? Yes, I think that idiot will mouth a proper prophecy. And, if the Kor-King is not impressed thereby, there will be means to make it clear to him that a new day dawns on Vallek."

"If he comes—"

The stranger swung around to face Suward. "Is there any doubt of that?" he asked sharply.

"He might not come at Orm's summons. But if he thinks he marches to free Kenric. . . . Maltus has the cloak we took from Kenric and other things, as well as a good tale. And the Lady Yarakoma will do all she can. If he will not move to Orm's call, he will to the other—" he repeated.

"If we still had Kenric we would be on safer ground."

Suward laughed. "If his body is not huddled somewhere in the Place of Ancient Stones, it is certainly sundried out in the waste. There is no way any man can cover the desert on foot without water. Even if he walks shoulder to shoulder with a sorceress. There being a limit to her power also."

"But it will be your business, my friend, to make sure, very sure, that the King does march."

Suward replied sullenly. "Do I not know it? Be sure—he will come."

"I trust so," said the other and left as abruptly as the Rover.

Kenric let fall the peephole shutter. He had heard plenty. If the worm priests, Yarakoma, the Kawyn, the Rovers and the enigmatic stranger had made so uneasy an alliance, then there was still hope. Already the stranger and Suward had agreed to the blotting out of the Rovers when their usefulness was over. And he did not doubt the Rovers nursed private plans against their allies, too.

But as uneasy as that alliance was, if it held long enough to break the Kor-King it would in turn break Vallek. Was the oracle really important now? The Orm priests needed the oracle to fire them, true enough. But the others already privately discounted that goad—their schemes depended upon the lure of Kenric himself.

Therefore the priorities had now shifted. It was no longer the oracle that mattered but a warning to the King. Were his enemies unable to trap him in the wastes, they might turn on one another. The resulting chaos could only favor the Kor-King.

Perhaps it had not been so misdirected after all, his awakening in this body. The Kor-King might not have been influenced by any prophecy but he would listen to his son. And, though the compulsion of the briefing ran deep, Kenric could break it. Now he must reach the Kor-King with news of what brewed here, must ready Lanascol before the pot boiled over.

As he descended the stairs at the best pace the steep fall allowed him, Kenric was already planning. The conspirators were right. A journey over the desert could not be made afoot—not with Rovers scouting in the heavens for anything moving. Besides, there had to be means to carry water and supplies.

Which left—the fire worms! Some were saddled; ergo, they had been ridden. And what other men could ride, so could—so must—Kenric now.

Arriving back at the chair ledge he paused, another thought coming to mind. He was as certain as if he had been told it during briefing that the plate of energy material, against which the head of the oracle must rest, had something to do with the prophecy. Could that material be damaged, slowing so the march of events?

There was, he decided, only one way of dealing with it and that would mean the devastation would be visible to the priests at once. Still—if the trouble pointed in turn to one of their allies—

He grinned. A good trick. The means perhaps of accomplishing double result—defeating the oracle and sowing discord among the enemy.

His descent to the floor below was quick and then he ran for the mouth of the tunnel where Niccolae should be waiting. Then he saw her moving out to meet him.

"Give me—" He snatched the weapon out of her hands, turned back.

"Are they after you?" She ran behind him.

He sighted on the tall back of the chair. He pressed the button. A ray of brilliant white crisped through the air, centering on the target.

Only an instant did he hold it so, astounded by the resulting violence. The chair exploded with a roar, erupting fragments of stone riven and blackened as if the plate had covered some cache of high explosive.

Kenric was momentarily deafened, then alarmed. He tried

to protect the girl with his body, snatching her back to the tunnel mouth as by a miracle they escaped the rain of stones.

"That noise will bring guards on us. We must take action fast!" Quickly he explained his reason for blasting the chair and his contemplated course. "I wonder what is the method of controlling the riding worms," he finished.

Once more she brought out her orm ore sphere. "This gives one a measure of control over the human mind, facilitating hypnotic suggestion. Whether it will work with a worm, I cannot tell. But I can try it."

"If they have borne riders in their saddles, there must be some way of reaching the beast. Let us find one."

"Suppose we do," she said. "Where then do we ride it?"

"To find the Kor-King." Swiftly he outlined what he had overheard. "If he is warned—"

"Then those plotters will ask who is responsible for their betrayal—each suspecting the other. A new way to win a war!" She laughed.

"Only if it works." He throttled down the excitement that might threaten a clear head. "There are many chances for failure. We must find a worm, must take it out of here, must cross the desert safely in spite of the Rover scouts, must locate the Kor-King in time—"

"There is your first requirement," Niccolae said, pointing to the tunnel leading to the open-air worm pen.

Kenric lifted his gaze. A hugh three-eyed head had appeared in the archway. The jaw tentacles were working in spasmodic jerks as if the creature were dangerous. Probably the explosion had alarmed it. Seen from ground level, the worm as it emerged from the tunnel mouth looked formidable enough to tense Kenric's grip on the blazer. In its fear and rage, would it attack the two who proposed to ride it?

Niccolae raised the sphere to her lips, breathed upon it three times. After staring into it intently, she tossed it aloft. It flew through the air and landed as a feeble spark of light on the pavement before the worm.

The creature stopped short, ugly head swinging from side to side. Then it lowered its head as if to sniff at the sphere. It froze so. The writhing tentacles at its mouth relaxed.

Niccolae touched Kenric's arm with pressure. He remained where he stood as she walked forward. But he held his weapon aligned on the middle eye of the worm in the event that skill failed.

Now she stood facing the worm, the sphere between them.

Her hands moved into the faint light, weaving a pattern in the air as if they manipulated threads of a netting. He guessed she so endeavored to imprison whatever mind the creature possessed.

Finally she stopped, surveying the worm closely. Then she clapped her hands. The limp tentacles curled up under the worm's chin. Ponderously it squatted, folding its jointed legs until it was belly flat on the pavement. Niccolae beckoned as she restored the sphere to its hiding place. Kenric boosted her into the wide saddle, took his seat before her and lifted the reins. As if that were a signal the worm recognized, it grunted and arose.

Kenric used the reins as he would control any mount, turning the giant worm toward the corridor down which they had originally come.

The worm bore them swiftly and truly. Occasionally its sides brushed the tunnel walls, adding another touch of smoothness to surfaces thus smoothed by generations of worms. When they reached the dark pool below the stairway, they dismounted to drink deeply. The worm drank also. Unfortunately they had no way to take water with them.

To negotiate the stairs, they were obliged to remain dismounted. Niccolae walked first with the sphere as a beacon. Kenric followed, the reins of the worm looped about his arm. Last went the creature, grunting dolefully as if it found the climb taxing. Taxing? A great weight of fatigue lay on Kenric also. What must it be, he thought, for the girl? Since they had awakened in the desert after their kidnapping, they had had no sleep. In fact, here below, time had not been divided into night and day, hour and minute. Even thinking of rest weighed his feet, made him feel as if he were wading ankle deep through shifting sand.

When he caught up to her, she forced herself to lurch forward. Though she kept one hand to the wall for support, she fell. As she tried to struggle up. Kenric moved to her, managed to get her back in the saddle. But he could not raise himself after her. Instead he caught at the edge of one of the worm's armor plates and allowed the creature to both support and lead him. It was as if that last climb up the stairs had drained all but the dregs of strength from him.

The wall-carvings moved past as if they walked through a dream. And Kenric was never sure afterward that he did not doze on his feet, as he had heard it said the wearied soldiers were able to do. But he roused into full consciousness when the huge worm came to a halt.

He looked about him. There were no carved and lighted walls now, only a dim, grayish light high up. And before them a barrier of rocky debris.

They were back at the crumbled pit in the desert through which they first entered the passage.

Kenric fought for a clear mind. He pulled at the girl who had fallen forward in the saddle so that she lolled against the double horn—carrying the pack made up of her robe. He croaked her name. "Niccolae!"

She stirred, whimpered, tried to resist his tugging. With a grunt, the worm squatted, as if expecting its inert rider to now dismount.

She rolled off the worm, lay still but with her eyes half opened. Probably she was as parched as he. Water. Where would they get water? In despair he beat his hands against the plated side of the worm. Where had his mind been? They would have to go back, down into the burrows, try to find another way. . . .

Kenric slipped, fell to the drifted sand. The girl's eyes fully closed. The great worm grunted and went limp.

Man, maid and monster slept.

He roused groggily. His head was thumping against rock as someone shook his shoulders, called out to awaken him. He blinked, tried to raise his hand to shield his eyes.

A glare of light was thrusting in through a gaping hole not too far away.

He saw Niccolae leaning over him. She sighed with relief and let go her hold on his shoulders.

She turned to pick up something, held it out to him. It was half of one of those ball fruits from which juice trickled to splash on his face.

He came fully awake at the sight of that. Burying his face in the soft pulp, he chewed to allay both hunger and thirst.

As he scooped the tough rind with his teeth, he looked about for a second piece. She shook her head.

"But little remains now. For the worm must eat also. Food was the inducement for it to clear our way." She pointed to the ragged hole in the debris of the landslide.

"Food? Not the sphere?"

Her grim face sketched a caricature of a smile. "One of these too ripe for our eating." She was stowing their remaining fruits back into the bag of her robe, save for a side sorting which already showed a sprouting of mold or gave forth a putrid smell. This she shoveled onto a tattered square rug, and got up to hurl the stinking mess through the opening. "I climbed up and poked the bait into a deep crevice. The worm crashed the barrier to get it." She peered through the hole. Now it eats the rest of its dinner."

So simple a solution. Kenric drew a deep breath. In his fatigue and male preoccupation he had even forgotten that Niccolae still possessed that pack of food.

"We need not fear its leaving us," she told him. "It feeds upon that too rotten for our eating. And I think that these worms have a long history of dependence upon men for sustenance."

"How long did I sleep?"

She shrugged. "I don't know. I slept also. But it was night when I awoke, and now it is late day. Since night would cloak us while we travel, it might be well we start now—"

He nodded.

They emerged through the jagged exit into the desert outside. There the worm still chomped at the stuff she had thrown to it. But at the sight of them it kneeled. Once more they settled in its saddle. Niccoale pointed to a distant blue rock spur making a leaning point against the sky.

"That I remember. The men who left us turned their backs upon it when they went. The question is—were they returning to Lanascol or going to Orm Temple? We do not want to take the wrong direction."

"Let the stars rise," she told him, "and I shall have guides in plenty. Reading the stars is part of my sorcery and I know those that hang above Lanascol well. But for now—I cannot say this is the right way, or that—"

The worm stirred uneasily, as if it wanted to be on the move. Kenric hesitated. There were landmarks in plenty—fantastic outcroppings all about them—to keep them from wandering in circles. But which way to start out?

"Fortune has been fair to us so far," he said. "I see no better way than to start by chance. Let us believe that those who took us were to return to Lanascol."

He set the worm going with a twitch of rein.

Their mount was plainly a desert creature. While this particular one might not have run the sands since it was hatched, its body was designed to travel here, the broad padded feet at the ends of those segmented legs finding a good surface even on sand.

They left the ruins behind them, threading in and out among standing rocks until they came to a section that was mainly shifting sand dunes. Only a rocky outcrop here and there showed, like broken teeth in the jaw of a sun-bleached skull. The sun, which had been a torment at their start, faded in force. The gathering of dusk began.

Kenric steered for a set of rocks he thought on a direct line with their progress so far. Beyond those he picked another goal ahead. He hoped it would not be long before the stars appeared.

Soon the dark was too deep to see a guide ahead. However, the baking heat was gone with the light. There was a cold wind blowing, making Kenric long for a cloak. He knew that Niccolae, having sacrificed her outer robe, must feel the chill even more.

"Cling close to me," he ordered. "At least we can warm each other."

She clung. But her eyes were searching the heavens, in which the first glimmers were appearing.

"Mark that star! Ah, we were right to trust fortune. Angle a little to the left—do you not see that bright gleam? It is the apex of a triangle with two lesser lights at its foot—"

The constellation was easy enough to distinguish.

"The Arrow of Attu," said Niccolae. "It will bring us to Lanascol."

Eventually the wind died. No longer did they have to breathe the gritty particles.

Still the worm padded on tirelessly. At times the creature detoured right or left to avoid some rocky ridge, but always it obeyed Kenric's rein signal to correct course. Clinging to Kenric, Niccolae slept. He was glad for her.

He was not aware of dawn until the sky was pale lemon, slowly darkening to the bright orange-yellow of full day, bringing back the heat. Now at last the worm was slowing. Against Kenric's back, Niccolae moved. Her hands gave up their tight hold on him.

"Let the beast eat." Her voice was a husky whisper.

She was right. If they did not satisfy the worm, it might refuse to serve them.

He loosened rein and immediately the worm squatted. It began to grunt in what to Kendric seemed a demanding fashion. Its riders promptly dismounted. Niccolae tottered a little away and kneeled to open the bundle of food.

The smell of it was rank. The worm's head swung around, its tentacles uncoiled and working, plainly avid for the rotten stuff. The girl picked over what lay there, chose one of the balls. This she split with a pointed rock, showing too-soft inner pulp. Kenric nevertheless was ready to share it. Niccolae threw to the worm most of the mass, retaining only a small portion.

"The rest in the pack has all gone bad," she told him bleakly. "We shall keep a little for the worm to feed again. But for us—"

"Wait!" He threw out a hand to silence her staring about him. There was nothing here for shelter, not even a sizable rocky spire. And those dots he saw in the sky, growing larger every second—were they Rovers?

There was a ridge ahead. Could they reach it in time?

"Mount up!" He caught her and shoved her toward the worm.

VI

The creature protested in coughing grunts. But it got to its feet and obeyed the signal to move out. There was no way to spur it to a faster pace. Not until, out of the sky, sounded a ripping screech.

The scaled body jumped in a convulsive indraw for a moment. Then it lengthened out again as the creature went into a rocking gallop while its riders fought to keep in the saddle.

That screech sounded again—louder and nearer. A Rover patrol right enough. Kenric could easily see now the reptilian forms of the flyers with the smaller figures of men mounted between their leather wings. The leader of the flight was planing down.

"Take the reins!" Kenric thrust them at Niccolae as he lifted his weapon.

He fired. A blinding beam of radiance speared. The flyer disappeared in the burst of flame.

A second flyer was too close on the leader to pull up and Kenric fired again. This time a sudden movement of the worm threw him off aim. Screeching, the flyer veered. But the edge of the blast must have singed its wing for it flapped away heavily not soaring as its flock mates did.

Kenric had no idea of the weapon's range. He fired again

at a more distant flyer. It remained untouched. Then to the left and ahead geysered a blast of sand and gravel. The dust and grit billowed to fill his eyes. He could not see to aim again.

The bombardment from above continued, ringing them with flying sand and earth. Thus blinded, they had no chance to find the doubtful protection of the ridge. The worm twisted its body, flung up its head. Suddenly it halted, went flat with a jolt that shook them out of the saddle into the storm of sand.

Kenric leaped back in the direction of the worm, now only a shadow in the cloud of grit. He clung to its bulk, one hand anchored to a plate trying to see. The three-eyed head was sinking into the sand, and he could feel the legs moving—the worm was digging in!

Reins—but he did not have the reins! Niccolae had been holding those. Was the creature to dig in and leave them here half-buried, easy prey for the Rovers?

"Niccolae!" His mouth filled with sand as he called but he was answered.

"Here!"

He glimpsed Niccolae crouched on the other side of the worm, her body taut as she pulled with all her strength on the reins. He joined her, setting the blazer between his knees, pulling on the reins with her to check the worm. Twice he stopped to raise the weapon and blast Rovers out of the sky.

That taught them caution. The attack ceased and with it the sandstorm raised by the bombardment. He could see them still, but they circled too high to reach now.

Heat came with the rising sun. Their worm-mount with its self-burial might well have the best idea for more than one kind of escape. Should they remain where they now were, they would be dead by day's end. The enemy need only pin them in place to win a one-sided battle.

Since the worm appeared quiet, half in the ground, half out, Kenric relaxed somewhat.

"Can you hold?" he asked the girl.

"If it continues to lie thus, yes. What do you do?"

"I want to see what they dropped to churn the sand."

With the blazer under his arm, he zigzagged to the core of tumbled earth and sand from which one of those miniature whirlwinds had risen. There was a pit scooped out, a space bare of even the finest shifting of sand, and sun glinted on metal. Kenric edged closed, used the butt of his weapon to turn the thing over that he might see it more clearly.

He would swear that this was not made on Vallek. It was a slim disk which had a bulbous end, a more slender portion pointing up. On that was a flexible round of small blades that whirled as the thing moved under his prodding. He had heard rumors of such a weapon somewhere in the galaxy—called, if he remembered rightly, an ovid.

Those slight blades must be incredibly strong to have sent soaring such volumes of sand and earth. Kenric frowned. So the Rovers were armed with what would bring the most confusion to desert travelers, allowing the attackers to stay at a safe distance.

What had been used to harry the two worm-riders into a kind of captivity could easily be turned against an army in this waste. Suppose such were hurled about the Kor-King's force until those comprising it were so separated and storm-blinded that a land-based enemy, waiting in reserve, could overrun them?

The ovid fell on its side. Instantly those blades began to spin, cutting into a small drift of sand, sending the dust up so Kenric jumped back, his arm raised to shield his face and eyes.

"What is it?" he heard Niccolae cry out.

Kenric backed away, wreathed in dust clouds. Then he bumped against the worm and crouched low as the sand continued to fountain up as if the ovid had rolled to where it had new earth to cut into. Screening his eyes he looked around. The one fountain was matched by a second now—but they were both dying down now. And he did not know how many more there were.

He crawled to where Niccolae lay in the lee of the half-buried worm. Quickly he explained his find.

"So the Rovers are armed with an off-world device."

"If they are really off-worlders." Though he no longer doubted that. There was a high and alien level of technology behind what he had seen.

The spouting of sand thinned, ceased. But nothing would shut off the sun. Above the Rovers continued to circle, though there were fewer of them now. He counted only three.

But they need only play the waiting game up there and the desert would do the rest for them. He could see no way out of the trap. He heard an exclamation from Niccolae.

"Look here!" She had scooped sand away from the body of the worm. A strong odor violated the air. About the lower plates of the creature's body oozed a sticky substance that trickled down to the sand. Where it moistened the loose particles they hardened into a shell, making a small wall.

Quickly Kenric did some digging of his own, to discover a wall along the length of his side of the worm's body. It was evidently able to build a secure tunnel as it went. If there were some way of controlling its direction underground—

"The sphere!" Niccolae brought out that most precious of her possessions. "But even if it digs a way—how can we be sure that it heads in the right direction?"

"We can't," he said. "But we can gain protection from the sun and from those over us. We can buy a little time." The thought revived his spirit.

Sphere in hand, the girl crept to the head of the monster. When they had checked its dig-in it had already sunk close to the level of its eyes. But those three unblinking globes were still above the sand surface, enough to see what she held. Now she placed the sphere there. Could she again impress her will?

Perhaps she was unsure of her form of communication. For at first she only huddled there, looking more to the sphere than the worm. Then she reached out both hands, not to pick up the globe but rather to use her hooked fingers to dig into the sand, achieving so a shallow depression. Obviously she was attempting hypnotic suggestion.

Finally she picked up the sphere, returned to Kenric's side. "I do not know—" she was saying when, with almost the same force as one of the digging ovids, the worm went into action.

Kenric pulled her away from a whirlwind of debris. The worm was digging in all right, at a far greater speed than earlier. As if all the energy gained during its enforced rest was being called upon to get it underground as speedily as possible.

Debris was shooting out now in another direction. The worm was out of sight. Only the stream of earth spiraling up to mound about a hole marked its going. Could the Rovers see what was happening? If it brought them in to make sure —Kenric fingered the stock of the blazer. A thin hope, but he clung to it.

Kenric wriggled up the mound to look down into a pit. Below the outer ring of loose earth and sand were the slick walls glued by the excretion of the worm's body. On one side was the entrance to a tunnel.

So—here was a hiding hole, screened from sun and overhead observation. He called to Niccolae, then slipped cautiously over the treacherous rim of the pit. He held up his arms to steady her as the girl followed. The entrance to the worm's tunnel was not much larger than the bulk of its body but it afforded them room to crawl in. And the mere fact they had shade was an instant relief.

Kenric pushed on, only to sight the hunched, drawn-in form of the creature. He backed away carefully, not wanting to incite it to digging again and run the danger of being smothered by a backfire of earth and sand.

They were buying time, but how much? They had no water, none of the fruit which had been their stay before. He tried to think.

"It no longer digs?" Niccolae asked.

"No. Try to sleep," he suggested. "At nightfall we can—"

"If still we live," she interrupted tonelessly.

"We have this chance. Having lost sight of us, the Rovers may come nearer. If we can meet them closer to ground level—"

Her eyes closed. She breathed shallowly, as if not to hurt her laboring lungs. And he thought that she might not have heard, or chosen to hear, his words.

Then she answered without opening her eyes.

"Men have lived on dreams before, Lord Kor Kenric. And sometimes even proven them true. So let us dream—"

But if she took refuge in sleep, he must play sentry. Not that he dared expect the coming of anyone: foe—or remotely, friend. Yet he would be ready.

It was hard to fight the stupor creeping over him. It was hard to think coherently. He tried to recall all that had happened to him since his arrival on Vallek. Those at HQ must have learned long ago that he was not the oracle. But would they know who he was? And if so—could a return fix ever be set up? To his own knowledge, not since the early experimental days had a sending misplaced an agent. He would be at least a footnote now in the confidential history tapes stored in ZAT.

Having failed with him were they trying to send another agent? If so, would that fail because of the blasted chair now in the worm walk? How had the priests used that plate in the seat back, anyway? How had—?

Kenric roused. He saw, out in the pit, what had snapped him out of his dreamy state. A cascade of sand hissed down its wall. Someone stood on the top of the mound of excavated sand. Kenric shouldered closer to Niccolae. One hand covered her lips lest she make some sound, the other shook her awake. When he saw her eyes open and focus intelligently, Kenric motioned to the pit. The sand had ceased trickling; perhaps who moved above was listening, too.

Suddenly one of the ovids was lobbed into the pit, its fan beating up a storm in such earth as the worm secretion had not glued.

The flying cloud was thin and it did not reach into the tunnel. But it might be cover for another form of attack. Weapon ready, Kenric waited grimly.

The wait ended as a dark figure leaped down, kicking the still revolving disrupter out of the way. There was a spurt of flame, but Kenric had fired at the same time—with better aim. The attacker exploded into shredded flesh. Niccolae cried out, beating against Kenric's shoulder, tearing loose smoldering strips of tunic where the other's ray had ignited fabric and seared skin. But Kenric was alive and the other dead.

They would try again. Kenric sped into the open, swept the top of the mound without taking direct ray, spraying the blazer's fire in a wide sweep as he pivoted.

The very fury of that move won. There was a scream of anguish. He saw a man who had stood directly above the tunnel entrance stagger back, his hands flung up to hide his face.

Kenric identified him as a Rover. But the other who lay in a singed heap in the pit was not. Kenric went to the dead man. His face had escaped the blast, and he was not a Kawyn, nor of Lanascol either. His skin was faintly greenish and the hair, still remaining was of a mottled gray—humanoid, but alien. The remains of his clothing suggested a space uniform. Kenric forced himself to search the body.

He found little, mainly the charred remnants of a belt to which various tools or instruments had been slung, most of which were now melted into unidentifiable blobs. Of his origin there was no clue. However, his death, in addition to saving their lives, provided them with a second weapon. It was a hand arm, short barreled, lacking the telescopic sights of the first. He picked it up to bring back to Niccolae.

What interested him now was how those men had reached

them. It could only be that the Rover must have landed his
mount somewhere near. And perhaps that flying thing could
signal trouble to any of the flock still aloft.

The only answer was to turn defense into offense again.
The force of that spray he had used on the mound top had
fused some of the sand into a slick surface which might be
hard to climb. He spoke to Niccolae, who was examining the
hand blazer.

"Try a quick blast here—and here—"

She obeyed. The flash hollowed hand and foot holds. Then
the girl stationed herself below, watching the rim while Kenric swung up.

He sprawled belly down on the top, his blazer ready. And
he was just in time to see a Rover mount waddling awk-
wardly for a takeoff—a man in the saddle between its wings,
clinging to the straps there while his body swayed weakly to
and fro.

Kenric fired, but his burst was short though he kept his finger on the button. He pressed again. This time there was no
flash at all. At the worst possible time the weapon needed
recharging.

He had missed the darting head, had only frightened or ir-
ritated the flying creature into a frenzy. It somersaulted vio-
lently, throwing off its rider, then pecked him to death with
two or three strokes of its great beak. Then it swept around
and, with more speed than Kenric thought its clumsy gait on
the ground would allow, it headed straight for him.

He threw himself backward, slid down into the pit.

The monstrous flying reptile scrabbled on the mound, and
the fanning of its huge wingspread raised almost as much
dust as might an ovid. With the girl, Kenric crouched in the
tunnel. The walls of the pit were cracking, giving away under
the thump of legs and body as the thing balanced, shooting
out its long neck, trying to reach the two below.

Kenric was feeling for the smaller weapon when Niccolae
fired it. The lance of flame brought a deafening screech from
the flyer. It flopped forward, falling into the pit and filling
most of it.

At the same time came a tremor in the earth. The worm,
quiet so long they had all but forgotten it, began to move. It
was digging again. Earth and sand flew all over them. They
plastered themselves to the wall. Outside the flyer screamed
and heaved, blocking any escape. They were fast being
buried.

A mighty shaking followed, as if an earthquake moved. The ground around the mouth of the tunnel was being kicked in by the flyer. A beaklike mouth stabbed at them. They could only push back into the newly turned soil behind. Again that beak thrust, this time grazing Niccolae's shoulder, leaving an ooze of blood.

Somehow Kenric pushed the girl behind him, tried to get ready to meet a third attack by the beak. But he was tossed by another tremor of earth. And the attack he awaited with no hope of escaping did not come.

Instead a wild squawking sounded. The body of the flyer heaved and fought as if it tried to find standing room beyond the pit entrapping it.

Kenric used the precious moment of respite to crowd yet farther back into the fresh debris. Then Niccolae pulled at him until he turned his head a little.

"Look!"

VII

A burst of sunlight there showed the worm gone. As it had buried itself, so it now must have attained the surface again. On hands and knees, through the choking earth, Kenric and the girl followed.

They emerged into a haze of sand as thick as that thrown up by the ovids. But through it they caught glimpses of massive bodies in battle. The huge fire worm was now seeking to bury the flyer in the pit. Kenric and Niccolae scrambled away from the sandstorm. By all the evidence they had seen, the worms were not carnivorous. But perhaps the flying reptiles were, and this was a defense against an old enemy delivered into the worm's reach.

Finally the swirl of high-flung sand subsided. Now they saw the worm clearly, crouched, its head bent, tentacles working feverishly as it watched a feeble movement under a thick mound of sand.

For the first time Kenric looked aloft. There were no Rovers in the sky. It might have been that the one who had landed had been left on guard while the others went elsewhere. Elsewere! To try their bombing tactics against the Kor-King's force?

When he said as much, Niccolae brought out the sphere. "The worm—if we can ride—"

"We must!" Though he was not sure they could control the

worm after its battle with the flyer. The heaving had subsided and the mound was now quiet. But the worm still crouched as if over an enemy.

The reins in his hand shook as the worm's head came up. The tentacles again hung loose to form a limp beard. Then the creature folded its legs under it so they could mount.

Kenric used the reins to point it once more toward the ridge he had selected just before they had been attacked. The flat pad-pad of the worm's jolting walk began again.

In this heat, Kenric could almost believe both eye and brain were cooked to the point of imagining things. But, squinting against the glare of the sun, suddenly he saw something he thought no trick of light could produce. A flashing came from their right, sparking from near the top of one of the rocky pinnacles. Around its base arose sand swirls he knew only too well—though there were no flyers visible aloft.

"A signal!" Niccolae's fingers dug into his shoulder.

"So I thought," he rasped.

"But you do not understand—it is a signal of Lanascol!"

"Where there are traitors—" He spoke so, though he wanted to believe.

He longed for the security of the blazer, now swinging empty in the saddle scabbard, as he weighed the hand beamer. But wanting and having were poles apart. He brought the worm's head around and bore toward the wink of light.

The sandstorm about the base of that rock was dying. It was plain the ovids could run only for a limited time. And, when they reached the peak, none were discharging grit into the air. So the haze was thin and the men who leaped from the stone to face them were easy to recognize.

"Lord Kor!" The one in the lead was ploughing through the sand toward the worm. He stared at Kenric and the giant worm as if he could hardly believe his eyes.

"They say men sight illusions in the desert," he began. "But I do not believe you are one."

"Nor am I." Kenric twitched the reins and the worm folded its legs. "Tell me, Girant, does the Kor-King ride this way?"

"Yes. He is behind—we are scouting. But there are Rovers aloft and they have the power to raise the sands to fight for them. They trapped us here but a short time ago—then flew on. We can only hope our talking mirror relayed the warning to the Kor-King's men. But Lord Kor, where have you been?

What is this monster you ride? The Kor-King's Eyes in the city discovered you had been tricked by a sorceress—" For the first time he turned his stare on the girl.

"Not tricked by the Lady Niccolae," Kenric corrected him. "She was taken captive with me. There are traitors in Lanascol, right enough. But they are of a different calling than sorceress. Have you mounts?"

"We had. When the sand wind arose they stampeded."

"I must reach the Kor-King. Yet to leave you here—"

"We have a goodly fort in these rocks, such as can hold off even the snake necks of the Rovers should they attack. And anyone coming on foot will meet a warm welcome."

"There are those with the Rovers with new and deadlier arms," Kenric warned. "They blast afar with fire. If you see any which look so," he slapped the scabbarded weapon, "take good cover behind the rocks."

Girant nodded. "Perhaps some will also come riding monsters such as you have?"

"True. Ours came from their stable. But I shall send aid as soon as I can."

"There is no need for such a promise, Lord Kor. We know of old the manner of man we serve." Girant touched two fingers to his forehead. "May fortune ride with you!"

"In what direction? I am hasty to be gone, but where?"

"See the rock wall to the south there—the double gap with the projection in the middle? Bear on that, Lord Kor, for our camp last night lay beneath it."

The worm began its tireless trot. Kenric looked often to the sky and felt an odd shrinking between his shoulder blades, as if he were presenting his back to some fatal attack. Yet there was still no sign of Rovers.

Nor did there appear to be any disturbance of sand ahead. If they were bombing the Kor-King's men, that battle was yet out of sight. Heat bore down. Kenric thought of water, food. Should he have begged both from Girant?

Niccolae pressed to him tightly. Her head rested on his shoulder. He thought how she too must be suffering for water.

Kenric had early discovered that distances in the waste were deceptive. Now it seemed that the longer they traveled, the farther off stood the hills Girant had pointed out. Did a haze now lie between?

He heard a gasp from Niccolae. Suddenly the surface of the open ground before them was heaving, turning up, coming alive—with the emerging heads and bodies of worms. Just as their own mount had earlier dug free, so were others breaking from the burrows in which they must have traveled.

And each was carrying double—a rider controlling the worm, an armed fighter with him. Kenric tried to rein in, found he could do nothing. The worm they rode was intent upon joining its fellows.

They need only be sighted by one of those other riders to be flamed to a crisp, Kenric thought. Then, eyeing the squad carefully, he realized that none carried blazers. Theirs were only the conventional weapons of Vallek: black tubes that directed small paralyzing darts, long lances, battle swords. Where were the blazers? Were there too few of them to arm such a company? Or did the suppliers of such weapons not trust these allies? Perhaps the sight of the worms alone was intended to demoralize the Lanascol forces.

The worm they bestrode showed no sign of weariness. Instead it forged ahead through the rear guard of the squad, pushing for the van. The attackers rode in loose formation, one worm well apart from his fellows. No one took notice of the newcomers.

"Lean low as you can," Kenric ordered Niccolae.

He bent himself nearly double across the bar of the saddle. The coarse hair of the worm whipped him, its odor stinging his eyes and nostrils. It was all Kenric and the girl could to to hold on. For the pace of the worm, plainly excited by its company, became a rocking gallop, threatening their grasp, bruising them back and front, whipping them with the steel-harsh strands of hair.

Kenric did not dare to raise his head to look at the riders around them. He could only cling and hope that the impetus of their charge would carry them through.

The worm rocked on. Kenric heard shouting, and then about them was the fury of driven sand. They were in the attack area. He shut his eyes and clung the tighter to his insecure seat. The worm skidded to a halt, dropped so that they sprawled out of the saddle, Niccolae still clinging to him, while sand arose about them. Kenric loosened hold on the reins, squirmed away, dimly aware than once more the worm was digging in and that they must not be engulfed by debris. He pulled Niccolae around. Then, with his arm upflung to shield his sand-rasped face, he staggered away.

Only to come up against a rock, a firm anchorage in this

world of swirling grit. There he clung, the girl pressed against him, both with eyes closed, trying to breathe.

How long that lasted he did not know. But he could hear shouting. And some of those shouts were battle cries of Lanascol. Someone caught at his shoulder, strove to loosen him from the rock. He tried to free himself without surrendering either the girl or his hold. But it was no use. He was hauled away.

Then he no longer felt the pelting sand. He opened his eyes.

He recognized the breast badges. The Kor-King's guard. Kenric tried to speak and produced only a dull croak. Someone lifted a water bottle to his lips. He sucked avidly.

His hands hung limp. Where was the girl? Realization that she was gone brought back his mind. He managed to straighten, supported on either side by guardsmen.

"Niccolae?"

"She is here, Lord Kor. See you—" They turned him a little and he did see. She lay on the ground as one of the guard dribbled water cautiously into her mouth. The man nodded to him.

"She lives, Lord Kor. This is only a swoon."

"The Kor-King?" Kenric said, "I have news of import—"

"He comes now, Lord Kor—" Again they aided him to turn, this time to face the tall man wearing half armor, the helm set with a jeweled device.

The last swirl of sand had subsided. It was close to sunset. There were many ledges on the rise of the rock cliff which might have been chiseled on purpose to provide seats for the waiting men. Kenric leaned back and looked to the right where the Kor-King was similarly enthroned. They could still see, on the floor of the waste, those humps which marked the dug-in worms, apparently quiescent underground. Of their late riders, those who had not died during the attack or been entrapped when their mounts began to tunnel, there were a score under guard and already being questioned by the Kor-King's officers.

"It would seem," the King observed, "that they entered battle woefully ignorant if they did not know their mounts' proclivity for seeking safety underground during sandstorms. That is ill planning. A natural result of what you have told me of their jealousies. And this defeat will not make for good feeling among them, either."

"Since I blasted the oracle throne with a weapon belonging to the strangers, they may be suspect. And as these other new weapons—these ovids—have brought defeat instead of victory, I should think any faith they have in strangers is sorely shaken. Still, it is those weapons we have most to fear."

"That and the treachery at our own core." The Kor-King took off his helm and rubbed his temples as if the weight of that headgear were too much. He was of the same general breed of all the Lanascol men, red-brown of skin, dark red of hair. Save above each ear was a patch of silver two fingers in breadth. But for that he showed no sign of age, his regular features bearing only those marks set by a vigorous life of much responsibility.

Kenric studied him as the King continued to look out over the desert. He wore well, did this Kor-King whose rule should remain intact if Vallek was not going to end a charred cinder in a future so far ahead of this twilight that the reckoning of it must be left to the machines of men of another world and age. He had accepted Kenric's wild tale with sober attention. Yet he might well have had doubts—seeing that a son who had long lain witless blurted it out while in a semidaze. Here was evidence that the real Kenric had been one in whom men could root confidence and not have it wither.

"These off-worlders wish to deal with the priests for the ore. We have long known it has certain unique properties. Sorceresses can make use of it. Just as the superstitious Kawyn grind it into useless powder, lest it be turned against them. And speaking of sorceresses, Kenric, it would seem this Niccolae has wrought well for our line. Let her ask of us what she would—if it be within our power to grant—" He made a gesture with his hands.

"I do not think she will claim any reward."

The Kor-King laughed softly. "That may be. But rewards come at the end. And there is another woman who had also wrought some twists and turns in this matter. You have said nothing of the Lady Yarakoma save that her man, or one purporting to be her man, was in the council of priests. Your forbearance is strange. She has said much of you these past days—"

"I do not wonder at that."

"No, I suppose you do not. She has said among other things that you are still brainsick from your wound. And that while so weakened you have fallen under the spell of a sorceress who uses you for her own foul purposes."

"And these words were believed?" Kenric could read nothing in the Kor-King's level voice. Could it be that Yarakoma still had some measure of influence?

"They had logic. My eyes reported some facts apparently bearing them out. Only, I have other, still more secret eyes. And one of them I had set on certain path of prying when word first came to me that you had suffered so badly in that border clash. It is meet that sometimes I be thought more blind than the Overgods decreed I be. The Lady Yarakoma has been scant friend to you in the past—why was it that she wished to watch so closely by your bedside when you lay without much more than breath left in you? Though she never did so alone."

Kenric smiled. "For which fact perhaps I should be devoutly thankful."

He heard the Kor-King chuckle, the dusk now veiling the other's face. "Your brother has never been noted for seeing beyond a pretty face when we would go courting. Therefore I speak no ill of him. In his way he is a valiant and worthy son. But should he come to wear this—" The King held out his helm, only a dark shadow now—"then I have fears for what might follow in Lanascol. The Lady Yarakoma cannot be denounced openly, lest she rive the kingdom top to bottom. She has many who listen while she spills well-chosen words. But it is meet that your brother be sent to hold the western marches and deal with the sea peoples. I have good reason to believe the worm priests have been meddling there. Since he will be gone for at least two years, and into a rough and dangerous country, he cannot take his loving lady with him. She will express an earnest desire to retire to the Tower of Seven Silences during that time, to find among the Wise Women there consolation and support."

Kenric lacked any knowledge of the place. But the Kor-King had taken the best precautions to control a treacherous daughter-in-law, Kenric did not doubt.

"So much for the Lady. What of the priests, these strangers, the alliance with the Rovers and the Kawyn?"

"We shall hope your initial sowing of discord will root. I have my eyes on duty and they have their orders to muddy waters, throw fuel on fires, generally make themselves useful. The Rovers may try to assault Lanascol, though I doubt it. The worm priests, without their oracle are deeply wounded for the time. And your detailed account will be widely repeated—mainly it will state that the oracle cannot any longer be inspired in the burrows. In fact, your tale will make a saga that will enhance our house and its rule. As for the strangers—we must learn more of them. Some of our eyes will move in that direction. And we have learned that the worm-animals have their uses. We have never been free of the desert because of its nature and ours. But if we can now mount our scouts on worms, that lack will be remedied."

Kenric nodded. The Kor-King spoke on.

"I do not say that all will be easy and one small battle wins a war. You are border-seasoned enough to know that is not so. But I do think their dark alliance will not hold now. And enemies who come to us singly we can handle. I think for Lanascol we have done well this day. Thanks to Girant who blinked us warning—and your message. There is always a way for brave men, or so I have found. We shall return now to Lanascol, leaving only a screen of scouts, perhaps mounted on these worms. There we shall await the return of our Eyes, preparing against Rover raids or trouble from the strangers. When has it not always been so? Man thinks of what lies ahead—the prudent try to foresee. Which makes me think once more of this sorceress of yours. I find her of note. Such we would do well to bind to us."

Kenric felt the Kor-King was looking at him now with meaning. But he was suddenly too tired to care what thought might lie behind the words. He might not have completed his mission in the manner the Service had intended, but at least Lanascol still was sturdily defended and he was sure the Kor-King would rule on.

Kenric stood just within the hangings. This room was somewhat larger than that in which Niccolae received her clients, but not by much. The scent of herbs clung to the fabric.

"We're only getting in deeper," he said without turning to look at her. "The Kor-King deserves better. He looks upon me as a partner in his plans. If I am recalled and he has left but a senseless clod—or a dead body!—that will cause someone as keen-witted as he to be suspicious. You might report that. It should shake up even ZAT."

"It has," she answered.

"Oh, has it?" he swung around. But she was standing in the dimmest corner of the room and he could not see her expression. Or was she presenting him with the same smooth mask she assumed for her clients?

"ZAT has confessed—if you can call it that."

"Confessed? To what?"

"That the last-minute switch in the sending was its responsibility."

Kenric stepped away from the drape. "Do you know what you are saying?" he demanded. He did not want to believe her—it approached too near to an old fear of his, once long existing on the fringe of his thoughts. The fear that some day the computer would not be following the orders of men to achieve a solution but would begin working on its own.

"ZAT came to the conclusion that the oracle was not the key. ZAT reports that the Kor-King needs the backing our operative could give. Knowing that, ZAT prepared a different sending—"

"So I was elected. Did Goddard know?"

"No one knew—until after you were sent. They then learned ZAT had arranged no recall."

"What!"

"The shift came by some circuit they can't trace—yet. And so you can't return safely. To try it might end in an abort. I presume you don't want to risk that."

"Of course not," he answered almost absently, trying to think out what ZAT had done to him. It was well in the realm of possibility that they would be a long time finding that circuit. ZAT could conceal it.

"Another thing," she said. "ZAT broke connections with me today when I was asking progress. Contact now will have to come from the other side if ZAT continues the break."

He was over the first shock, able to think steadily. "It's as if I volunteered for Permanent Agent. I think I'll have to see it that way."

"You take it well." She moved into the window light to stand watching him closely. The ravages of their days in the desert were largely gone from her face.

"No use calling down the wrath of any gods of Vallek on ZAT." He tried to laugh and found the sound he produced passable. "All right—I forget Creed Trapnell, and am truly Lord Kor Kenric. Well, there is plenty to do under that name."

"That being?"

"The Kor-King wants you in the family. Last night he gave me one of those straight talks of his. I can understand his concern. Yarakoma is hardly to be listed as a credit to the clan. He would like a hand in picking the next woman to be marriage-linked with the Kor blood."

Kenric grinned at her. Her face remained placid, but not her eyes. They glowed like orm ore. He moved toward her, and on the way he said:

"He's shrewd and he's right. I think I would set him up even against ZAT!"

Then he stopped talking, for a good reason.

Andre Norton:
Loss of Faith

By RICK BROOKS

THE impression that a regular reader of Andre Norton's books might have is that of growing pessimism. From light hearted adventure stories like *Star Rangers* and *Sargasso of Space,* she has gone to books like *Dread Companion* and *Dark Piper* that give the feeling at the conclusion that it is best not to see or even guess what lies ahead.

While Miss Norton has never seemed too comfortable in the here-and-now, it seems that now the future that once beckoned has become another area for distrust. Even the latest Solar Queen story, *Postmarked the Stars,* is more sub-dued and grim in tone. The Patrol, a largely unsullied organization, comes in for its lumps in *The Zero Stone* and its sequel, *Uncharted Stars.* In *Ice Crown,* the Service makes no move to help those under a planetwide conditioning program. As a correspondent, children's librarian Devra Langsam remarked:

> . . . more and more it is the organized cultural groups, like the Patrol, and in this case, the Service (cultural-anthropology?) who are the villains. . . . I suppose that this was foreshadowed in her Solar Queen stories, but it's still surprising . . . and she's a bit old to be getting this anti-establishment thing.

But are these impressions correct? Has Miss Norton lost faith in the future? After reading her books over the last few

187

weeks, I see the answer as yes ... and no. She has definitely lost some of her optimism—but haven't we all? In novels like *Dread Companion* and *Dark Piper,* she is trying for deeper characterization. This slows down the action and gives one more time to spot her usual lack of blind faith in the future.

Star Man's Son, her first science fiction novel, was written after warming up with a couple of short stories (as Andrew North) in *Fantasy Book,* two historical novels, and "Adapting" the myth of Huon of the Horn. Since Miss Norton "wastes" little in previous writings, in 1965, *Steel Magic,* a juvenile sequel to *Huon of the Horn,* came out.

Star Man's Son takes place in a post-nuclear-war world. While the ending is upbeat with the hope of a rebirth of civilization, most of the story is rather bleak. This novel sees the birth of a theme that runs through all Norton's books—tolerance for other races.

Star Rangers (her first of many Ace Books, published in 1955) extends this theme to non-humans and introduces the reptilian race of Zacan (the Zacathans) which have become almost a fixture in her later far future novels. The mighty stellar empire of Central Control seen at a much earlier stage is collapsing later in *Star Guard,* and a battered Patrol ship limps back to Terra, now long forgotten, to start anew. The upbeat ending again overshadows the brutal future pictured with a hardening of hereditary stratification in all groups, even the Patrol, and bloody power struggles in which entire worlds with all their people are burnt off with little apparent concern. The character's rather matter of fact acceptance of the latter is quite chilling.

The Stars Are Ours starts on another post-destruction Terra, this time by a satellite burn-off which triggers a program against Free Scientists. A few escape to Astra under cold sleep. The bleak repressive Terra miraculously gives way to the vividly drawn Astra. With this, Miss Norton comes into her major strength, the portrayal of other worlds. The switch between bleak winter on Terra and the verdant growing season on Astra seems to mark a turning point in Norton's writing.

She now has a more optimistic tone as she explores the glory of other worlds. In *Sargasso of Space,* the planet Limbo has been partially burnt off, but in a long gone Forerunner war. *Star Guard* sees an attempt to set human mercenaries against each other, but no killings of non-combatants. *The Crossroads of Time* does show some brutal alternate presents. *Plague Ship* features a run-in with the Patrol and the danger of being shot on sight as plague carriers. *Sea Siege* is a downbeat near-future tale where radioactive mutated sea life and a nuclear war endanger humanity. *Star Born* features a clash with Those Others, the vicious native race of Astra. While there still is a lot of violence, the characters' attitude has changed from passive acceptance of it as a part of life to downright loathing.

Star Gate is a rather unique book as it concerns the alternate histories of another world. With the exception of Norton's later "Toys of Tamisan," this is the only science fiction that comes to mind covering both star travel and travel *sideways* in time. Creating an alien world is usually considered enough, without creating a history to go with it.

Andre Norton seems to have suffered a rough period in 1961-62. *Star Hunter* has the Patrol ignoring the mental conditioning of a young drifter so that a Veep can be nabbed. In *The Defiant Agents*, a group of Indians are mentally conditioned and sent off to occupy Topaz before the Reds can. The optimism of *Galactic Derelict*, where the universe and its wonders had been opened to man, have in its sequel turned to dread of the weapons of the earlier galactic empire in human hands. *Eye of the Monster* is Norton's most xenophobic story by far. The previous *Storm over Warlock* had a very nasty portrayal of the Throgs, but humans still try to make peace. Here there is no thought of peace. In all other stories, evil aliens are the result of forbidden researches. Here the crocs are vicious barbarians that suddenly start butchering all off-worlders. Several racial characteristics are adversely mentioned, especially odor. In all other Norton novels, aliens are evil for what they do, not what they are. Despite provocation, no other Norton hero has reacted by a hatred that could be classified as racial. This momentary failure underlines her usual tolerance for living beings.

Outside of these three novels, not much distinguished one Norton novel from another during the late fifties and most of the sixties except a little more polish in writing of later ones. With *Dark Piper* (1968), a lessening of optimism is again visible.

One of the most fascinating things about Andre Norton has been her consistency with respect to certain ideas and themes while totally ignoring consistency where most authors wouldn't. As Ralph Waldo Emerson said:

A foolish consistency is the hobgoblin of little minds . . .
with consistency a great soul has simply nothing to
do. . . . Speak what you think today in words as hard as
cannon-balls, and to-morrow speak what to-morrow
thinks in hard words again, though it contradict every
thing you said today.

At least one fan has waged a titanic struggle in trying to
sort out a consistent "future history" from Norton's books
when she never has bothered with one. However, most of her
stories do fall within a loose framework. It is almost like
such terms as *Free Traders, Forerunners, First Ship, Patrol,
Jack, Veep, First-in Scout,* and *Combine* fit so well that she
doesn't bother to coin others. Races such as the Zacathans
and planets such as Astra receive mention in many stories, as
does the game of Stars and Comets. Whether this is a matter
of sentiment, laziness, or practicality (it is work to create an
entire world for just one story, let along several worlds) is a
point that can be argued.

Miss Norton, instead of being bound by a future history,
has created a series of alternate universes that largely over-
lap. All her interplanetary stories, with the exception of *Star
Gate* (though a planet Gorth is mentioned in *Moon of
Three Rings*), *Secret of the Lost Race,* "Long Live Lord
Kor!" and *Dark Piper* have interlocking references. The latter is probably to emphasize the isolation of the research
planet of Beltane from the rest of the galaxy. I think that it
is significant that the two novels date from 1958 and 1959,
while the other is a novelette. Since Miss Norton's references to previous books have become more numerous in
her last group of books, it would seem that certain races,
planets, and things have become touchstones for her.

In *Unchartered Stars,* the sequel to *The Zero Stone,* she
runs wild with references to *The Zero Stone,* a Salarik (pp.
13, 72; the feline race of Sargol in *Plague Ship*), a male
Wyvern of Warlock (p. 114; *Ordeal in Otherwhere*), a Trystian (p. 117), Zacathans (pp. 117, 176), a Faltharian (p.
166; three races prominent in *Star Rangers*), ". . . the Cav-
erns of Arzor and of that Sargasso planet of Limbo . . ." (p.
140; *The Beast Master* and *Sargasso of Space*), and koro
stones (p. 173; *Plague Ship*). References to many other races
and many other gem stones are mentioned in passing.

This is a good thing and gives depth to a story, but occasionally Miss Norton goofs in choosing a "spear-carrier"

from an earlier story. The worst example is the Salarik who tended bar in *Star Hunter*. He could not have taken the odors of the place without protection.

Miss Norton's stories are born in many ways. *Star Rangers* started from the story of the Roman Emperor who ordered a legion eastward across Asia to the end of the world. Childe Roland and the Dark Tower became *Warlock of the Witch World*. *The Year of the Unicorn* owed its origin to the folk tale of "Beauty and the Beast." Even more obvious are the links between *Dark Piper* and the Pied Piper. However, few would realize that *Night of Masks* was sparked by the "powerful descriptions" of William Hope Hodgson's classic *The Night Land*.

"Long Live Lord Kor!" was written around an unused cover that showed the couple mounted on a giant fire worm firing at a flying thing. The title was originally "Worm Walk." Running things—by human default was a giant super computer called ZAT ". . . whose limitations had yet to be discovered." (*Worlds of Fantasy* No. 2, p. 53). *X Factor* is dedicated to "Helen Hoover whose weasel-fisher people gave me the Brothers-In-Fur." Helen has a series of excellent nature books illustrated by her husband Adrian (whose illustrations remind me of Ernest Thompson Seton's, who was a very early idol of mine. But Adrian's are much better.)

The stories are shaped by references to an "extensive personal library of natural history, archaeology, anthropology, native religions, folklore, and travel in off-beat sections of the world." The ". . . forests of Janus and *The Zero Stone* are both taken from the great forests of the Matto Grosso." And of course history plays an important part.

History, by the way, is not weapons (which are again a form of machines) but human beings—the fact that some ruler was ill on a certain day and so made a decision he might not have done otherwise—the fact that some personal animosity moved action can be seen over and over again. Until we read it from the viewpoint of the people, who were worked upon by the strains and stresses of their times which again may be alien to our present thinking, we do not read real history. I wish the students in school would study diaries and the volumes of contemporary letters of the period they are seeking to study rather than read the texts (which cannot help but be influenced by the personal tastes of their writers).

From such sources they would learn what moved these people three, four, five hundred years ago to behave as they did. One volume of Pepys' diary can give one a vivid impression of Restoration England of far more value to the student than any list of dates and decisions of Parliament of that period.

To which, I agree heartily. To create an alien culture, it is a big help to understand one. Which means just about all previous cultures as well as the present one. Our command of technology separates us from the cultures of the past. The Founding Fathers had more in common with the Classical civilization members of Greece and Rome than they do with us. But have we lost something?

Descartes' dicotomy had given modern man a philosophical basis for getting rid of the belief in witches, and this contributed considerably to the actual overcoming of witchcraft in the eighteenth century. Everyone would agree that this was a great gain. But we likewise got rid of the fairies, elves, trolls, and all of the demicreatures of the woods and earth. It is generally assumed that this, too, was a gain, since it helped sweep man's mind clear of 'superstition' and 'magic.' But I believe that this is an error. Actually what we did in getting rid of the fairies and the elves and their ilk was to impoverish our lives; and impoverishment is not the lasting way to clear men's minds of superstition. There is a sound truth in the old parable of the man who swept the evil spirit out of his house, but the spirit, noticing that the house stood clean and vacant, returned, bringing seven more evil spirits with him; and the second state of the man was worse than the first. For it is the empty and vacant people who seize on the new and more destructive forms of our latter-day superstitions, such as beliefs in the totalitarian mythologies, engrams, miracles like the day the sun stood still, and so on. Our world has become disenchanted, and it leaves us not only out of tune with nature but with ourselves as well. (*Man's Search for Himself* by Rollo May, Signet, pp. 62-3)

So in the end, the chief value of Andre Norton's writing may not lie in entertainment or social commentary, but in her "re-enchanting" us with her creations that renew our linkages to all life. One might say of her writing that

> . . . there was much she said beyond my understanding, references to events and people unknown, such hints only making me wistful to go through the doors they represented and see what lay on the far side. (*Moon of Three Rings*, Ace, p. 103)

But Norton falls into a much more rigid pattern in her view of the complex technological future that largely ignores the individual. Her sympathies can be easily seen as the Norton hero or heroine never seems to fit into their society and often are outright misfits. In *Night of Masks*, Nik Kolkerne has a badly mutilated face and a personality to match. Diskan Fentress is a clumsy oaf crashing through the faerie world of Vaanchard in *The X Factor*. Ross Murdock is an alienated criminal when he becomes part of a time traveling team in *The Time Traders*. Roane Hume in *Ice Crown* finds the medieval life of Clio draws her from her relatives who treat her like an extra pair of hands.

Miss Norton seems to be fond of the medieval period. *Moon of Three Rings* was deliberately based on the culture of the European Middle Ages. (Dark Ages is a misnomer, for an age that saw the inventions of the horsecollar, the windmill, and stirrups. These allowed men to harness horsepower and windpower for the first time and to weld man and horse into a battle unit. See Lynn White's book on medieval technology. Miss Norton would stress the Guilds and other human factors.) All six Witch World novels, *Key Out of Time*, *Star Gate*, *Star Guard*, "Toys of Tamisan," "Wizard's World," and to some extent *Plague Ship* feature a medieval-like culture. Some writers use such a culture regularly because they are too lazy to work out another, but Miss Norton sees important values that we bypassed in the medieval period.

Another major feature is the stressing of the bond between man and animal (and Iftin and tree if the Janus series). In *Star Man's Son*, Fors of the Puma clan had Lura, the mutant cat, as a companion. In *Star Rangers* occurs the following:

> Fylh's crest lifted. He raised his face to the sky and poured out a liquid run of notes, so pure and heart tear-

ing a melody that Kartr held his breath in wonder. Was this Fylh's form of happy release from emotion?

Then came the birds, wheeling and fluttering. Kartr stiffened into statue stillness, afraid to break the spell. As Fylh's carols rose, died, rose again, more and more of the fliers gathered, with flashes of red feathers, blue, yellow, white, green. They hopped before the Trystian's feet, perched on his shoulders, his arms, circled around his head.

Kartr had seen Fylh entice winged things to him before but never just this way. It appeared to his bewildered eyes that the whole campsite was a maze of fluttering wings and rainbow feathers.

The trills of song died away and the birds arose, a flock of color. Three times they circled Fylh, hiding his head and shoulders from sight with the tapestry of tints they wove in flight. Then they were gone—up into the morning. Kartr could not move, his eyes remained fixed on Fylh. For the Trystian was on his feet, his arms outstretched, straining upward as if he would have followed the others up and out. And for the first time, dimly, the sergeant sensed what longings must be born in Fylh's people since they had lost their wings. Had that loss been good—should they have traded wings for intelligence? Did Fylh wonder about that? (Ace, 1955, p. 166)

In view of this, it is also hardly surprising that the survivors of the Patrol choose to go out into the wilderness and live off nature instead of seeking another abandoned city to live in at the book's end.

Star Rangers also introduces the theme of telepathy. In *The Beast Master* (1959) the two are fused together and we have Hosteen Storm, the Beast Master, and his team of African Black Eagle, Meerkats, and dune cat all telepathically linked. But like Diskan Fentress in *The X Factor*, his talent just covers animals. Kartr in *Star Rangers* as well as Zinga the Zacacathan can communicate telepathically with animals, but do not try for an emotional bond or work with them.

Murray Leinster's "Exploration Team" (Astounding Science Fiction magazine, March 1956, "Combat Team" in *Colonial Survey*) had a team of man, eagle, and giant bears. They manage to save a colony that was supposed to be protected by robots. It could have influenced Norton, but since she was heading that way anyway, I doubt it. Besides, she makes a point of not reading other sf when she is writing so it won't influence her. The treatment of robots is about the same (the robots in Leinster's story were computer controlled as I remember). Andre Norton's only favorable mention of robots is in *Star Rangers* where one had been a member of the crew and ". . . he was good with engines—being one himself." (Ace, 1955, p. 20).

In *Moon of Three Rings*, Maelen the Moon Singer can telepathically communicate with her animals that work together for her traveling show. Travis Fox and the mutant coyotes work together and communicate on Topaz in *The Defiant Agents*. *Key Out of Time* features Karara Trehern telepathically linked with dolphins. Shann Lantree and his wolverines mentally share information and work together in *Storm Over Warlock*.

Catseye carries the idea the next logical step. Troy Horan, once son of a Range Master on Norden, becomes an equal partner with a kinkajou, two foxes and two cats that have been mutated for greater intelligence. Rerne, the ranger of the wilds, asks:

"Always we. Why, Horan?" Rerne rubbed his wrists.

"Men have used animals as tools." Troy said slowly, trying to fit into words something he did not wholly understand himself. "Now some men, somewhere, have made better tools, tools so good that they can turn and cut the maker. But that is not the fault of the tools—that they are no longer tools but—"

"Perhaps companions?" Rerne ended for him, his fingers still stroking his ridged flesh, but his eyes very intent on Troy.

"How did you know?" the younger man was startled into demanding.

"Let me say that I am also a workman who can admire fine tools, even when they have ceased, as you point out, to be any longer tools."

Troy grasped at that hint of sympathy. "You understand—"

"Only too well. Most of our breed want tools, not companions. And the age-old fear of man, that he will lose his supremacy, will bring down all the hawks and hunters of the galaxy down on your trail, Horan. Do not expect any aid from your own species when it is threatened by powers it cannot and does not want to understand . . ." (Ace, pp. 141-2)

In Eric Frank Russell's "The Undecided" (*Astounding Science Fiction* magazine, April 1949, *Deep Space*) he handles the same theme of equality between man and our "little brothers." As he sums it up:

> For all had passed through the many cons. Some had leaped ahead, some lagged behind. But several of the laggers had put on last moment spurts—because of late functioning of natural laws—and the impact upon their various kinds of the one kind called Man.
> Until they had breasted the tape together. (Bantam, p. 53)

Or, as Miss Norton puts it in *Catseye:*
"We are of one kind, plains rider." Then Rerne looked beyond the man to the animals. "So shall we all be in the end." (Ace, p. 176)
Judgment on Janus (which begins in the Dipple of Korwar, as does *Catseye*) has a working agreement between the Iftin and the quarrin, a vaguely owl-like bird that can communicate mentally with the Iftin. In *The X Factor,* Diskan Fentress seems to almost fall under the domination of the "Brothers-in-Fur," and their communication is rather uncertain.
Ordeal in Otherwhere, the sequel to *Storm Over Warlock,* takes things a step further than equality. Shann Lantee and the wolverine Taggi (Togi is busy with the kids) are joined by Charis Nordholm and Tsstu, the curl-cat. Together they form a unit (almost the same as the mental fusion in Doc Smith's *The Children of The Lens,* Astounding Science Fiction magazine, November, December 1947, January, February 1948) that can withstand all that the Power of the Wyverns can throw at them. (But even in the unit, the man is still "first among equals.")
In places, Norton's consistency is disturbing as she insists on attacking the computer of ten or fifteen years ago. But Miss Norton is true to her daemon wherever it leads her. She sees a nuclear war as our probable future and it or the threat of it is a part of all her near future stories except *The Stars Are Ours*. The crosstime series, the time trader series, and *Operation Time Search* take place in the calm before the

storm and this blights *The Defiant Agents.* Both *Star Guard*
and *Plague Ship* note the changes wrought on Terra by such
a war several hundred years past.

But her afterview is much too optimistic. Our civilization
has delved deeply into the earth for the resources we now
use. Let civilization collapse for very long and some of the
resources needed to rebuild it will be out of reach. This is
our main chance. Muff it, and most likely the stars will forever remain no more than points of light in the night sky.

However, Miss Norton's main thrust is not in the area of
science and technology, but in that of human society. While
all her stories are good entertainment, most contain more.
Most of the writers now considered great, from Shakespeare
on, have considered it necessary to entertain as well as say
something, but for some reason that is out of style today.

> No writer writes out of his having found the answer
> to the problem; he writes rather out of his having the
> problem and wanting a solution. The solution consists
> not of a resolution. It consists of the deeper and wider
> dimensions of conscience to which the writer is carried
> by virtue of his wrestling with the problem. We create
> out of a problem; the writer and the artist are not
> presenting answers but creating as an experience of
> something in themselves trying to work—'to seek, to find
> and not to yield.' The contribution which is given to the
> world by the painting or the book is the process of the
> search. (*Love and Will*, Rollo May, pp. 170-1)

Miss Norton's main problem seems to be that of the rela-
tionship between man and his machines. And her attitude is
fairly obvious. I'd hardly expect a Norton story featuring a
planet-bound misfit who finally realizes his dream of becoming a star ship mechanic. There have been sympathetic characters that have dealt with machines, but not recently. Since
Galactic Derelick (1959) only Ali Kamil from the engine
room of the Solar Queen in *Postmarked the Stars* comes to
mind. And he had played a strong part in the first two books
of the series.

Miss Norton is rather unacquainted with the "hard
sciences" and her earlier books suffer a bit with her attempts
to go into detail. This was especially true of astronomy. Sol is
off the charts, yet the "Sirius Worlds" are mentioned as a
familiar part of history (*The Last Planet/Star Rangers*, Ace,

1955, pp. 158, 170) while the ship is the "Vegan Starfire" (p. 183) and the Hall of Leave-Taking was supposed to be on Alpha Centauri (p. 171). Norton's *Star Atlas* gives Vega as 26 light years away, Sirius 9, and Alpha Centauri 4.3. With a galaxy around 100,000 light years wide, these are literally in our lap. And only Proxima Centauri is now closer than Alpha Centauri.

By *The Stars Are Ours* and following books, Miss Norton avoids the trap most beginning sf writers fall into, and coins most of her planet names, mostly from mythology.

Even this early, Miss Norton showed a marked distrust of what Gene Marine in *America the Raped* termed the engineering mentality. Those Others who inhabit a part of Astra and almost wiped themselves out were rather evil. In *Star Born* (1957), Astra is visited by Terran space travelers generations after the events of the first book.

> To Raf, the straight highways suggested something else. Master engineering, certainly. But a ruthlessness too, as if the builders, who refused to accept any modifications of their original plans from nature, might be as arrogant in other ways. (Ace, p. 39)

In the battle between technology and nature, Miss Norton took a stand long before the great majority of us had any doubts. Miss Norton has little knowledge of technology and rarely tries to explain the scientific wonders in her stories. John Campbell, whose death has left us all the poorer, once said something like, "If we really could explain it, we'd patent it." The less explanation, the less likely the science of the story is to date. But Andre Norton doesn't go into detail because she doesn't care. Technology is a necessary evil to get there for the adventure and to get some of the story to work. And the adventure is as much to mold her universe to her views as to entertain.

Two of the most extreme nature vs. technology novels are *Judgment on Janus* and its sequel, *Victory on Janus*. In this story the Iftin race have left "traps" that change humans sympathetic to nature into Iftin. Their lives are bound with nature and the massive trees. Technology becomes very distasteful. The chief villain turns out to be an alien computer.

The same type of villain turns up in *Star Hunter*, while a human built computer is the main evil in *Ice Crown*. In both *The Stars Are Ours* and *Dark Piper* where the computer performs a useful function, it isn't allowed any more scope than yesterday's model. In *Star Rangers,* a city computer directs a robot to destroy the heroes.

No, Norton does not like computers. Which is really a pity. Out of all the tools that man has created, the computer may well prove to be even better than the scientific method. Its potential is barely scratched today.

In Florida, Miss Norton lives on the border of two counties. She has been charged by both for local taxes due to a "computer error" (a term used to cover a computer operator or computer programmer error). She was told that it was too much trouble to correct the programming and to ignore the wrong tax. Which could have led to legal problems. ". . . It is this sort of thing which arouses hatred of having a machine in control."

But the point is that the machine is in control only in the way that it is told to be. In *Star Rangers,* the computer was programmed to shoot any trespassers (Ace, 1955, p. 68). All that people blame on the computer, which is getting to be a symbol of technological oppression, is due to lazy programming. A computer can be made responsive enough so that every child can have a private tutor to supplement his teacher. But the programming barring a breakthrough would take a vast effort. Is the machine to blame for our refusing to take the time and expense to make it responsive?

Miss Norton sees no marriage of science and human powers. "One had to be anti-tech to be a Beast Master." (*Lord of Thunder,* p. 120) "But even so much a modification as a dart gun—that meant careful preparation in thinking patterns. We could not ally with a machine!" (*Sorceress of the Witch World,* p. 126) So it should not be a surprise after traversing all the magical horrors the Witch World universe has to offer to find that the ultimate depth is a world from an environmentalist's nightmare where a degenerate humanity fights against men incorporated with machines both using weapons of advanced technology.

An interesting treatment of the theme occurs in Roger Zelazny's *Jack of Shadows* where technology is relatively untainted and human powers largely harnessed to evil ends. Jack of Shadows runs afoul of the Lord of Bats and he retreats to tap dayside technology (again, a computer) and harness it to his magic. In doing so, he destroys his world so that a better one can be rebuilt on its foundations, utilizing technology.

Even the biological technologies are usually not for Miss Norton. In *Three Against the Witch World,* delving too deeply in magic (?) to create humanoid races and to gain knowledge is condemned. In *Warlock of the Witch World,* one of the characters is still considered within the pale since he ". . . had for a tutor in his childhood one of the few remaining miracle workers who had set a limit on his own studies." (p. 27) But Dinzil went on from there and he turns out to be the chief villain of the story.

In her only fall from grace, *Star Guard* (1955) has the bodies of the mercenary group being adapted to the conditions of the Planet Fronn while in flight to that world. Yet they show no discomfort on returning to Terra, despite no mention of reverse conditioning. After this, she ignores adverse planetary conditions.

After considering the possibilities set forth in Gordon Rattray Taylor's *The Biological Time Bomb,* one is tempted to agree that there are things the human race shouldn't mess with at its present level of maturity.

> Science and our social habits are out of step. And the cure is no deeper either. We must learn to match them. And there is no way of learning this unless we learn to understand both . . . So however we might sigh for Samuel Butler's panacea in *Erewhon,* simply to give up all machines, there is no point in talking about it . . . It is just not practical, nationally or internationally. ("Science, the Destroyer or Creator" by J. Bronowski in *Man Alone: Alienation in Modern Society,* edited by Eric & Mary Josephson, p. 284)

Going back to nature has its temptations. But it would mean that at present 2 or 2½ billion people would probably starve—most of them in the cities. That is a rather high price to pay.

Miss Norton's reasons for disliking machines tie in with her liking for medieval settings. In her words:

> Yes, I am anti-machine. The more research I do, the more I am convinced that when western civilization turned to machines so heartily with the Industrial Revolution in the early nineteenth century, they threw away some parts of life which are now missing and which the lack of leads to much of our present frustration. When a

man had pride in the work of his own hands, when he could see the complete product he had made before him, he had a satisfaction which no joys of easier machine existence could or can give.

Why all the accent on hobbies and do-it-yourself projects now—so many of them futile? Simply because in his productive work a man can no longer take any pride. Read some of the accounts of the old Guilds and I think you can see what I mean. Before a man could practice any trade then, he had to prove to his peers that he could do it. Very few people now have any pride in what they do—they are slip-shod in a piece of labor because they cannot see that good workmanship in the day of the machine means anything more than poor.

This extends on now from the work itself—there is a wave of bad manners, of outright discourtesy in stores and businesses—no worker identifies with his job enough to actually want to produce something better—he feels a part of a machine, vast, impersonal, not the master of it. And the more we deal so with machines—for example the more computers are brought in to rule our lives— with their horrible mistakes and no one to appeal to to correct them—then the more alienated man will become.

So I make my machines the villains—because I believe that they are so; that man was happier—if less geared to a swift overproductive life—when he used his own personal skills and did not depend upon a machine. And I fear what is going to happen if more and more computers take over ruling us.

This will doubtless seem like rank heresy to you who are training to use such machines—but with the growth of the impersonal attitude towards life which these foster, there is going to be more and more anger and frustration. And where it will all end perhaps not even a writer of sf can foresee.

This is indeed a damning indictment of our age, and there is enough truth in it so that it bites deeply. It is over-reacting—and placing the blame in the wrong place. We have definitely lost something, but this is the fault of those who lacked foresight and took the easy way of fitting the much more adaptable man to the machine. "Now some men ... have made better tools, tools so good that they can turn and

cut the maker. But that is not the fault of the tools . . ."
(*Catseye*, Ace, p. 141)

"The enemy is not a devil out there called technology—he
is Man, the creature we are trying to save. Only because he
has become more conscious of his powers is he capable of
so much folly and evil." (*The Children of Frankenstein: A
Primer on Modern Technology and Human Values* by Herbert J. Muller, p. 331)

The Third Force by Frank Goble concerns the theories of
"humanistic psychology," mainly those of Abraham Maslow.
Behaviorism and Freudian psychology are both looks at a
limited part of man; humanistic psychology tries to view the
whole man. Instead of studying people who have mental
problems, Maslow started with "self-actualizing" people
whom he felt had adjusted the best to living. The second part
of this excellent popularization is concerned with proof of
these theories.

The President of an electronic manufacturing company challenged Dr. Argyris to prove his contention that
the average worker was giving the company only about
a third of his full capability. Argyris set up a one year
experiment in which twelve female electronics assemblers were given individual responsibility for assembling
an entire electronic unit. Instead of efficiency experts
telling the assemblers how to do the job, they were free
to develop their own methods. Furthermore, each of
the twelve girls was to inspect the finished product, sign
her name to the product, and then handle related correspondence and complaints from customers.

The first month of the experiment was not encouraging. Productivity dropped 30% below that of the traditional assembly-line method, and worker morale was
also low. It was not until the end of the eighth week
that production started up. But by the end of the fifteenth week production was higher than ever before,
and overhead costs of inspection, packing, supervision,
and engineering were way down. Production continued
significantly higher than that of assembly-line methods
for the balance of the one year experiment. Re-work
costs dropped 94%, and customer complaints dropped
from 75% a year to only 3%.

. . . When the twelve girls were returned to the routine
assembly line, three of them were relieved by the de-

crease in responsibility. The remaining nine found it hard to adjust to the old routine; they missed the challenge of greater freedom with greater responsibility. (Pocket Books, p. 186-7)

Other cases with about the same results were also covered. The most significant point is not the economic factors—our culture vastly overstresses economic values—but the improvement in workmanship. With almost complete control over what they were doing and the faith in them showed by giving them responsibility for the product, the women seemed to care about what they were doing and felt that it—and they—were of value. Of course, this will not work with very complex products. But they can and probably should be broken into sub-assemblies. One auto plant is totally automated at the moment. All should be.

While the Society for Creative Anachronism wastes most of their energy on costuming and mock duels, they have the right idea in trying to select out of that bygone era what we need today. "Time was and it was all time up to 200 years ago, when the whole of life went forward in the family, in a circle of loved, familiar faces, known and fondled objects, all to human size. That time has gone forever. It makes us very different from our ancestors." ("The World We Have Lost" by Peter Laslett in *Man Alone,* p. 93) (While overstated and overlooking the brutality of the period, and "tyranny of the family," the point is certainly valid.)

In a society of hereditary privilege, an individual of humble position might not have been wholly happy with his lot, but he had never had reason to look forward to any other fate. Never having had prospects of betterment, he could hardly be disillusioned. He entertained no hopes, but neither was he nagged by ambition. When the new democracies removed the ceiling on expectations, nothing could have been more satisfying for those with the energy, ability and emotional balance to meet the challenge. But to the individual lacking in these qualities, the new system was fraught with danger. Lack of ability, lack of energy or lack of aggresiveness led to frustration and failure. Obsessive ambition led to emotional breakdown. Unrealistic ambitions led to bitter defeats.

No system which issues an open invitation to every

youngster to 'shoot high' can avoid facing the fact that room at the top is limited. Donald Paterson reports that four-fifths of our young people aspire to high-level jobs, of which there are only enough to occupy one-fifth of our labor force. Such figures conceal a tremendous amount of human disappointment. (*Excellence: Can We Be Equal and Excellent Too?* by John Gardner (now head of Common Cause), pp. 19-20)

Here is a major social problem that has little to do with machines. Worrying about machines is worrying about an effect rather than a cause. The answer is remodeling society. Gardner's solution to the problem he stated above is for our society to cultivate excellence in all walks of life.

An excellent plumber is infinitely more admirable than an incompetent philosopher. The society which scorns excellence in plumbing because plumbing is a humble activity and tolerates shoddiness in philosophy because it is an exalted activity will have neither good plumbing nor good philosophy. Neither its pipes not its theories will hold water. (*Excellence*, p. 86)

Our culture is also burdened by what Alvin Toffler called "Future Shock" in the book of the same name. Just the rate of change that an individual faces will have an adverse effect on his health if it increases (pp. 291-6). He also points out that technology can free man. "This is the point that our social critics—most of whom are technologically naive—fail to understand: It is only primitive technology that imposes standardization. Automation, in contrast, frees the path to endless, blinding, mind-numbing diversity" (p. 236). For example, the computer designed apartment house, Watergate East, in Washington, D.C., has no continuous straight lines, no two floors alike and 167 different floor plans for 240 apartments (p. 237).

Just as Norton's computers are a parody of the ones we now have, so are the people of the future's attitude toward machines.

The assigner sent him and it was supposed to be always right in its selection. (Troy Horan in *Catseye*, p. 9)

All his life, he had relied on machines operating, of course, under the competent domination of men trained to use them properly. He understood the process of the verifier, had seen it at work. At the Guild headquarters there were no records of its failure; he was willing to believe it was infallible. (Ras Hume in *Star Hunter*, p. 29)

Naturally with that kind of build-up, the verifier fouls up royally.

Star Hunter, while just apparently written so that Ace would have a short novel to fit opposite the abridged *Beast Master*, is a meaty book for attitudes. Besides rubbing our noses in the fallibility of "infallible" machines, we get her feelings on computers. Such phrases as "mechanical life of a computer tender" (page 15) and "but to sit pressing buttons when a light flashed hour after hour—" (page 85) bring out her limited view. There is another reference to button pushing in response to flashing lights in the ultra-scientific hell of the Witch World. (pp. 131-2)

Star Hunter also has the Patrol winking at the mental conditioning of Vye Lansor so that they can net the Veep, Wass. Afterward, of course, he is offered compensation. In *Ice Crown*, morality extends to not interfering with the conditioned people of Clio, but no attempt is made to release them from conditioning. In this the successors of the Psychocrats are as bad since they also keep the people of Clio for observation. In *The Zero Stone*, Murdoc Jern notes that "the Patrol ever takes the view that the good of many is superior to the good of the individual." (Ace, p. 155)

Norton consistently views the future as one where the complexity of science and technology have reduced the value of the individual. But the good of many is in the long run the good of the individual. As John Gardner points out in *Self-Renewal: The Individual and The Innovative Society*, our cultures become rigid and decay when they cease to allow a wide range of freedom to the individual.

So Miss Norton is actually wrestling with the prime problem, that of human worth and purpose. The question of human purpose has led to reams and reams of prose, most of it junk. Miss Norton is right in saying that it is not to be machine tenders, but she is vague on what human purpose should be. Arthur C. Clarke in his "beautiful vision" of the future in *Profiles of the Future* feels that ". . . in the long run the only human activities really worthwhile are the search for knowledge, and the creation of beauty. This is beyond argument; the only point of debate is which comes first." (Bantam, p. 87)

Margaret Mead would certainly disagree. She states that automation should result in people doing only ". . . human tasks—caring for children, caring for plants and trees and animals, caring for the sick and the aged, the traveler and the stranger.") ("The Challenge of Automation to Education and Human Values" in *Automation, Education, and Human Values*, edited by W. W. Brickman and S. Lehrer, p. 69)

And I have little doubt which Miss Norton would side with. But either is too restrictive; we need a synthesis of the two. The important thing is to establish a society where all individuals can realize as much of their potential as possible. Since our society comes the closest—despite its many faults—we should start improving it.

As Herbert J. Muller points out (*The Children of Frankenstein*, pp. 369-83), utopias are out of style in this era as they tend to be too simplistic and too rigid. We get glimpses of a Norton utopia in *Judgment on Janus* and *Victory on Janus* as well as scattered places throughout her books. The most appealing might well be the Valley of Green Silences which we see very little considering that parts of three Witch World novels take place there. While all her desirable places are those of nature, it is well to remember that man might not be man as we know him without his links to nature.

In *Star Rangers*, they ponder the reason why the cities are deserted.

> "It seems to me," began Fylh, "that on this world there was once a decision to be made. And some men made it one way, and some another. Some went out"—his claws indicated the sky—"while others chose to remain—to live close to the earth and allow little to come between them and the wilds—"
>
> "Decadence—degeneracy—" broke in Smitt.
>
> But Zacita shook her head. "If one lives by machines, by the quest for power, for movement, yes. But perhaps to these it was only a moving on to what they thought a better way of life." (Ace, 1955, p. 169)

The question today is not whether we can do without technology, but how much we can compromise with nature. Like the Orbsleon in *Unchartered Stars* (p. 165), we shall have to learn to live by using technology to assist nature.

As Charis Nordholm explains to the Wyvern Gidaya in *Ordeal in Otherwhere,*

> Four have become one at will, and each time we so will it, that one made of four is stronger. Could you break the barrier we raised here while we were one, even though you must have sent against us the full Power? You are an old people, Wise One, and with much learning. Can it not be that some time, far and long ago, you took a turning into a road which limited your power in truth? Peoples are strong and grow when they search for new roads. When they say, "There is no road but this one which we know well, and always must we travel it," then they weaken themselves and dim their future.
>
> Four have made one and yet each of that four is unlike another. You are all of a kind in your Power. Have you never thought that it takes different threads to weave a real pattern—that you use different shapes to make the design of Power? (Ace, p. 188)

It is impossible as far as we are along the way of the machine to leave it without untold human misery and suffering. But we must traverse the byways that will make the most of our humanity.

In her horror at the machine forcing men to be its tenders, she overlooks that machines have taken much drudgery off our shoulders and can free us from more routine labor. When she turns her back on the machine, she ignores all the potential good that it can do us.

> The point was brought home to me recently when I visited an academic friend. He sat in an air-conditioned study. Behind him was a high-fidelity phonograph and record library that brought him the choicest music of three centuries. On his desk before him was the microfilm of an ancient Egyptian papyrus that he had obtained by a routine request through his university library. He described a ten day trip he had just taken to London, Paris and Cairo to confer on recent archaeological discoveries. In short, modern technology and social organization were serving him in spectacular ways. And what was he working on at the moment? An essay for a literary journal on the undiluted evil of modern technology and large-scale organization. (*Self-Renewal*, p. 62)

We must face the fact that while much of what we have is tainted, it is also much more on the positive side than any age before us has had. The potential is almost limitless. If we fail, it will not be because ". . . science, too, had its demons and dark powers," (*Victory on Janus*, Ace, p. 190), but because our nerve has failed us and we let technology run wild.

Even Arthur C. Clarke pauses in his optimistic view of the future to admit that

> . . . Sir George Darwin's prediction that ours would be a golden age compared with the aeons of poverty to follow, may well be perfectly correct. In this inconceivably enormous universe, we can never run out of energy or matter. But we can all too easily run out of brains. (*Profiles of the Future*, Bantam, p. 155)

And just as the potential exists for a heaven beyond our wildest dreams, so does the potential for a hell worse than our bleakest nightmares. Science and technology are amoral and we must fit the morals to them. If we fail, not only we will foot the bill but many generations to follow.

> If there is a long chance that we can replace brutality with reason, inequality with justice, ignorance with enlightenment, we must try. And our chances are better if we have not convinced ourselves that the cause is hopeless. All effective action is fueled by hope. Pessimism may be an acceptable attitude in literary and artistic circles, but in the world of action it is the soil in which desperate and extreme solutions germinate, among them reaction and brutal oppression.
> It is not given to man to know the worth of his efforts. It is arrogant of the individual to imagine that he has grasped the larger design of life and discovered that effort is worthless, especially is that effort is calculated to accomplish some immediate increment in the dignity of a fellow human. Who is he to say it is useless? His business as a man is to try. (*The Recovery of Confidence* by John W. Gardner, Pocket Books, pp. 84-5)

But no matter how deeply Miss Norton's despair in the present and the future is germinating, she never councils quitting or even considering it. "It is better not to be met by pessimism when the situation already looks dark." (*Unchart-*

ed Stars, p. 230) Her heroes and heroines do not tamely bow their heads and accept their lot in a society that does not fit them. Some, like Diskan Fentress, may not seem to be concerned with others, but come through when the chips are down. Even if Norton's future societies do not value the individual, her sympathetic characters do.

Norton's future societies usually combine high ideals with a lack of concern for the people in it, an extrapolation of today's society that seems to be more comfortable treating men largely as interchangeable parts. And as our society worsens, so does her view of the future. *Catseye* (1961) marked the rise of organized crime. By *Night of Masks* (1964), crime syndicates had gone interstellar. *The Zero Stone* (1968) and *Uncharted Stars* show the Patrol reacting by trampling individual rights in their efforts to stamp out crime.

In *Sargasso of Space,* the Free Traders were recruited from the trainees that the Combines depended upon. too. By *Dread Companion* (1970) and *Exiles of the Stars,* the Free Traders are almost a separate race, rigidly controlling themselves on the planets, with their women and the declining feline race kept on their asteroid bases. It is almost as though the cats began to die out as their masters became less human, less linked to nature.

In the future, most of Miss Norton's work will probably be mainly the more aware and less hopeful novels such as *Dark Piper* and *Dread Companion*. But I shall miss seeing more light-hearted optimistic adventures. After all, anyone can be aware. But few can give us an Astra or a Witch World.

Andre Norton Bibliography

BOOKS*

Android at Arms
  Harcourt Brace Jovanovich, 1971, 253 pp. Ace 02275.
    British: Gollancz, 1972. German: *Androiden im Einsatz*,
    Pabel, 1974.
  (S/f)
At Swords' Points
  Harcourt, Brace, 1954, 279 pp. Dutch: *Zijn lijk lag in
    Maastricht op straat*, Schoonderbeek, 1956.
  (Espionage—post-W.W. II; LORENS VAN NORREYS
    III)
The Beast Master
  Harcourt, Brace (Canada: Macmillan), 1959, 192 pp.
    Ace: *D-509 [abridged], F-315, 05161, 05162, 05163.
    British: Gollancz, 1966; Penguin, 1968. German: *Der
    Letzte der Navajos* (2 vols.), Moewig, 1963.
  (S/f, animal telempathy; HOSTEEN STORM I)
Breed to Come
  Viking, 1972, 285 pp. Ace 07895. British: Longman Young
    Books, 1972.
  (S/f)
Catseye
  Harcourt, Brace & World, 1961, 192 pp. Ace: F-167, G-
    654, 09266, 09267. British: Gollancz, 1962; Penguin,
    1967.
  (S/f, animal telempathy)
The Crossroads of Time
  Ace *D-164, 1956, 169 pp. Ace: D-546, F-391, 12311,
    12312.
  (S/f—alternate worlds; BLAKE WALKER I)

*Ace "Double" editions are marked with an asterisk before the book
number.

Crosstime Agent . . . see *Quest Crosstime*

The Crystal Gryphon
Atheneum, 1972, 234 pp. DAW #75 (UQ1076). British: Gollancz, 1973.
(Fantasy; WITCH WORLD VIII, High Halleck)

Dark Piper
Harcourt, Brace & World, 1968, 249 pp. Ace: 13795, 13796. British: Gollancz, 1969.
(S/f)

Daybreak—2250 A.D. . . . see *Star Man's Son, 2250 A.D.*

The Defiant Agents
World, 1962, 224 pp. Ace: F-183, 14231, 14232, 14233. German: *Schiffbruch der Zeitagenten*, Moewig, 1964.
(S/f; ROSS MURDOCK III)

Dragon Magic
Crowell, 1972, 213 pp. Ace 16647.
(Fantasy; juvenile)

Dread Companion
Harcourt Brace Jovanovich, 1970, 234 pp. Ace: 16669, 16670. British: Gollancz, 1972. German: *Die Welt der grünen Lady*, Pabel, 1972.
(Fantasy in an s/f frame)

Exiles of the Stars
Viking, 1971, 255 pp. Ace 22365. British: Longman, 1972. German: *Verfemte des Alls*, Pabel, 1972.
(S/f + some fantasy elements; MOON SINGER II)

Eye of the Monster
Ace *F-147, 1962, 80 pp. Ace 22375. German: *Im Dschungel von Ishkur*, Pabel, 1963.
(S/f)

Follow the Drum, being the ventures and misadventures of one Johanna Lovell, sometime lady of Catkept Manor in Kent county of Lord Baltimore's proprietary of Maryland, in the gracious reign of King Charles the Second
William Penn (Canada: McClelland & Stewart), 1942, 312 pp.
(Historical—American colonial)

Forerunner Foray
Viking, 1973, 288 pp. Science Fiction Book Club, 1973; Ace 24620. British: Longman Young Books, 1974.
(S/f + fantasy—psychometry; LANTEE III)

Fur Magic
World, 1968, 174 pp. British: Hamish Hamilton, 1969.
(Fantasy—Amerindian folklore; juvenile story frame)

Galactic Derelict
World, 1959, 224 pp. Ace: D-498, F-310, 27226, 27227.
German: *Spähtrupp in die Vergangenheit*, Moewig,
1964.
(S/f; ROSS MURDOCK II)

Gray Magic . . . see *Steel Magic*

Here Abide Monsters
Atheneum, 1973, 215 pp. DAW #121 (UY1134).
(Fantasy)

*Huon of the Horn, being a tale of that Duke of Bordeaux
who came to sorrow at the hand of Charlemagne and
yet won the favor of Oberon, the elf king, to his lasting
fame and great glory*
Harcourt, Brace, 1951, 208 pp. Ace: F-226, 35421, 35422.
(Fantasy, adaptation of chanson de geste; juvenile)

Ice Crown
Viking, 1970, 256 pp. Science Fiction Book Club, 1970;
Ace 35840. British: Longman Young Books, 1971. Ger-
man: *Die Eiskrone*, Pabel, 1972.
(S/f)

Iron Cage
Viking, 1974, 288 pp.
(S/f)

Island of the Lost . . . see *Sword in Sheath*

Jargoon Pard
Atheneum, 1974, 194 pp.
(Fantasy—Tarot, were-folk; WITCH WORLD IX, High
Halleck)

Judgment on Janus
Harcourt, Brace & World (Canada: Longmans), 1963, 220
pp. Ace: F-308, 41550, 41551, 41553. British: Gollancz,
1964.
(S/f + fantasy; JANUS I)

Key out of Time
World, 1963, 224 pp. Ace: F-287, 43671, 43672, 43673.
German: *Das Duell der Zeitagenten*, Moewig.
(S/f + some fantasy elements, animal telempathy; ROSS
MURDOCK IV)

Last Planet . . . see *Star Rangers*

Lavender Green Magic
Crowell, 1974, 241 pp.
(Fantasy—herb lore; juvenile)

Lord of Thunder
Harcourt, Brace & World (Canada: Longmans), 1962, 192

pp. Ace: F-243, 49236, 49237. British: Gollancz, 1966; Penguin, 1968.

(S/f, animal telempathy; HOSTEEN STORM II)

Merlin's Mirror

DAW #152 (UY1175), 1975, 205 pp.

(S/f treatment of Arthurian legend)

Moon of Three Rings

Viking (Canada: Macmillan), 1966, 316 pp. Ace: H-33, 54101, 54102; Junior Literary Guild, 1966. British: Longman Young Books, 1969. German: *Das Geheimnis der Mondsänger*, Moewig, 1969.

(S/f + some fantasy elements, animal telempathy; (MOON-SINGER I)

Night of Masks

Harcourt, Brace & World (Canada: Longmans), 1964, 191 pp. Ace: F-365, 57751, 57752. British: Gollancz, 1965; Brockhampton, 1970.

(S/f)

Octagon Magic

World, 1967, 189 pp. British: Hamish Hamilton, 1968.

(Fantasy; juvenile)

Operation Time Search

Harcourt, Brace & World (Canada: Longmans), 1967, 224 pp. Ace: 63410, 63411.

(S/f + some fantasy elements, Atlantis)

Ordeal in Otherwhere

Harcourt, Brace & World, 1964, 221 pp. Ace: F-325, 63821, 63822, 63823. German: *Im Bann der Träume*, Moewig, 1970.

(S/f + fantasy, animal telempathy; LANTEE II)

Outside

Walker, 1974, 126 pp.

(S/f + fantasy; juvenile derived from her short story "London Bridge")

Plague Ship [as Andrew North]

Gnome, 1956, 192 pp. Ace *D-345, F-291, 66831, 66832. British: Gollancz, 1971. German: *Gefährliche Landung*, Pabel, 1958. French: *Fusée en Quarantaine*, Ditis, 1960.

(S/f; DANE THORSON II)

Postmarked the Stars

Harcourt, Brace & World, 1969, 223 pp. Ace 67555. British: Gollancz, 1971.

(S/f: DANE THORSON IV)

The Prince Commands, being sundry adventures of Michael Karl, sometime crown prince & pretender to the throne of Morvania
  Appleton-Century (British: same), 1934, 296 pp. Danish: *Varulven*, Gyldendal, 1937.
  (Adventure—"Ruritanian")
Quest Crosstime
  Viking (Canada: Macmillan), 1965, 253 pp. Ace: G-595, 69681, 69682. British, as *Crosstime Agent*: Gollancz, 1975. German: *Hetzjagd der Zeitgardisten* (2 vols.) Moewig, 1967.
  (S/f—alternate worlds; BLAKE WALKER II)
Ralestone Luck
  Appleton-Century (British: same; Canada: Ryerson), 1938, 296 pp.
  (Adventure—then-contemporary 1930's)
Rebel Spurs
  World, 1962, 224 pp.
  (Historical—post-Civil War Southwest; DREW RENNIE II)
Ride Proud, Rebel!
  World, 1961, 255 pp.
  (Historical—Civil War; DREW RENNIE I)
Rogue Reynard, being a tale of the fortunes and misfortunes and divers misdeeds of that great villain, Baron Reynard, the fox, and how he was served with King Lion's justice
  Houghton Mifflin (Canada: Thomas Allen), 1947, 96 pp. Dell Yearling Books, 1972.
  (Adaptation of French beast saga; children's book)
Sargasso of Space [as Andrew North]
  Gnome, 1955, 185 pp. Ace: *D-249, F-279, 74981. British: Gollancz, 1970. German: *Die Raumschiff-Falle*, Pabel, 1958; *Der unheimliche Planet*, Boje-Verlag, 1972; German Book Club edition. French: *Les Naufrageurs de l'espace*, Ditis, 1960. Russian [as Endriu Norton]: *Sargassy v Kosmose*, Mir, 1969.
  (S/f; DANE THORSON I)
Scarface, being the story of one Justin Blade, late of the pirate isle of Tortuga, and how fate did justly deal with him, to his great profit
  Harcourt, Brace, 1948, 263 pp. Comet Books #28, 1949. British: Methuen, 1950.
  (Historical/pirate)

Sea Siege
> Harcourt, Brace, (Canada: Longmans), 1957, 216 pp. Ace: *F-147, 75695, 75696. German: *Gefangen auf Limbo* [as Andrew North], Pabel, 1963.
> (S/f)

Secret of the Lost Race
> Ace *D381, 1959, 132 pp. Ace: 75830, 75831. German: *Das Geheimnis der Verlorenen*, Pabel, 1960; Moewig, 1966.
> (S/f)

Shadow Hawk
> Harcourt, Brace, 1960, 237 pp. Ace: G-538, 75991. British: Gollancz, 1971. Arabic [as Andrayah Nūrtūn]: *Ṣaqr al-Hurrīyah, Awwal Thawrah fi-al-Tārikh didd al-istiᶜmar* [*Falcon of Freedom, history's first anti-imperialist revolution*], Arab Record, 1963.
> (Historical—ancient Egypt)

The Sioux Spaceman
> Ace *D-437, 1960, 133 pp. Ace: F-408, 76801. German: *Die Sklaven von Klor*, Pabel, 1960.
> (S/f)

Sorceress of the Witch World
> Ace H-84, 1968, 224 pp. Ace 77551. British: Tandem, 1970.
> (Fantasy; WITCH WORLD VI)

Stand to Horse
> Harcourt, Brace, 1956, 242 pp. Voyager Books.
> (Historical—American Southwest, 1859)

Star Born
> World (Canada: Nelson, Foster & Scott), 1957, 212 pp. Ace: *D-299, F-192, 78011. British: Gollancz, 1973. German: *Flammen über Astra*, Moewig, 1964.
> (S/f; ASTRA II)

Star Gate
> Harcourt, Brace (Canada: Longmans), 1958, 192 pp. Ace: F-231, 78071, 78072. British: Gollancz, 1970. German: *Blut der Sternengötter*, Pabel, 1973.
> (S/f—alternate worlds)

Star Guard
> Harcourt, Brace, 1955, 247 pp. Ace: *D-199, D-527, G-599, 78131. British: Gollancz, 1969. German: *Die Rebellen*, Pabel, 1958; *Die Rebellen von Terra*, Pabel, 1973. Italian: *Riscatto Cosmico*.
> (S/f)

Star Hunter

Ace *D-509, 1961, 96 pp. Ace: *G-723, *78192. German: *Das Geheimnis des Dschungel-Planeten*, Ullstein, 1974.

(S/f)

Star Man's Son, 2250 A.D.

Harcourt, Brace, 1952, 248 pp. Ace: [all as *Daybreak— 2250 A.D.*] *D-69, D-534, G-717, 13991, 13992, 13993. British: Staples, 1953; Gollancz, 1968. German: *Das grosse Abenteuer des Mutanten*, Moewig, 1965.

(S/f)

Star Rangers

Harcourt, Brace (Canada: McLeod), 1953, 280 pp. Ace: [all as *Last Planet*] *D-96, D-96, D-542, M-151, 47161, 47162. British: Gollancz, 1968. German: *Weltraum-Ranger greifen ein.*

(S/f)

The Stars are Ours!

World, 1954, 237 pp. Ace: *D-121, F-207, 78431. German: *Ad Astra* (2 vols.), Moewig, 1956; *Die Sterne gehören uns*, Ullstein, 1974. Italian: *Addio alla Terra*, Urania.

(S/f; ASTRA I)

Steel Magic

World, 1965, 155 pp. As *Gray Magic*, Scholastic, 1967. British: Hamish Hamilton, 1967.

(Fantasy; juvenile)

Storm over Warlock

World, 1960, 251 pp. Ace: F-109, 78741, 78742. German: *Sturm über Warlock*, Ullstein, 1974.

(S/f + some fantasy elements, animal telempathy; LANTEE I)

Sword in Sheath

Harcourt, Brace, 1949, 246 pp. British, as *Island of the Lost*: Staples, 1953; World Distributors, 1957.

(Espionage—post-W.W. II; LORENS VAN NORREYS II)

The Sword is Drawn

Houghton Mifflin (Canada: Thomas Allen), 1944, 178 pp. Junior Literary Guild, 1944. British [and Canada]: Oxford Univ. Press, 1946.

(Espionage—Holland in W.W. II; LORENS VAN NORREYS I)

Three Against the Witch World
    Ace F-332, 1965, 189 pp. Ace: F-357, 80800, 80801,
        80802. British: Tandem, 1970.
    (Fantasy; WITCH WORLD IV)
The Time Traders
    World, 1958, 219 pp. Ace: D-461, F-386, 81251, 81252.
        German: *Operation Vergangenheit*, Moewig, 1964.
    (S/f—time travel; ROSS MURDOCK I)
Uncharted Stars
    Viking, 1969, 253 pp. Ace: 84000, 84001. British: Gol-
        lancz, 1974. German: *Sterne ohne Namen*, Moewig,
        1970.
    (S/f; MURDOC JERN II)
Victory on Janus
    Harcourt, Brace & World (Canada: Longmans), 1966, 224
        pp. Ace: G-703, 86321. British: Gollancz, 1967.
    (S/f + fantasy: JANUS II)
Voodoo Planet [as Andrew North]
    Ace *D-345, 1959, 78 pp. Ace: *G-723, *78192.
    (S/f + some fantasy elements; DANE THORSON III)
Warlock of the Witch World
    Ace G-630, 1967, 222 pp. Ace: 87319, 87321. British:
        Tandem, 1970.
    (Fantasy; WITCH WORLD V)
Web of the Witch World
    Ace F-263, 1964, 192 pp. Ace: G-716, 87871, 87873.
        British: Tandem, 1970.
    (Fantasy; WITCH WORLD II)
White Jade Fox
    Dutton (Canada: Clarke, Irwin), 1975, 230 pp.
    (Gothic romance fantasy elements, including I Ching)
Witch World
    Ace F-197, 1963, 222 pp. Ace: 89701. British: Tandem,
        1970. Portuguese: *Mundo Diabolico*, Editora La Selva
        S.P. (Brazil).
    (Fantasy; WITCH WORLD I)
The X Factor
    Harcourt, Brace & World, 1965, 191 pp. Ace: G-646,
        92551, 92553. British: Gollancz, 1967. German: *Der
        Faktor X*, Pabel, 1973.
    (S/f + some fantasy elements)
Yankee Privateer
    World, 1955, 300 pp.
    (Historical—American Revolution)

Year of the Unicorn
Ace F-357, 1965, 224 pp. Ace: 94251, 94252. British: Tandem, 1970.
(Fantasy—were-folk; WITCH WORLD III, High Halleck)
The Zero Stone
Viking, 1968, 286 pp. Ace: 95960, 95961, 95962. British: Gollancz, 1974. German: *Der Schlüssel zur Sternen- macht*, Moewig, 1969.
(S/f; MURDOC JERN I)

COLLABORATIONS

Bertie and May [with Bertha Stemm Norton]
World, 1969, 174 pp. British: Hamish Hamilton, 1971.
(Rural family life, 1870's; children's book)
Day of the Ness [with Michael Gilbert]
Walker, 1975, 119 pp.
(S/f; juvenile)
Murders for Sale [as "Allen Weston", with Grace Allen Hogarth]
Hammond, Hammond (British), 1954, 240 pp.
(Mystery)

SHORT STORY COLLECTIONS

Garan the Eternal
Fantasy Pub. Co., 1972, 199 pp. Daw #45 (UQ1045).
German: *Garan, der Ewige*, Pabel, 1974.
(Fantasy)
High Sorcery
Ace 33700, 1970, 156 pp. Ace 33701.
(Fantasy)
Spell of the Witch World
DAW #1 (UQ1001), 1972, 159 pp. DAW (UY1179).
(Fantasy; WITCH WORLD VII)
also:
The Many Worlds of Andre Norton [ed. by Roger Elwood]
Chilton (Canada: Thomas Nelson), 1974, 208 pp. DAW # (UY1198). as *The Book of Andre Norton*, DAW: #165 (UY1198)
(Fantasy + some s/f)

SHORTER FICTION

"All Cats are Gray" Herein, and—
  Fantastic Universe Aug.-Sept., 1953.
  Many Worlds of Science Fiction (Ben Bova, ed.), Dutton, 1971.
"Amber out of Quayth", in *Spell of the Witch World*, q.v.
"The Boy and the Ogre"
  Golden Magazine Sept., 1966.
"By a Hair" Herein, and—
  Phantom Magazine (England) July, 1958.
"Desirable Lakeside Residence"
  Saving Worlds (Roger Elwood and Virginia Kidd, eds.), Doubleday, 1973.
"Dream Smith", in *Spell of the Witch World*, q.v.
"Dragon Scale Magic", in *Spell of the Witch World*, q.v.
"Garan of Yu-Lac", in *Garan the Eternal*, q.v., and— *Spaceways Science-Fiction* Sept.-Oct., 1969, and June, 1970.
"Garin of Tav" . . . same as "People of the Crater", q.v.
"The Gifts of Asti" Herein, and—
  Fantasy Book No. 3, 1949.
  Griffin Booklet 1 (Basil Wells and Andrew North, eds.), Griffin, 1949.
  The Time Curve (Roger Elwood, ed.), Tower 43-986, 1968.
"Legacy from Sorn Fen", in *Garan the Eternal*, q.v.
"London Bridge" Herein, and—
  Magazine of Fantasy and Science Fiction Oct., 1973.
"Long Live Kord Kor!" Herein, and—
  Worlds of Fantasy vol. 1, no. 2, 1970.
"The Long Night of Waiting" Herein, and—
  Long Night of Waiting . . . and Other Stories (Roger Elwood, ed.), Aurora, 1974.
"Mousetrap" Herein, and—
  Magazine of Fantasy and Science Fiction June, 1954.
  Best Science Fiction Stories and Novels, 1955 (T. E. Ditky, ed.), Fell, 1956.
"One Spell Wizard", in *Garan the Eternal*, q.v.
"People of the Crater", in *Garan the Eternal*, q.v., and—
  Fantasy Book vol. 1, no. 1, 1947.
  Swordsmen in the Sky (Donald Wollheim, ed.), Ace, 1964.
  Alien Earth (Roger Elwood, ed.), Macfadden Book 75-219.

"The Toads of Grimmerdale" Herein, and—
  Flashing Swords Vol. 2 (Lin Carter, ed.), Science Fiction
     Book Club, 1973. Dell, 1974.
"Toymaker's Snuffbox"
  Golden Magazine Aug., 1966.
"Toys of Tamisan", in *High Sorcery*, q.v., and—
  Worlds of If April-May, 1969.
"Through the Needle's Eye", in *High Sorcery*, q.v.
"Ully the Piper", in *High Sorcery*, q.v.
"Wizard's World", in *High Sorcery*, q.v., and—
  Worlds of If June, 1967.
  Galaxie (French) no. 75, 1970.

ANTHOLOGIES EDITED

Bullard of the Space Patrol [stories by Malcolm Jameson]
  World, 1951. 255 pp. (S/f)
Gates to Tomorrow [with Ernestine Donaldy]
  Atheneum, 1973, 264 pp. (S/f)
Small Shadows Creep
  Dutton, 1974, 195 pp. (Ghost stories; juvenile)
Space Pioneers
  World, 1954, 294 pp. (S/f)
Space Police
  World, 1956, 255 pp. (S/f)
Space Service
  World, 1953, 277 pp. (S/f)

NONFICTION

"Ghost Tour"
  Witchcraft and Sorcery vol. 1, no. 5, Jan-Feb., 1971.
"Living in 1980 Plus—"
  Library Journal vol. 77, Sept. 15, 1952.
"On Writing Fantasy" Herein, and—
  Dipple Chronicle [fanzine] Oct.-Dec., 1971.

ALAN BURT AKERS—The first five great novels of
Dray Prescot is The Delian Cycle:

☐ **TRANSIT TO SCORPIO.** The thrilling saga of Prescot
of Antares among the wizards and nomads of Kregen.
Book I.   (#UY1169—$1.25)

☐ **THE SUNS OF SCORPIO.** Among the colossus-builders
and sea raiders of Kregen. Book II. (#UY1191—$1.25)

☐ **WARRIOR OF SCORPIO.** Across the forbidden lands and
the cities of madmen and fierce beasts. Book III.
                                   (#UY1212—$1.25)

☐ **SWORDSHIPS OF SCORPIO.** Prescot allies himself with a
pirate queen to rescue Vallia's traditional foes! Book IV.
                                   (#UY1231—$1.25)

☐ **PRINCE OF SCORPIO.** Outlaw or crown prince—which was
to be the fate of Prescot in the Empire of Vallia? Book V.
                                   (#UY1251—$1.25)

DAW BOOKS are represented by the publishers of Signet
and Mentor Books, THE NEW AMERICAN LIBRARY, INC.